Contents

THE GLASGOW SUBWAY MURDERS

By

Will Cameron

The Glasgow Subway Murders

This book is a work of fiction. Any resemblance to actual persons, living or dead, is entirely coincidental.

For Karen

Every Moment of Every Day

Chapter 1

The Warmth of a Cold Glasgow

Cheryl Kerr walked out the side entrance of Glasgow Central Station and into the bustling crowds on Union Street like she was slotting into a conga line. It was the last Saturday of November 2008, but by the number of people in town, you would have thought it was the last Saturday before Christmas. Even the bitter wind wasn't a deterrent, as it blew along the streets, reddening everyone's faces, chilling their hands and feet.

Cheryl, though, wasn't aware of the cold. She was only aware of her luxurious, blissful happiness wrapped around her like her long green scarf. She now knew for certain Ryan was the one. Of course, deep down, she always knew Ryan was the one.

Her blonde bob was topped with a black beret, pulled down at an angle over her forehead. She wore it with a style Claire Grogan would have been proud of. Among the crowds' bobbing heads, she stood out for a fashion and beauty she effortlessly wore along with her beret, tight faded denim jeans, and ankle leather boots. With her modest canvas travel bag slung over her shoulder, her hands were plunged into a black and white checked coat which, like her beret, was more stylish than practical for this weather.

Cheryl continued to shuffle along the pavement, trying to keep in step with those around her. With head bowed, she watched the heels of the woman in front trundle through the sludge with truncated steps. All the while, Cheryl could hear the city's comforting blanket of familiar sounds around her— chatter, laughter, snippets of conversation in local and non-local accents.

It was good to be home.

Cheryl looked to her left to see silhouetted, immobile heads inside the steamed-up windows of a traffic-jammed, double-decker bus. On some windows were rubbed rough, small portholes of clearer glass by curious commuters inside. Suddenly realising the rare opportunity to cross the road, Cheryl seized the day and darted behind one car, in front of another, and then behind a double-decker bus like she was playing real-life Frogger. Now, she was in another slow-moving mass of people moving along the pavement, only this time on the other side of the road.

Ryan. Beautiful Ryan. It wasn't just that Ryan said he loved her. It was the way he said it. The way he looked into her eyes when he said it.

She could actually see his love as well as feel it. It was like 3D love, you could say— all so real — absolute pure emotion.

Delayed by cross-border snow, Cheryl's train from Sheffield hadn't arrived at Central until 4:10 pm. Now, with fast darkening sky, the shop windows on the left appeared to have a relatively brighter glow, bathing the Christmas crowds in a pale yellow light that gave the illusion of warmth.

Ryan said he loved her.

Once again, this thought banished away the cold as Cheryl passed people crammed in tight groups at a line of bus stops like penguins huddled together against the freezing wind.

Different conversations drifted in and out of earshot. 'What about Aunt Jean...' 'I'm no going in there, too expensive...' 'ma feet are freezing' 'I'm dying for ma tea...' Cheryl loved her hometown. She loved Glasgow.

Cheryl turned left when she reached Boots Corner, where Union Street met Argyle Street. She listened to the infinite noise of people being people, the rustling of voices and lives mixing with the echo of wet footfall and the grumbling of non-moving buses, cars, and taxi engines. Traffic on Argyle Street was as immobile as Renfield Street, and grateful for another traffic crossing opportunity, Cheryl skipped across to the other side of the road. She now walked hurriedly along the outside of the pavement, regularly stepping onto the road like she was Gene Kelly singing in the sludge. She was now making good progress towards her goal, St Enoch subway station.

Suddenly Cheryl began to feel tired and was more aware of the sharp, piercing cold around her. The day's excitement was fast wearing off, and now she just couldn't wait to get back to her flat in Bank Street. Thank God for the subway. A bus journey would have taken forever to get her back home. Even a taxi would have taken ages in this traffic. The subway was a real blessing at times.

Before turning right towards the subway station entrance, Cheryl stopped and, glancing to her left, looked up Buchanan Street. In the dim light, she could still make out another mass of bobbling, bubbling people stretching all the way up to the Royal Concert Hall in the distance. Aye, returning to the warmth of a cold Glasgow was the perfect end to a perfect week.

Cheryl passed under the curved subway arch, once again slotting into a line of people and feet moving onto the escalator. She heard constant chatter around her, but this time it was mixed with the escalator's mechanical whirring, grind, and screech. Cheryl was aware at that moment that she was happier than she had ever been. She let herself be slowly guided downwards by the dirty silver-griddled stairs descending ever deeper beneath the ground and into the depths of St Enoch subway station.

*

Cheryl Kerr lay on the ground, her naked body shaking uncontrollably through fear and freezing cold. Was this really happening? Please, God, let it be some sort of vivid nightmare she would wake up from at any second. Yet the pain was all too real. The cold was real. The penetrations, the beatings, and the torture were real. She wanted to scream, but the tape across her mouth stopped her, just as the tape across her eyes prevented her from seeing. Everything was black, pitch black.

Cheryl never realised such pain was possible. At regular intervals, something smashed against her legs, knees, hips, thighs, stomach, arms, chest, shoulders, feet... Overwhelming agony from every inch of her body sent desperate signals of distress to her brain.

Was this how her life ended? Not yet, surely not now. She was only twenty-two years old. She didn't want to die. She wanted to live. *Please, God, if you can hear me, please spare me. Let me live. I'm begging you, just let me live; I'll do anything. I don't want to die! Not yet. Please, not yet. Please, not now.*

Such incredible bitter cold, pain, fear— Part

of her wanted to live, yet another part just wanted it all to end.

Cheryl heard soft footsteps on the crisp ground once again. A lot more bad things would happen, even worse than before, even worse than Cheryl could have possibly imagined.

Chapter 2

A Doubtful Return

Detective Chief Inspector Michael Patterson had a peculiar feeling as he walked up the stairs to the main office at Partick Police Station. It was a feeling of returning to school. How old was he now? Forty-eight? And yet, this sensation was so vivid; it was like being transported back in time.

Patterson stopped for a moment and took a deep breath before walking into the main office. He was glad to see it was still empty, apart from one person, Detective Inspector Claire Pettigrew sitting at her desk.

For Pettigrew, seeing her boss walk into the office was a welcome sight. When he had last walked out of the office in mid-October, Patterson had seemed a beaten man. It was clear to those who knew him well that Patterson desperately needed extended time away from work. The worry Pettigrew had was that the temporary break would become a permanent one. Yet, here he was, back at work on the first day of December.

Patterson was tall, of slim build, with short, tidy grey hair combed to one side. His silver-rimmed glasses adorned a youthful and quite handsome face. If you were judging by appearances, you would say this was an intelligent and thoughtful man, and, in this case, you'd be right to judge the book by the cover. Patterson had an old-fashioned quality to him. It wasn't just his preference for wearing corduroy trousers and v-neck jumpers with his shirt and tie. His overall colour was grey like he was wearing camouflage for the rainy Glasgow skies.

Reassuringly, for Pettigrew this morning, Patterson looked as he always looked. Uncertain, as if he had wandered into the wrong room.

'Morning, sir,' Pettigrew cheerily called across the open plan office. Patterson cautiously raised a hand in greeting as if he was in two minds about hailing a cab.

'Morning Claire,' Patterson replied as he walked towards her desk. 'How's things?'

'Oh, you know, the usual, no rest for the wicked and all that. Good to see ye back.'

'Good to be back,' Patterson said unconvincingly as he surveyed the office once more. It had its all too familiar aroma of paper, desk, and carpet. The bright, soulless strip lights contrasted with the Glasgow winter darkness outside. He felt a slight knot in his stomach.

What was that? Dread? Anxiety? His anxiety had been as under control these last few weeks as it had ever been. His time away had really helped him in that respect. Yet, had the anxiety simply been waiting for him to return to work? Whatever that uncomfortable feeling was, he tried to ignore its tapping finger.

Pettigrew noticed Patterson's pensive mood and, wanting to disrupt negative thoughts, asked, 'You're looking well, been anywhere nice while you were away?'

'I went with Stephanie to the Maldives. Just got back on Saturday.'

'Ooh, the Maldives, eh. Sound nice. I hope you had a good time.'

Patterson contemplated whether he did have a good time, quickly concluded he did and that Stephanie also enjoyed the break. More importantly, she managed to keep her promise to stay off the drink.

'Yes, we did have a good time, thanks. It was good to get away - very relaxing.'

'Good to hear,' Pettigrew said, smiling while arranging papers on her desk.

Once more, Patterson looked around the office. That gnawing feeling of apprehension was still there, an interior monologue of doubt about whether he really wanted to be back at Partick Police Station.

'I see you're the first one in, as always. Are Simpson and McKinnon due in later?' asked

Patterson.

'Aye, the whole gang is still here. No holidays in the Maldives for us.'

Pettigrew was a dark-haired woman with a fuller figure, which meant she constantly had to fight the prevalent, what was the word, *fatism*? as well as sexism on an almost daily basis. Many a man and woman mistook her helpful and friendly nature as a weakness, but Pettigrew didn't suffer fools gladly. No one made the mistake of commenting on her size or tried to take advantage of her good nature twice. As well as being the hardest-working officer in Patterson's team, she was one of the nicest. If Patterson did leave the force, perhaps the one colleague he would miss more than any other would be DI Claire Pettigrew.

'Tell you what, why not grab us both a coffee, Claire, then come in my office, and you can fill me in on what's been happening these past few weeks.'

'Will do,' Pettigrew said with a smile. She rose from her desk and made towards the cafetiere as Patterson headed down to his small office at the end of the room.

Five minutes later, Pettigrew was sitting in front of Patterson's desk, placing the mug of coffee before him as he studied the memos placed haphazardly on his desk.

He took a sip of the warm coffee - it was never hot - and looked up at Pettigrew. 'So, tell us the latest.'

'Well, it's actually been relatively quiet since you went away; everyone must have known you were away on holiday.'

'Aye, that'll be why.'

'At the moment, everything is focused on a missing person's case.'

'Is she the woman who went missing on Saturday?'

Pettigrew nodded. 'Aye, you heard about that? Cheryl Kerr. It's only been a couple of days, but it's well out of character, apparently.'

'And still no indication where she could be?'

'Nope. She was last seen exiting Kelvinbridge subway station on Saturday afternoon and then zilch.'

'It doesn't sound good,' Patterson said quietly.

'Not good at all.'

'Who's in charge of the case?'

'DCI Weaver,' Pettigrew replied.

'Weaver? What the hell is he doing back?'

'Dunard called him in. It's only temporary to help with Cheryl's disappearance.'

'Weaver, eh? It must be two years since he left here.'

'Aye, but Dunard thought since Weaver was successful in finding Abigail McDonald, he was just the man to help us find Cheryl. Speaking of which, Weaver's having a briefing this morning on the disappearance, and Dunard wants you to be there.'

'What time?'

'Nine.'

Patterson felt that knot in his stomach get slightly tighter.

'So anyway, how's yourself?'

'I've been fine, thanks,' Pettigrew said with a smile. 'I've moved address. Bought this place in Jordanhill.'

'Oh aye?'

'Aye, it's OK, they sold it to me as this Swiss chalet in the heart of Glasgow. It's really just got a wooden balcony and cute windows, but I like it.'

'And how's Simpson and McKinnon.'

'Simpson's his usual self. Actually, he's been brilliant since you left. Working away, putting in extra hours. Really stepped up to the plate. Don't tell him I said that.'

'I won't. And McKinnon?'

'Fine, you know McKinnon, he just gets on with it. Actually, he's on a keep fit mission at the moment.'

'You mean he's cut down on the digestives?'

'Naw, it's the real deal. He goes to the gym twice a week, and, get this, he cycles to work.'

'I don't think I can imagine Brian McKinnon riding a bike.'

'I know, neither could I, but he's got all the gear and a right fancy bike. You'll see him when he gets in.'

'Well, can't say I'll be joining him, but fair

play.'

'Aye, I suppose so.' Pettigrew drank up the last of her coffee. 'Anyway, I best be getting on with things.' Pettigrew rose from her chair. 'I'll see you later at the briefing.'

Patterson nodded. The thought of the briefing and seeing Weaver again didn't exactly fill him with joy.

'Oh, and sir, it really is good to see you back again,' Pettigrew added.

Patterson smiled, a smile that quickly faded as he looked down at all the memos on his desk. He realised he, too, had a lot to be getting on with.

Chapter 3

My Perfect Cousin

Patterson knew his attitude towards DCI Rafe Weaver wasn't justified. Despite that, it didn't matter. Weaver always managed to get under Patterson's skin. For one thing, Inspector Weaver was always so confident. He had none of the insecurities or anxiety Patterson had. He also had a natural ability to connect with anyone and everyone. Something Patterson never managed to do.

DCI Weaver was also an artist. An actual artist that is. Which is why his nickname was Raphael. His work was frequently exhibited in galleries across Glasgow and further afield. One thing Patterson had to concede was that Weaver couldn't help looking like a stereotypical hero. Thick, brown hair complemented piercing green eyes. Sharp cheekbones complemented a strong jaw, and he had a moustache that could have easily seen him star in a 1930s thriller about thwarting an enemy spy ring. Then there was Weaver's recent success in the Abigail McDonald kidnap. Weaver had found six-year-old Abigail Macdonald relatively quickly when all hope of doing so was fading fast. It seemed that Weaver had a gilded touch. It was why Patterson often thought of Weaver as My Perfect Cousin. The force's little golden boy who could do no wrong.

Just before nine, Patterson slowly walked through to the main briefing room for the morning update. He made his way past the rows of chairs and officers to the back of the room, trying to keep as low a profile as possible. He was helped in this quest by the incident room filling up quickly with colleagues. As Patterson sat, twiddling with his watch, he could sense the buzz from colleagues as if they were waiting for the headliner act to appear at a rock concert.

When Weaver did appear and stood in front of the incident board, there was a lot of pointing and winking from Weaver as he spotted colleagues in the 'crowd'. Patterson took off his glasses and pinched his eyes with his fingers – he could feel a headache coming on.

Weaver clapped his hands together, acknowledging his reception with a calming motion as if he was half-heartedly worshipping Allah.

'Guys, guys, calm down, shall we? Now I know you're all excited because our much-loved DCI Patterson is back,'— there was ironic laughter as everyone turned around and stared at Patterson, who gave a small wave trying unsuccessfully to be part of the banter –'but we have a very important missing person's enquiry to be getting on with.' Eventually, the noise abated.

'Seriously though,' Weaver continued,' Welcome back, chief; it's good to have you back.'

This was said with such sincerity it made Patterson wince.

'OK,' Weaver started, clapping his hands together once again, 'partly for our benefit and for the benefit of DCI Patterson here, I am going to go over all the aspects of the Cheryl Kerr case that we know of so far. And as always, if you have any questions, don't be afraid to ask. Weaver took a drink of fizzy water from a bottle. 'OK, now, the enquiry. As said, for everyone's benefit,' Weaver pointed at Patterson again, this time with two-hand gun style. Was Weaver deliberately trying to annoy Patterson? 'I'm going to start at the beginning, state what we know for certain, what we can assume, then presume and speculate. All of which will hopefully bring us to where we are now and where we mean to go from this point onwards. I hope there's no need to remind you all just how vital time is, so let's crack on. OK. Cheryl Kerr.' Weaver pointed to a passport-style photo of a pretty young woman with blonde hair. 'Twenty-two years old. Local girl, she lives in a shared flat in Bank Street with two student friends from Strathclyde Uni. On Monday, the 24th of November, Cheryl travelled to visit her boyfriend, Ryan Maxwell, in Sheffield. By all accounts, she has a lovely time before returning to Glasgow five days later on Saturday, the 29th of November, that's to say, two days ago. Due to heavy snow, Cheryl's train didn't arrive at Glasgow Central until late afternoon, 4:10 pm to be precise. She then walks down from Central to St Enoch subway station, gets on a train, and then gets off at Kelvinbridge. At 4:42 pm, Cheryl is seen exiting Kelvinbridge station—Weaver points to a CCTV still of Cheryl pushing through the subway turnstile —and that's the last anyone has seen of her. Now I know a couple of days isn't that long, but the circumstances of Cheryl's disappearance naturally give cause for concern, a lot of concern.'

As Patterson listened to this, he forgot any other thoughts about Weaver and concentrated on the disappearance.

'Now,' Weaver continued, 'there is more than one exit from Kelvinbridge. One, via the escalators, leads up to Great Western Road, and another, at ground level, leads onto South Woodside Road. Otherwise, from ground level, you could cross the bridge over the River Kelvin towards the stairs leading up to Caledonia Crescent. Meanwhile, from South Woodside Road, Cheryl could have gone in various directions. However, CCTV is scarce in most directions, especially towards Maryhill. We know this ground-level exit is the one Cheryl took to leave the station from the CCTV we do have.'

A hand rose in the air.

'Yes, Jane.'

DS Millar lowered her hand. 'Sir, As I understand it, if her flat is on Bank Street, wouldn't the quickest way home be via going up the escalator onto Great Western Road and then walking straight up to Bank St? Or else onto Caledonia Crescent? Why would she walk in the other direction?'

Weaver nodded. 'You're right. Almost. Strictly speaking, the quickest way to her flat is going onto Great Western Road or via Caledonia Crescent and walking straight up to Bank St, as you say. However, you can still get to Bank St via Gibson St, and there isn't really that much of a time difference in regards to getting there. A possible explanation for her going that way is a subscription to a magazine she usually picked up from a newsagent on Gibson St on a Saturday. Having said that, we have no CCTV of her in said shop nor any CCTV of her at all in Gibson St. Likewise, there is no CCTV of her anywhere else after she leaves the subway station.'

Pettigrew spoke up. 'So, it's possible she turned left and walked up South Woodside Road towards Maryhill or turned right then left towards Park Road?'

Weaver nodded. 'These are all possibilities,

but unfortunately, there is no CCTV in these directions for us to verify that. Another possibility is she, again, for whatever reason, walked down the side of the River Kelvin, down the path which leads to Kelvingrove Park. Once more, there is no CCTV to verify this, but it is certainly a possibility.'

Before continuing, Weaver took another slug of his drink. He kept hold of the bottle, screwing the top back on as he talked further. 'Now, there is one more clear and obvious destination Cheryl could have gone, and that's into the River Kelvin itself. As you know, it runs right past the subway station. It's fenced off in most places or has a chest-height wall acting as a barrier, but it's still possible she went too close to the river and somehow ended up falling into it. There is no evidence that Cheryl had been drinking, and as far as we know, she isn't on any medication. There is also no suggestion that she is depressed or has any mental health issues. We have made a preliminary search of the river from Wyndford down to the Clyde. Nothing of note, and no one has been found. Of course, she could have been swept further out into the Clyde, but if that's the case, we can only wait and see if she washes up somewhere.'

It was DC Derek Jackson's turn to speak up. 'Is there not quite a lot of debris in the Kelvin around Kelvinbridge? Trees and logs, and so forth. If she had gone into the river, wouldn't it be as likely she would get snagged on something near the subway station instead of being washed all the way down the river and into the Clyde?'

'There is, but over the weekend, there was a lot of water, as in melting snow, coming down from the Campsies at the time. By all accounts, the river had been fast-flowing over the weekend. Similarly, supposing she did go into the water, the freezing temperatures mean she probably wouldn't have lasted long, unfortunately. Of course, we shouldn't get too fixated on the idea she went into the river. Even if that's our most likely explanation for her disappearance, for now. As we speak, search teams are still being deployed as far as Dumbarton in the hope, if that's the right word, that we find her.

'Now, we had no signal from Cheryl's mobile since she was on the train and sent a message to her flatmates to say she was on her way home. Cheryl was carrying a small canvas bag over her shoulder, as seen from the CCTV here as she left Central. Her bank and credit cards are unused, with no sign of any activity whatsoever or any clue as to where she might be. Before I go on, I'd like to get the thoughts of DCI Patterson. Have you any questions, Mike?'

'Have you traced any vehicles parked in or around the station and in the car park?' Patterson asked.

'We have. Most vehicles in the station

car park and South Woodside Road have been accounted for. So far, nothing of significance to report. We'll be checking up on the remaining vehicles as the day progresses. However, you're right. If Cheryl didn't go into the river, she might have been driven away somewhere. Anything else, Mike?'

'Door-to-door enquiries have brought up nothing?'

'Nope, nothing so far. No one has reported seeing or hearing anything unusual, but we have a few no-answers to follow up. It was quite dark when Cheryl left the subway station, and the street lighting around the station isn't great.'

'What about family?' Patterson asked.

'Cheryl has a mother and father who live in Helensburgh. They're currently staying with a friend in Bishopbriggs.'

Patterson nodded as Weaver continued talking.

'OK, for now, we keep searching and following up on any leads. I'm splitting you all into teams of two, and I'll hand out the details shortly. Remember, this is still a missing person's enquiry. Cheryl is still alive, and we need to find her ASAP, so let's just do that.'

Patterson rose with everyone else and, like everyone else, knew it was more than likely Cheryl Kerr was already dead.

Chapter 4

The Most Likely Explanation

As Patterson walked out of the briefing room, Weaver called him over.

'Hey, Mike, how have you been?'

'Good, good, yersel?'

'Fine. Bet it was a surprise seeing me back here.'

'Aye, you could say that. This missing person enquiry doesn't look good.'

'It does not. Actually, there are a couple of things I wanted to run by you if you have the time.'

'Sure, I'd be delighted,' Patterson lied. 'Actually, I have to see Dunard first. Give me half an hour, and I'll be right with you.'

'OK,' Weaver replied smiling, 'I've been given room three as my office. Just pop in when you can.'

Patterson nodded and then headed back to his own office. Saying he had to see Superintendant Dunard had also been a lie.

However, when Patterson returned to his office, there was a note informing him that Dunard did indeed want to see him.

Patterson walked upstairs and knocked on Dunard's door. After being given permission to enter, he did just that.

'Mike, come in, take a seat.' Patterson again did as he was told. 'I just wanted to welcome you back. How are you feeling?'

Dunard was a small, intense man who always gave the impression he was out of his depth, mainly because he was out of his depth.

'Good,' replied Patterson, 'I've been learning more about the Cheryl Kerr case.'

'Yes, that's what I wanted to see you about. For the moment, if you can help Weaver with the case, that would be great. Did you have a nice holiday?'

Yes, I did, thanks. I went with Stephanie to the Maldives.'

'Oooh, the Maldives, eh? Sounds nice.'

'Yes, it was.'

'And Stephanie? How's she keeping?'

Patterson knew the question had a hidden meaning since his boss was more than aware of Stephanie's battle with alcoholism. Patterson's answer had as much hidden meaning as the question.

'Fine, she's been very disciplined.'

'That's good to hear. As I said, it's just to let you know Weaver is the SIO on this disappearance. I thought it best to get him in after his success with Abigail MacDonald.'

'Yes, I heard.'

'Of course, use your own judgement as well.'

'OK, I'll do that, sir,' said Patterson as he rose from his chair.

'And give my love to Steph.'

'Will do,'

Patterson left Dunard's office and walked down to Weaver's temporary office along the corridor from the main incident room. On knocking and entering, Weaver looked up and smiled.

'Mike, didn't think you could make it so soon. Take a seat. I'll just be a moment; got to finish writing this press release.' Waiting for Weaver to finish what he was doing, Patterson noticed how neat everything was on Weaver's desk and around the room, such contrast to Patterson's desk.

Once finished, Weaver looked up. 'Sorry for that; I'm in front of the cameras later. So, did the boss have anything interesting to say?'

'He was just confirming you're in charge, and I should give you as much help as you need.'

'Good, it will be nice to have a helping hand from someone who knows what they are doing.'

'So what're your thoughts on Cheryl Kerr, then?' asked Patterson. 'You think the river is the best bet?'

'I do. How or why remains to be seen, but alas, I feel that is the most likely explanation. It could be as simple as Cheryl leaning over, looking at the river. Glad to be home and all that. Ends up leaning too far over and falls in. Maybe she tripped. Lost her balance. Of course, Cheryl could have been abducted, but it's unlikely. So far, there's no indication of foul play. What are your own thoughts?'

'We know Cheryl couldn't have just vanished into thin air. Something must have happened between leaving the subway station and returning to the flat. If she did fall into the river, I would have expected the diving teams to find some belongings from her canvas bag, the bag itself, or the scarf I believe she was wearing. In my view, if she didn't fall into the river, the most likely explanation is an abduction. I don't believe she would voluntarily disappear. You said you've checked most of the cars in the car park?'

'Most owners have been checked, and there's no one of immediate interest. At least, no one with relevant previous.'

'And nothing at all from her phone?'

'Her last text was sent just before arriving at Central. To her flatmates, saying she would be home soon. Nothing after that.'

'What about her flat? No signs at all she made it back?

'None whatsoever. Besides, Cheryl would have been picked up by CCTV somewhere on the way home, regardless of what way she went.'

'What about the flatmates?'

'They say they were waiting for Cheryl to come home all afternoon and evening.'

'And you trust what they're saying?'

'There's no reason to doubt them. They've both been checked out. They come across as a couple of everyday students.'

Patterson thought it over. If Cheryl didn't end up in the river, and if she wasn't abducted, then she would have returned to the flat. That was the third most likely explanation. Weaver interrupted his thoughts.

'Cheryl's boyfriend, Ryan, is travelling up from Sheffield later this week, by the way.'

'He's not travelling up sooner?'

'Apparently, he can't. Work commitments or something. Anyway, as Dunard says, you have a free rein on this one. Anything you need, just ask. Where would you like to start?'

'I think I'd like to start by visiting her flat in Bank Street. I know you've checked it, but it might give me a better idea of who Cheryl is.'

Weaver pulled open a drawer and took out a set of keys. 'You better have these then. This fob is for the street entrance, the bronze key is for the main door of the flat, and this smaller silver one is for her room. Of course, we've searched the place thoroughly, but see if you can find anything we've missed.'

'What about her computer or laptop?'

'Her computer is still being checked, but so far, most of her online activity was either to do with her studies or her boyfriend down south. From what we can tell so far, her social media activity was surprisingly limited.'

'I'd like to interview the flatmates at some point. What're their names?'

Weaver opened a folder on his desk. Their names are...Jonathan Dunbar and Jenna Taylor. They'll probably be at university this morning, but I can arrange an interview sometime.'

'I'd like that. What are you doing yourself?' Patterson asked.

'I'm reviewing witness statements to see if we could have missed something, and I've got that presser at midday. I'm also going to give Robin Garvey in Anniesland a visit.'

'Robin Garvey? I thought he was locked up.'

'So did I. I just found out he was released from Barlinnie a few weeks back. These pervs seem to be getting out earlier and earlier.'

'Robin Garvey, eh? That could be interesting.'

'I know. He better have a cast-iron alibi for the weekend.'

There was a knock on the door, and a petite, dark-haired woman entered. She walked up to Weaver's desk, looking at a piece of paper she was holding but, on noticing Patterson, she looked at him warily.

'Oh, Leanne, I'd like you to meet DCI Mike

Patterson; I used to work with Mike at this station. Mike, this is DI Davies, Leanne, a trusted colleague I've brought from Cathcart. Patterson gave a small nod towards her while Leanne Davies gave a limited smile in return.

'What can I do for you, Leanne?' asked Weaver.

'It's just to confirm the search areas for today. I can start arranging search teams once these are confirmed. We've got the use of a helicopter for the whole day. I've directed it towards the Clyde downstream unless you want different.' Davies said this with a slight Welsh lilt to her voice. She handed Weaver a couple of sheets of paper which her superior scanned and then signed. 'Yes, that's fine; go ahead and arrange it, thanks.'

Davies nodded and gave a hesitant nod towards Patterson before leaving the office.

'She's one of the best, is Leanne. Such a help on every case.'

'Yes, you need colleagues you can trust 100%. OK, well, as I said, I'll head down to Bank Street. I'll take Simpson with me.'

Patterson stood up and was followed to the door by Weaver. 'Oh, and I meant what I said earlier Mike; it's good to have you back.'

'Likewise, and it's good to be back.' Patterson said, realising he didn't feel it was good to be back one little bit.

Chapter 5

Bank Street

Bank St was a narrow thoroughfare between Great Western Road and University Avenue. It could be described as residential, quaint or sleazy, depending on what mood you were in or what mood the street was in.

On one part of the road were two-storey homes that unsuccessfully asked to be called townhouses. Cheryl's flat was further along, in the middle part of the street that housed tenements on either side. The entrance to Cheryl's tenement inevitably had a security door that added nothing to the aesthetic of the building or to the security of the building either.

Patterson climbed the stairs of the close, Glasgow's inexplicable name for a stairwell, with Simpson following behind. DI Jack Simpson was a well-built man in his mid-twenties with a natural non-threatening demeanour. Although muscular, Simpson was slightly smaller than

Patterson. However, that wasn't surprising given Patterson's six-foot and relatively slim build.

Simpson looked like someone you could trust. Someone you would seek out in a crowd when asking for directions or something more important. His face wasn't one of character but straightforward openness. A native of Manchester, he had been in Glasgow for over three years.

The close was pleasant enough and, by its clean appearance, appeared to have a weekly or fortnightly cleaner. On the first floor, Patterson got the keys out. Although Weaver told him Cheryl's flatmates would probably be at university, Patterson knocked on the door just in case. As expected, there was no answer. However, as Patterson was about to put the bronze Yale key in the lock, the door opened, and there stood a young man in red polka-dot boxer shorts, an unbuttoned white shirt, and a flushed face.

'Oh, hello,' Patterson said, slightly surprised, 'I'm DCI Patterson, Partick CID,' Patterson showed his ID. 'And this is DS Simpson. We're here to look around Cheryl's room.'

The young man didn't react but stared back at the two men as if he didn't understand English. Perhaps he was trying to decide whether they really were policemen regardless of Patterson showing his ID. Eventually, though, and still not saying anything, the young man pulled the door open further to let the two policemen in.

They entered a hallway which was pleasant enough. Not much decoration, but it was clean and reasonably big. The one submission to décor was a tall rubber plant that respectively stood in a cream vase in a far corner of the hallway. Patterson was aware of a strong smell of lavender which was, if not mistaken, possibly hurriedly sprayed air freshener.

Five doors, all in pale yellow, led off the hallway. Presumably, the entrances to three bedsits plus a bathroom and kitchen. Only one of the doors was open, which was undoubtedly the bedsit of the cautious inhabitant who had opened the front door.

The young man was almost good-looking. He had long, thin dark hair that came down in angled lines towards his eyes. The eyes on either side of the long, thin nose were blue and perceptive, scanning the two policemen thoroughly and methodically. He wore black-rimmed glasses, which were designed with the geek in mind.

'I take it you're Jonathan Dunbar?' Simpson asked.

'How do you know that?' Dunbar replied defensively. As he spoke for the first time, his accent was well-spoken and had a tinge of the east coast about it.

'Oh, we know everything,' Simpson said light-heartedly. Dunbar appeared to take the remark seriously. 'I'm joking,' Simpson added quickly. 'From our enquiries, you're obviously one of the flatmates, and unless you're called Jenna Taylor, I take it you must be Jonathan Dunbar. We're not detectives for nothing, you know.'

'You're English,' Dunbar said in a monotone statement kind of way. Simpson had learned not to jump to conclusions on hearing this statement.

'You're obviously a bit of a detective yourself.'

'Whereabouts?' Dunbar asked again in a monotone voice.

'Whereabouts what?' asked Simpson.

'Whereabouts in England you from?'

'Manchester. Born and bred.'

'I've been to Manchester,' Dunbar replied, still in his matter-of-fact way. 'All the best bands come from Manchester.'

Simpson could have used this as an opening to start a conversation with Dunbar and gain his confidence. Yet, Simpson had no interest in or knowledge of music.

'Do they?' was Simpson's best reply. Instead of an opening into a conversation, the question was an opening into an awkward silence which Patterson decided to put to bed.

'Right,' Patterson said, 'I hate to break up a budding friendship, but if you could just tell us which is Cheryl's room, Jonathan, that would be great.'

'I haven't got the key,' Dunbar replied.

'That's all right; I've got a key.' Patterson held up the silver key between his thumb and forefinger. 'Now, which room is Cheryl's?'

Before Dunbar could answer, a young woman appeared from the open doorway, leaned against the door frame and crossed her arms. She was covered in an oversized yellow and blue tartan pyjama top that just reached below her thighs. She had long dark hair and even darker eyes giving a tinge of Latino about her.

'Hello!' she said, bright and breezy. 'I couldn't help overhearing. If you're looking for Cheryl's room, it's that one in the middle.' She nodded in the direction of the door across from her. 'I'm Jenna, by the way, Jenna Taylor. Mr charisma here and myself are Cheryl's flatmates.'

'We thought you'd both be at uni today,' Simpson said. He was instantly curious about her, although he couldn't say why at that point.

'We took the day off, what with everything going on and stuff.' Jenna replied, smiling, and she looked at him as if weighing him up for what could have been a multitude of reasons.

'As you also probably heard, we're going to look around Cheryl's room,' Patterson explained, 'but since you're here, we'd like a chat with you both afterwards, if you don't mind.'

'We've already talked to the police, your colleagues, ' said Jenna. If Patterson wasn't mistaken, she said, *your colleagues* in a slightly sarcastic way.

'Yes, but we'd just like to go over a couple of things,'

'No sweat,' Jenna said. Her voice was more Glasgow West End than East End. 'Come along, Jonathan, let's allow the policemen to get on with their job.' She pronounced *job* in a slightly mocking way again. It appeared to be Jenna's manner to always talk in this fashion.

Both flatmates turned, entered Dunbar's room and shut the door.

Patterson and Simpson looked at each other, with Simpson raising an eyebrow before Patterson walked across and placed the key into the lock of the indicated door. With a turn and a click, the door opened.

Cheryl's room was unremarkable, a typical student's bedsit, neither completely neat nor messy. The air was noticeably cold. The room had a single bed with a yellow duvet imprinted with green birds. There was a large cupboard, a small work desk, and a bookcase filled with mostly technical and chemistry books. Another smaller bookcase was filled with well-read fiction books. Some ornaments and plants were placed around the rather small room. A conspicuous space was apparent on one of the tables, presumably where Cheryl's computer was once set. As other officers had already gone through the accommodation, Patterson didn't expect to find anything of interest.

There were a couple of posters on the wall, one with a polar bear, the other with a sunset and both with an environmental message. There were also a couple of framed photos on the work desk; one of a middle-aged couple, presumably Cheryl's parents, and one of a cat. All very normal and expected. The window, which looked down onto the backcourt, was slightly open, and it was this that gave the room a chill. It also meant that the hum of traffic could be heard from Great Western Road.

Simpson pulled open a drawer. There were some stationery bits, ticket stubs to concerts and clubs, batteries, hair clips and pens, and some scribbled on scraps of paper. Patterson read through the scraps, but there was nothing of interest.

Simpson bent down and looked under the bed, which resulted in his superior giving him a wary look.

'Really?'

'Well, it has been known to happen,' Simpson replied, smiling, as he stood up again. Patterson had to agree, and he now looked closer at the large, old-fashioned wardrobe, which along with the bed, dominated the small room. He turned the dark copper key poking out of the lock and then tried to pull open the doors, but they remained shut. He pulled again, but the doors remained jammed.

'Go into the kitchen and get a knife so I can prise these doors open,' Patterson instructed, and Simpson left before coming back with a small but strong-looking knife.

Patterson positioned the knife between the doors and tried to wedge them open, but they still refused to budge. Why wouldn't the doors open? Patterson tried again, this time with more force and less consideration about breaking the lock. The doors loudly sprung open, and both officers looked down at what was in the wardrobe.

In a small wicker basket were assorted shoes, sandals, trainers and a couple of handbags. Mostly bright coloured dresses, blouses, jeans and trousers hung from hangers. Patterson looked through the clothes and shoes but again saw nothing of interest.

Patterson shut the door as best he could to hide his damaging DIY. 'Come on, Let's go talk to Pinky and Perky.'

Both officers walked out of Cheryl's room, closed and locked the door, and then knocked on the door of Dunbar's room.

Dunbar opened the door with the same non-expression expression he had before.

'It's only us,' Simpson said cheerfully. 'May we come in?' Patterson added, and only then did Jonathan Dunbar slowly open the door fully for both officers to enter.

Simpson and Patterson entered and found

themselves standing in a messy, slightly foul-smelling room. Here, the lavender air freshener had been beaten into submission by other heavyweight odours. What was that smell? Patterson thought. It seemed a mix of sweat and something else it was probably best not to identify.

The room seemed much bigger than Cheryl's, and the impression of space was helped by large bay windows in front of which a large battered-looking tan settee was placed.

The grate of a once-working coal fire of Victorian times was now filled by a run-of-the-mill gas fire. A single bed was in the back corner of the room next to the door. Above this, a bookshelf ran the length of one wall. It was filled with an array of technical manuals, hardbacks, tattered paperbacks, toy figures and a variety of junk.

Jenna Taylor was already sitting on the bed while Jonathan went and sat down on one arm of the battered-looking couch. Simpson brought out a notepad and noticed a slight mocking look from Jenna as he did this.

'We would just like to go over some details about Cheryl,' said Patterson. 'I know you've already given my colleagues information, but we just want to clarify a few things.'

Simpson decided to wander towards the window where he waited with notepad and pen, ready for Patterson to ask the first question.

'When was the last time you saw Cheryl?' asked Patterson.

Patterson was looking at Dunbar when he asked this first question, but Taylor answered before Dunbar could.

'The last time we saw her was the morning she left for Sheffield. Last Monday. Her train was leaving at just after eight. I think Cheryl must have gotten up around six. She was so excited, bless her. I got up to make her breakfast, but Cheryl said she only wanted some toast, butter, and a coffee.'

'Is that what you remember as well, Jonathan?' Again, before Dunbar could answer, Taylor answered for him. 'Jonathan was still in bed. He didn't see Cheryl that morning.'

'If you don't mind, Jenna, I'd prefer Jonathan answered for himself.'

Jenna's smile didn't waver, but she was clearly a bit miffed at being told what to do.

'Yes, that's right,' Dunbar answered. 'I was sleeping; I didn't see her leave.'

'So, the last time you actually saw her was when?'

'The night before. We were just in here. Chilling out, listening to music and stuff.'

'And when was the last time you heard from her? Did she phone while she was away?' The question was again directed at Dunbar.

Dunbar looked across at Taylor before answering. 'I think she phoned on the Thursday,

Thursday night, I think it was. She spoke to Jenna, though.'

'Yes, that's right,' Jenna confirmed. 'She phoned on Thursday night to say she was returning on Saturday. She said she would see us in the afternoon sometime, and I told her we could get a takeaway that night, on the Saturday night, I mean.'

'So that was the last time you talked to her?'

'Talked yes. She texted us a few times as well. Just daft stuff. Saying hi, nothing important.'

'When she phoned, how did Cheryl seem?'

Taylor shrugged. 'Fine. Excited. She said she had some news to tell us.'

'News? What sort of news?'

'She didn't say. She said she'd tell me later on.'

'And you have no idea what she could have meant?'

'No.'

'What about you, Jonathan? Any ideas?'

'No, I guess it was something about Ryan.'

'When did you first realise something was wrong with Cheryl not turning up?'

'I would say it was later on Saturday she was due back,' replied Jenna. 'She texted us from the train to say it was just pulling into Motherwell, so it would be in Glasgow within the next hour. I mean, we had been waiting for her to arrive all afternoon, and she didn't turn up, but then I looked online and saw the train was late, and I knew it was snowing heavily down south, so at first, I thought it was no big deal.'

'What time was this? When she texted from the train?'

'Must have been about three.'

'Have you got your phone here? Have you still got her texts?'

'I deleted them.'

'Deleted them? So soon?'

'The memory on my phone is shit, scuse my language, so I usually delete my messages as soon as.'

'So, did you not call her? See where she was?'

'I did. Once. I called her mobile, but there was no answer.'

'When did you call her, exactly?'

'I think it was just after six. I sent a text message too. Asked her where she was, but there was no reply. I assumed she must have had her phone in her bag and didn't hear or see it.'

'You still weren't overly worried at that time?'

'A little, but like I said, I knew the train was delayed, so even though it later said the train had arrived, I assumed it had still been delayed again or something. When it got to around seven, then I started to wonder where Cheryl could have got to. It doesn't take that long to get here from Central. But, then, I just thought she may have gone somewhere else first.'

'Where?' Simpson asked.

'Dunno, really. I just thought she could have met someone from uni and gone for a drink or something, but even then, I did find it strange she hadn't phoned or texted to let us know.'

'Is that the same for you, Jonathan?'

Jonathan looked across at Jenna again before answering. 'Yeah. I didn't really think anything of it, either. Jenna was more worried than I was.'

'You didn't call the police?'

'And say what? Of course, we didn't call the police,' Jenna answered, 'At that time, she was just a bit late, that's all. She could have gone anywhere, and anyway, there was not much we could say.'

'What about Ryan? You didn't think to call him?'

'Ryan? What could he do? He was in Sheffield. To be honest, I didn't know what we should do. When it got to after ten, I got really worried.' Patterson noticed that Jenna was constantly smiling as she spoke and listened.

'So, what did you do in the meantime?' Patterson looked at Dunbar.

'As Jenna said, there was not much we could do, so we just watched the telly and waited. We were going to get a takeaway but didn't want to get one before Cheryl arrived. So we sat around hoping Cheryl would turn up, drunk or something.'

'For the record, what did you watch?'

'Watch?'

'Yes, watch. What did you watch while you were waiting?'

Dunbar looked at Jenna again.

'It was...that thing. Oh, I forget its name.' Jenna said.

'What thing?' Patterson queried further.

'I can't remember now. My mind wasn't really focusing. I was too worried about Cheryl.' Jonathan said.

'I thought you said you weren't really worried?'

'Yes and no,' Jonathan answered, 'I guess I was worried as time went on.'

'So, you can't remember any programme you watched?'

Jonathan shook his head. 'Well, no, does it matter? I don't see what that has to do with anything.'

Patterson looked at Simpson. 'OK, no matter. That's all for now. We'll probably be in touch again. If you can think of anywhere Cheryl may have gone, of course, anything at all, let us know immediately. Hopefully, there's an explanation for all this, and Cheryl will turn up safe and sound. Thanks for your time, for now.'

Jonathan rose from the edge of the settee as both policemen walked towards the door.

'There's no need to get up; we'll see

ourselves out, thanks.' Patterson said, and Jonathan dutifully sat down again.

Patterson and Simpson left the room, then the flat, and went down the close. Once back in their car. Simpson looked at Patterson and asked. 'Well, what do we think?'

'They're lying.'

'You think?' asked Simpson, slightly surprised at this conclusion.

'At the very least, I think they're hiding something. The way Dunbar kept looking across at Taylor before answering any question as if he was scared to give a wrong answer and considering her flatmate is missing, I found Jenna smiling all the time, strange.'

'Well, they've been thoroughly checked out,' said Simpson, 'and nothing has turned up in their past or present to suggest they have anything to hide.'

'Aye, maybe,' Patterson said, 'Anyway, let's get back to the station and see if there have been any developments.'

Chapter 6

Homecoming

On returning to Partick station, Patterson and Simpson were lost in their thoughts about the two flatmates. As they headed up University Avenue, Patterson turned towards Simpson again.

'So you're telling me you didn't think there was anything curious about those two?'

'I didn't say that,' Simpson replied. 'As it happens, I thought there was a lot curious about those two. As you said, Jenna seemed strangely unperturbed about the disappearance of Cheryl. Of course, she may have just been putting on a brave face, but it was almost as if she knew Cheryl was safe.'

'That's what I was thinking.'

'Yeah?' said Simpson as the car headed down the other side of University Avenue towards the busy junction with Byres Road.

'Let's just say that Cheryl made it back to the flat,' Patterson said.

As the car pulled up to the traffic lights, Simpson looked at his superior, 'That's unlikely; we've checked every CCTV camera around Bank St. There is no sign of Cheryl approaching her flat from any direction.'

'It's unlikely but not impossible. CCTV doesn't cover every square inch of the route back. Cheryl could have made it to Bank St without getting caught by a camera. There must be several blind spots on the way.'

'So what are you suggesting? Cheryl made it back to the flat, and Jonathan and Jenna have something to do with Cheryl's disappearance? If that's the case, why don't we take them down the station? Interview them formally.'

'Because it's just a thought at the moment. For now, I want you to go over their statements for me. See, if they have said anything today which doesn't tally with what they have said before.'

Back at the station, there were no new developments regarding Cheryl's disappearance. Search parties were still combing areas where Cheryl had been known to have gone in the past, friends past and present located, but nothing, no one, was found. A quick chat with Weaver revealed that his visit to Robin Garvey hadn't brought any joy. For the whole weekend, Garvey had been in Dundee to watch Rangers play Dundee United. He had stayed overnight at a mate's house in the Tayside city for a drinking session, all of which was verified by the homeowner and other travelling mates.

So, for the remainder of the day, Patterson caught up with more paperwork that had wound its way onto his desk. Meanwhile, Simpson went over Dunbar and Taylor's past statements looking for chinks in consistency.

It was nearing six o'clock when Weaver came in and told everyone to call it a night and start again in the morning. Patterson walked up to Simpson to ask if he had found anything worthwhile regarding Dunbar and Taylor.

'Nothing,' said Simpson. 'The statements they've already given are basically the same as what they said to us. When Cheryl was due back, they were in the house watching TV. Still doesn't say what they were watching, but I guess it's a small point.'

'You think?' Patterson sighed, but he knew Simpson was right.

Patterson was accompanied by Pettigrew out of the building. 'So, how was your first day back?'

'As good as can be expected. It would be even better if we could get a lead on this Cheryl case.'

'Too right,' said Pettigrew, knowing that every hour she was gone, it was less likely she would be found alive.

As Patterson stepped outside into the freezing night air, the ground frost reflected the orange sodium streetlights, and everyone's breath became visible clouds of warm air. The officers hurried to their respective cars and switched on the heating. Through the car park gates, a steady stream of dipped headlights could be seen passing by on the main road.

Patterson sat in his car, waiting for the heating to get up to speed, and his thoughts again drifted to Cheryl's flatmates. Experience told him that if something was bugging him, it was usually bugging him for a reason. Was it something they said? Something in their relationship? What were the dynamics of Dunbar and Taylor being an item and Cheryl sharing a flat with them? Could something have happened in that respect? Jealousy? An affair?

Patterson continued to ask countless questions as he drove out of the car park gates and slipped into the conveyor belt of traffic on Dumbarton Road. He knew there was more to learn about those two flatmates.

Patterson switched on the drivetime radio show. 2008 had been a difficult year for many, and the news reflected this. It still talked about cutbacks and hardship, with the financial crisis earlier in the year still having a long way to run. One news item featured a speech by the newly elected US President, Barack Obama. In many ways, though, the news never changed. People struggled, politicians were elected or resigned but still made the same promises that were never kept. Patterson's thoughts wandered over the news to Stephanie and getting home, and another question struck him. Would Stephanie be sober? He immediately chastised himself for asking that question. Yet, he couldn't help it. Yes, Stephanie had managed to stay sober for over two months now. However, in spite of himself, he always wondered how long it would last. Patterson forced himself to focus on the remainder of the drivetime show. Apparently, Scotland had lost a football match. Again, in many ways, the news never changed.

Once home, as soon as Patterson opened the door and entered the hallway, he knew Stephanie was still sober. For one thing, there was an acceptable level of noise; the radio was quietly playing. A drunk Stephanie would be accompanied by loud music or a foreboding silence. He could also smell the welcoming aroma of dinner being made and hear the tea-time sounds of plates clinking and water boiling.

Patterson opened the kitchen door further, and Stephanie embraced him as she always did these past few weeks. As if she, too, was pleased she had made it through the day sober till her husband returned. Patterson held Stephanie tight and kissed her on the cheek.

He took his jacket off and loosened his tie as he sat at the table. His wife handed him a glass of orange squash, his aperitif of choice. Patterson immediately relaxed, and tiredness crawled over him like an impatient child who had been waiting for him to come home.

'So,' Stephanie asked, 'how was your day?'

'Aye, OK. Just the usual. Well, almost the usual. Rafe Weaver's back.'

'Rafe Weaver? How come he's back?'

'We've got a missing person enquiry. Remember on the news this morning they talked about that young woman who went missing at Kelvinbridge?'

'Aye,'

'Well, that one. Weaver's in charge of it. I've been seconded to help him, as it were.'

'So, she's still not been found, then? That's not good.'

'No, it's not good at all. That's why Dunard wants everyone available to try and find her. There is still a chance she's alive. After all, it's only been two days. A lot of other stuff has been put on the back burner till she's located.'

'So is Rafe back permanent then?'

'No, as far as I know, it's only temporary until this woman is found.'

'What's her name again?'

'Cheryl Kerr. Disappeared after leaving Kelvinbridge Subway station on Saturday, not far from her home. I had a chat with her flatmates today. Bit of a strange pair.'

'In what way, strange?'

'Not too sure, to be honest. Just their manner. Something about them.' Again,

Patterson pondered what it was about the pair that bothered him. 'Apart from that, everything is the same as usual. Though Claire was telling me she's moved address, bought her own place.'

'Good for her. Where's she staying now?'

'Jordanhill.'

'Well, remind me to get a home warming gift for her.'

'Aye.'

'I've got some news myself,' said Stephanie.

'Oh?' replied Patterson apprehensively.

'Aisling and Callum are coming home for Christmas.'

'Really? That's great news. Both of them?'

'Yes, both. Aisling called me. They're travelling up together on the twenty-third. She said they'll be staying till New Year.'

Patterson and Stephanie had two children, Aisling and Callum. Both were at university in England, Aisling at Southampton and Callum at Norwich. Aisling was in her late teens and Callum in his early twenties.

'It'll be nice having them here for Christmas,' Patterson said.

'Won't it just.'

'Anyway, what's for dinner? I'm famished.'

'Well, since it's your first day back at work, I've made your favourite, a roast chicken dinner.'

'With stuffing?' Patterson asked hopefully.

'With stuffing,' Stephanie confirmed.

Patterson smiled. It was good to have his

wife, his real and original wife, back. It was something he appreciated every day.

Chapter 7

The Chase

Tommy Beaton sat bolt upright, taking a sharp intake of breath as if violently shocked into life by lightning. He frantically looked around in the dark, trying to figure out where he was before realising he was at home and in his own bed. Gradually, his breathing and his pulse slowed. Thank heavens. It had just been a nightmare, just another vivid nightmare.

Tommy had dreamt he was being chased. It was the same every night. He was always being chased. At first, he didn't know who or what exactly was chasing him. All he knew was he had to run and run as fast as he could. He had to run for his life.

The problem was that the faster he tried to run, the slower he seemed to go. As his pursuer gradually gained on him, the panic set in. Nevertheless, Tommy would try even harder and try to run faster and faster. Alas, it was to no avail. Tommy would always end up going slower and slower. There would inevitably come a moment when he could feel his pursuer upon his shoulder, reaching out to grab him. At that moment, the fear would be unbearable, and Tommy knew he had to turn around and see who or what was chasing him.

Tonight it was Phillip Schofield.

Every night it was the same nightmare. Yet every night, he had a different pursuer. One night his pursuer would be Claudia Winkleman. Next would be Graham Norton, then Bradley Walsh, Piers Morgan, Gordon Ramsey, Anne Robinson, Gary Lineker...

Tommy gradually calmed down, wiping the sweat off his forehead with the edge of the duvet. Looking at the digital clock, he could see it was 3:21 AM. He leaned over and clicked on the bedside light before pulling the duvet off his legs and getting up off the bed. God, he had to get a grip. Were all these nightmares simply about the fear of being caught?

Tommy walked slowly through to the kitchenette, his bare feet freezing on the linoleum floor. He opened the door to the fridge and took out a carton of orange juice, its corner roughly torn off. Taking loud gulps of the cold, thick liquid, Tommy soon felt better. He understood he was just letting his fears get the better of him. He had nothing to worry about—he had covered his tracks. The chances of him getting caught were – well, slim.

Tommy put the orange carton back in the fridge and walked back to the bedroom. He lay down on the bed, conscious of the cold, his sweat-covered skin making him feel even colder. Tommy switched off the bedside light and laid his head back on the pillow before pulling the duvet up to his shoulders.

Then from somewhere in the room, he heard a growl.

It was a faint growl at first before the noise gradually got louder and louder. As the noise became more apparent, Tommy now found it comforting instead of frightening as he realised what the sound was—the low rumble of the night maintenance train passing underneath from the subway deep below ground. As regular as his nightmares, during the wee small hours, if awake, Tommy would usually hear the passing of the battery-powered vehicle laboriously trundling over the subway tracks as it checked for faults.

The sound of the night train slowly faded into the distance, and Tommy began to feel sleepy again. As he let sleep overcome him, he reassured himself that everything would be all right. He had nothing to worry about—nothing at all. Then he suddenly opened his eyes again.

Cheryl Kerr. That was her name. On the news, they said her name was Cheryl Kerr. God almighty, what had he done?

Chapter 8

Riverside

Pettigrew stirred in the early morning dawn. It was so nice under the comforting cover of duvet and darkness: yet there was a persistent noise pulling her from sleep—a ringing noise demanding that she open her eyes.

Pettigrew eventually gave in, and the noise, she realised as she slowly gained consciousness, was her mobile ringing, vibrating across the sideboard like a baby screaming for attention. Pettigrew reached across and grabbed it, waking it from its nightmare. She pressed the answer button, put the phone to her ear and heard Patterson's voice.

'Get down to Benalder Street ASAP.'

'Sir?'

'They've just pulled a body from the River Kelvin.'

Forty minutes later, Pettigrew turned left into Benalder Street and found that the road was cordoned off just after Castle Street. She could see a fire and rescue engine further up the road, a couple of squad cars, plus various vehicles of official personnel who had woken up faster than Pettigrew. She parked up and got out of her car. The bitter morning cold was virtually unopposed as the sun was still wondering whether to rise, and Pettigrew shoved her hands deep into her coat pockets. After showing her warrant card to the uniformed officer doing traffic duty, she walked on.

She crossed through a gap in a grey metal fence covered in early morning frost like everything else in the vicinity. With her fur-lined boots, she hacked her way through thick, stubborn grass and weeds semi-luminous with a glaze of snow and made her way down an embankment towards the River Kelvin.

In the half-darkness of almost dawn, Pettigrew could still make out the tall thin silhouette of DCI Patterson and the smaller, bulkier DI Simpson. The outline of DCI Weaver was also visible nearby, giving instructions to a group of uniformed officers. The condensation from everyone's breath looked like they were having a smoking party. Most activity was closer to the river's edge, where a small group of firefighters stood in a huddle beneath a powerful, buzzing spotlight. They looked on at a couple of divers who stood half-submerged in the relatively fast-flowing, freezing waters surveying a long ago fallen tree trunk.

Alone and further up the embankment, and as if being ignored at its own party, was the body pulled from the river, covered by and zipped inside a dark green tarpaulin bag.

As Pettigrew walked up behind Simpson, she heard him mutter in his familiar Mancunian tones, 'It's bloody Baltic this morning.'

Pettigrew couldn't disagree. She came around into her colleague's line of view and gave a nod as way of saying hello.

'I take it it's Cheryl?' Pettigrew asked.

'Have a look for yourself,' Patterson replied, nodding in the direction of the lonely tarpaulin bag.

Pettigrew gingerly walked over the crisp ground and unzipped the top of the bag. With the aid of the spotlight illumination, Pettigrew found herself looking down at the face of a young woman who generally matched the description of Cheryl Kerr. Her face seemed remarkably fresh. Her eyes were closed, her blonde hair swept back, matted and wet. It gave her the look of a fashion model, a look her chalk-white skin and blue-tinged lips only enhanced. Pettigrew unzipped the bag a little more. Cheryl was wearing a black and white jacket with jeans and ankle-length tan leather boots. Pettigrew lifted the blouse and saw that Chery's body was covered in cuts, scratches and bruises. A relatively large ragged hole in the side of her blouse led to a relatively large puncture wound in the side of her waist, the skin hanging open and loose. Pettigrew zipped up the bag and walked back over to her colleagues.

'Well?' Patterson asked.

'Aye, it certainly looks like Cheryl, all right,' said Pettigrew. 'Has death been declared?'

'Yes. Doctor's been.' said Patterson.

'Pathologist?'

'On her way,' Simpson said.

'Looks like she's wearing the same clothes as when she disappeared,' Pettigrew said.

'Yeah, they also found a long green scarf nearby wrapped around a fallen log in the river.' Simpson added.

'Which suggests she may well have fallen in the river the day she disappeared,' said Pettigrew

'So you didn't notice, then?' said Patterson.

'Notice what?'

'The lines around her wrists and ankles. They seem to have been made by a ligature of some kind, a thin rope or cord,' said Simpson.

'No, I didn't,' Pettigrew said, surprised.

'They're quite fresh too,' added Patterson. It looks like she was tied up, and I'd say she was stripped naked and then dressed again after being murdered.'

'What makes you say that?' asked Pettigrew; she felt she was constantly trying to catch up with Patterson's thoughts.

'For one thing,' Patterson explained, 'her top is on back to front, and her body is covered in scratches made directly to the skin. Yet, apart from the large puncture wound and the hole in her blouse, her clothes are intact. There are also cuts and bruises on her legs under her jeans. I doubt all those injuries occurred when she was in the river. In my opinion, this wasn't an accidental death. Cheryl Kerr was murdered.'

'It doesn't look like she's been in the water that long, either,' said Simpson.

'No,' Patterson agreed. 'What's today's date?

'The 2nd,' replied Pettigrew.

'And she went missing when? Saturday, the 28th? No, it doesn't look like she's been in the water for over three days.'

'So you reckon she was dumped here?' Simpson asked.

'Or somewhere upstream,' Patterson replied, 'One of the divers said she was impaled on that tree trunk. So that wound in her side probably happened when she smashed into the thick stub sticking out. She would have been travelling at some speed in this current. As you said, Jack, it doesn't appear she's been in the water that long. In fact, it wouldn't surprise me either if her death happened in the last few hours.'

'If that's the case, why has she been missing for over three days?' asked Pettigrew.

'That's one of the first questions we need to answer,' said Patterson as all three officers started watching DCI Weaver walk towards them. Unlike everyone else, Weaver was only wearing a very light jacket. However, he didn't seem affected by the cold or suspected Patterson, he pretended he didn't.

'Morning, guys. How we all doing?' Weaver said in a chirpy voice.

'Who found her?' Pettigrew asked.

'That lady over there,' Weaver replied, pointing to a youngish-looking woman wrapped in a silver thermal blanket given by the fire service. 'She was jogging across the bridge just before six this morning, glanced over and noticed what looked like a dummy lodged on that fallen tree trunk. Curious, she came down to check and saw it was a body. Called the police, a patrol came down, then fire and rescue, and then the diving team to recover her.'

'So what happens now?' Pettigrew said.

'Well, once the pathologist comes down,' Patterson answered. 'Hopefully, she can give us an approximate time of death and any other titbits which may help us. It looks like Cheryl, but we'll need a couple of people to formally identify her at some point.'

'Best get the parents to do that,' Weaver said. 'You said they're staying in Bishopbriggs? Simpson, arrange for them to come down the mortuary sometime.'

'The poor parents. It's a cruel world sometimes,' Pettigrew said.

A silence fell upon the group. The hell the

parents were going through was going to reach a new level of anguish that would last the rest of their lives.

'Listen,' said Weaver. 'I'm the SIO. I'll break the news to the parents. Damn…' Weaver realised something, which made him pause for a moment. 'Of course, Henshaw's not available now, is she? We'll need to get in touch with a new FLO.'

Julie Henshaw was the family liaison officer who, until now, had been assisting Cheryl's parents during the missing person enquiry.

Julie Henshaw not being available was news to Patterson. 'What's wrong with Julie?' he asked.

'She had an accident yesterday; somebody rammed into the back of her car.'

'Is she all right?' said Patterson, concerned.

'Oh, she will be, thank God. She has some whiplash injuries, but luckily nothing more. Still bad enough for her to be off work for a while. The bugger who rammed into her drove off without stopping. I thought you knew,' said Weaver.

'No, I didn't. So Julie's not available then?' asked Patterson

'No,' said Weaver. He then spoke in the direction of Pettigrew. Didn't you say your regular FLO is coming back from sick leave? Booth, is it?'

'Yes,' said Pettigrew, 'Emma Booth, she

phoned yesterday to say she was available. Bit of good timing, really, now that Julie is indisposed.'

'Emma Booth?' asked Patterson.

'Yes, you know Booth, sir. Actually, she's been off work around the same amount of time you have; not sure what was up with her,' she said to Patterson before turning towards Weaver. 'You'll like her, sir. She can head up with you to the parents. In fact, I'll give her a call now.' Pettigrew walked a short distance from the group and brought out her mobile phone.

Patterson had managed to forget Emma Booth since he had returned to work. As such, he had managed to convince himself there was nothing to worry about regarding her. Yet....

Pettigrew came back. 'Emma Booth is available, sir. She says if you give her a call beforehand, she'll meet you outside the parents' house. I'll give you her number later.'

'Good,' said Weaver. 'I'll—'

'Morning!'

All four officers turned to see the pathologist Tasmina Rana walking toward them. 'Blooming freezing, innit?' she said. 'Traffic's murder, there's still them roadworks going on at Charing Cross. No workmen, though, as per usual.'

Tasmina Rana was a petite bundle of upbeat energy and enthusiasm. Even in the earliest stages of dawn, her dark skin and jet-black hair seemed to radiate good health.

'Tas, we've been eagerly awaiting your presence,' Weaver said.

Patterson looked at Weaver. *Tas?* He didn't realise Weaver knew Tasmina, let alone knew her well enough to call her Tas. In fact, no one, as far as Patterson was aware, called Tasmina Tas.

'Nice to be popular,' said the pathologist smiling, yet on spotting the body bag, Rana's smile faded as she was reminded why she was there. 'Just give us a chance to get set up,' said Rana as, with her large briefcase, she strode toward the body.

As Tasmina's colleagues waited for her to do her tests, they stood in a semi-circle freezing in the pre-dawn cold.

'We'll need this whole area cordoned off,' said Patterson.

'Already done. Cheryl, if it is Cheryl, was probably dumped up river though,' said Weaver.

'So she could have been dumped anywhere. The Kelvin goes all the way to the Campsies,' said Pettigrew.

'I doubt she was dumped that far up; I feel it would be unlikely she would travel this far down. She would have ended up snagged somewhere further up the river,' said Patterson.

'No, I would guess it was somewhere no further than Maryhill,' agreed Weaver.

The officers then discussed what preliminary actions should now be taken regarding the murder investigation. They didn't have to wait long before Rana stood up and walked back across to her colleagues.

'OK,' said Rana. 'What I can tell you initially is what you've probably worked out for yourselves. This was no accidental death. There is severe bruising and lacerations on her front and back, and indications, going by the bruising on the inside of her thighs, that she has been sexually assaulted or raped. She also appears to have multiple broken bones. There are also marks around her wrists and ankles made by some thin cord cutting into her skin. Impossible to tell the cause of her death, but at this stage, going by the severe beating she had, probably blunt force trauma, though don't quote me on that. If you want to know the time of death, that's tricky too. The cold water could have preserved her somewhat, but for a quick guesstimate, I would say she was murdered in the last six to twelve hours. She definitely hasn't been dead that long. I can give you a more definite time once the autopsy is done.'

'Any idea of when the autopsy will be?' asked Weaver.

'What's this, Tuesday? Probably won't be till Thursday, I'm afraid. Thursday afternoon, I'd say. We're chock a block at the minute.'

'Thursday? This is top priority Tas; don't suppose there's any chance of getting it done tomorrow?' asked Weaver.

'Tomorrow? Listen, I'll see what I can do

since it's for you, Rafe, but I'm sure you've more than enough to get on with in the meantime.'

Weaver nodded. 'OK, best get back to the station for now. '

'Aye, it looks like we have a murder investigation to begin,' said Patterson.

As Tasmina Rana began to walk back to the body bag and retrieve her instruments, the other officers turned to walk towards their cars.

'By the way,' added Rana turning to Weaver, 'Are you no' freezing with just that jacket on? Why don't you wear an overcoat like every other sane person around here?'

It was Patterson's turn to smile as Weaver didn't answer.

However, Patterson's smile faded as he glanced at the dark green tarpaulin bag on the river bank and thought of the human being inside. Cheryl Kerr was still that human being, no longer alive, a life that ended way before it should have ended. Patterson knew he would do everything possible to bring her murderer to justice.

Chapter 9

Changing Lives Forever

Tasmina Rana was right. Weaver and his team had more than enough to get on with until the autopsy took place. Weaver's first task was informing the parents of the news they had dreaded hearing since Cheryl had first gone missing.

A body had been found, and there was every indication it was their daughter, Cheryl.

Outside the modest home in Bishopbriggs where the parents were temporarily staying, Weaver met the new family liaison officer for the case, Emma Booth. He immediately liked her, as she did him. At the same time, they didn't say much to each other apart from quickly going over and acknowledging protocol. Pausing for a moment outside the front door, they looked at each other before Weaver chapped on the door. Mrs Kerr opened the door with Cheryl's father inquisitively looking over her shoulder.

In effect, the news of Cheryl's death was

informed with the combination of 'May we come in?' and the grim demeanour of the two officers.

As such, Mr and Mrs Kerr simply turned and silently walked away from the door. By the time the two officers entered the living room, both parents were sitting on the edge of the settee, holding each other's hands, bracing themselves for what was to come.

There were no screams or hysterics in response to the news. Mrs Kerr slowly let her head fall onto her husband's shoulder and then quietly began crying.

We're terribly sorry.

More words of condolence were spoken, along with answers to the father's polite questions. Where? How? When? Weaver patiently answered each question as best he could in a softly spoken voice matching that of the father. Booth, meanwhile, provided as much comfort to the parents as her experience and natural humanity had taught her.

Weaver asked if one or both could come to the mortuary later to formally identify Cheryl. For both parents, this immediately gave rise to a faint hope that perhaps the body found wasn't Cheryl and it was all just some kind of unfortunate coincidence. DCI Weaver then left as Booth stayed, giving more comfort and support before accompanying the parents to the mortuary later that afternoon.

At the mortuary, when the sheet was pulled

back, it was then that the screams started. The mother broke down, her legs giving way, awkwardly being held up by both Weaver and the father as Booth looked on. The father himself was now quietly sobbing. He looked at Weaver and nodded, a necessary act and an unnecessary one.

Their instant grief had been the true act of acknowledgement.

Back at the station, Weaver informed the team what they already knew; the woman found battered and bruised in the River Kelvin that morning was indeed Cheryl Kerr.

The incident room had a sombre mood for the rest of the day. Tasks were quietly assigned and carried out. The faint hope of finding Cheryl Kerr alive was gone. For that day, they were simply playing out time in a game that had already been lost.

At just after seven, taking note of the dejected mood in the office, Weaver called time and told everyone to come back in the morning. Along with his colleagues, Patterson was subdued as he finished up for the day. There was noticeably less talk on the way to the car park, no invitations to go for a drink or well-worn, in-house jokes between workmates.

Now, the task wasn't to find Cheryl Kerr; it was to find who murdered Cheryl Kerr.

Chapter 10

The Smell of Murder

Weaver asked Patterson if he would like to accompany him to the autopsy of Cheryl Kerr, and Patterson agreed. Walking through the double doors and entering the autopsy room, the two officers were surprised to find that Tasmina Rana wasn't there. In her place was Rob Cooper, a forensic pathologist with a reputation for being excellent at his job. By his side was the deputy pathologist, there to make sure Rob's findings were all present and correct.

The assistant pathologist was an older man in his forties whom the two officers hadn't seen before. Rob raised a hand in greeting as the two officers entered, 'Sorry, gentlemen, you've missed the action; I had to start early as we have a lot on today.'

Missing the autopsy wasn't a disappointment for either officer, as they were more interested in the result than seeing the game.

'Where's Tasmina?' Patterson asked.

'She's been called away to another case,' said Rob. 'We're stretched to the limit here. No Mean City is doing itself proud. This is John, by the way,' Rob said, introducing his assistant, who gave a friendly nod in their direction.' John has been brought in from Paisley to help. Help which is greatly appreciated, I may add.' Rob smiled in John's direction. 'Tasmina asked me to carry this one out for you. She also told me that if either of you gives me any problems, she'll have your guts for garters.'

Cooper had a very cheery demeanour. This wasn't unusual; in Patterson's experience, pathologists tended to be exceptionally upbeat and cheerful. No doubt it was some defence mechanism, or perhaps they just appreciated life more, seeing the reality of death every day.

The Glasgow City mortuary, perhaps ironically, had long outlived its sell-by date. It was a Victorian building near Glasgow Green that was barely adequate for its purpose. There was talk, there was always talk, about the forensic pathology department moving to a new, more modern site. Whether it would ever come to anything remained to be seen.

Cooper looked over at the two men once more. 'Be with you in a sec.'

The two detectives waited awkwardly in the relatively small room where the persistent smell of chemicals and disinfectant filled their nostrils as it permanently filled the corridors and spaces throughout the cramped building. It was ultimately the smell of death and, as with today, often the smell of murder.

As Cooper went through a checklist with his assistant, both visitors turned their attention to the star witness, who would hopefully reveal some secrets post-mortem. Cheryl Kerr lay on a long metal table in the middle of the room. Her body was covered, though her face remained uncovered.

Rob Cooper dried his hands and picked up a clipboard while his assistant went over to Cheryl to stitch up the body.

'So what was the cause of death, Rob, blunt force trauma?' asked Weaver impatiently.

'Drowning,' Rob answered as he moved closer to the two men, still looking down at his clipboard.

'You mean she was still alive when she went into the water?' Patterson asked.

'Yes, I would say Cheryl was only just alive when she hit the water but alive all the same. The water in her lungs indicates drowning, which, I admit, is surprising considering what happened to her before she went into the river.'

'What did happen to her beforehand?' Weaver asked.

'She had been severely beaten, though some of the bruises and lacerations you can see could have resulted from her being swept downriver. Having said that, almost all the injuries happened beforehand. Assuming she was abducted late Saturday afternoon, I would say Cheryl would have been constantly beaten over the following three and a half days. There are also indications she has been sexually assaulted. There is severe internal and external trauma around the vagina and anus.'

'Sexually assaulted? Not rape?' asked Patterson.

'Not rape, no. She was penetrated by an object rather than a penis. Possibly a dildo or similar object.'

'What kind of object?'

'Possibly a sex toy of some kind, anything hard, quite large. This object was thrust into her repeatedly, including her mouth. A couple of her back teeth have been knocked out, a couple of others dislodged. It's rare to see trauma as bad as this, at least in my experience. Cheryl must have suffered terribly, I'm afraid.'

Without his smile and cheery demeanour, Rob suddenly lost his boyish good looks and appeared much older than his 35 years. Depending on his mood, his apparent age varied between early twenties and late forties. Rob gazed towards the corpse of the young woman once more before continuing. 'She was also suffering from severe hypothermia, and that hypothermia took hold before she hit the water. As for other info, her last meal was a tuna sandwich. It's hard to say exactly, but it is the kind you would buy from a shop –'

'Or on a train,' said Patterson.

'Yes,' said Rob. 'It's unlikely she had anything to eat when held captive. Due to the hypothermia, I would also say she was held outdoors. Apart from the sexual assault, she was beaten by a heavy bat-type object, something like a baseball bat, and repeatedly punched. She has multiple broken bones. There was severe blunt force trauma to her sides and front. All in all, she was basically tortured for the whole time she was held captive.'

'The hypothermia, you're sure it's not a result of just being in the river?'

'No, this is longer-term, and besides, I would say Cheryl hadn't been in the river that long before she was found. A couple of hours, if that. As I say, she was in a very poor state when she went into the water. Close to death but still alive. Literally beaten to within an inch of her life. Initially, the shock of the freezing water could have made the poor woman more aware of what was happening. Still, at the same time, she would have quickly succumbed to the freezing temperature of the river. I believe the Kelvin was fast flowing at the time?' He looked over at the detectives, and Patterson nodded.

Cooper continued, 'Well, even though she would have been exhausted, starving, her bones broken and barely conscious, Cheryl still fought as best she could for her life. Her hands have numerous marks as if she was trying to grab onto something as she was swept downstream.'

'What about the wound in her side?' Weaver asked.

'Most probably done by a thick branch. I believe Cheryl was found caught up against a tree trunk. There are small shards of wood in the opening. One of those sharp branches probably ripped the skin and punctured her side.'

'Do you think the murderer would have known she was still alive when they put her in the river?'

'I would say so,' Rob said after a moment's thought. 'She would still have been moving, in pain obviously, moaning, semi-conscious, but I think the killer took a calculated risk knowing she would not be alive that much longer once in the river.'

'Why take that risk?' Patterson asked.

'That's your department, I think.' Rob said.

'So, for the time of death, you think she died not long before she was found?' asked Weaver.

'Yes. Cheryl's time of death would have been shortly after she entered the river. If she was found at around six, I would say her death was three or four in the morning. She hadn't been in the water much longer than that. As for any forensics, there isn't much to go on. We've still got quite a few tests to carry out, but I very much doubt we'll find any DNA. The river washed away anything we could use. However, quite a bit of dirt was jammed under her fingernails as if she had been clawing at dirt on the ground.'

'Would that not have been her grabbing at the river bank?'

'No, that dirt was there, jammed in hard before she was in the river.'

'So, what would be your explanation for that?'

'Well, this is speculation, of course, but as I say, the indications are that she was held on an outside piece of ground. If that was the case, I would say she was somehow tied down on her back, arms and legs apart. Rob stopped and looked into mid-air again as he tried to imagine the scenario of Cheryl's abduction. 'Yes, I would say she was held down on a piece of ground on her back, her wrists and ankles attached to something, perhaps like metal rods or spikes, pushed into the ground. Something like that would account for the ligature marks on her wrists and ankles. She was held like this for quite a while, again, days. The cuts to the skin on her wrists and ankles made by these ligatures are simply Cheryl constantly trying to break free.'

A silence ensued as all three men were lost in thought, imagining the circumstances of Cheryl's death both from an investigative and humanitarian point of view.

Patterson was the one to break the silence again. 'You say she was severely beaten, yet her face is relatively unmarked.'

'Yes, certainly more by design than accident. Our killer seems to have made a point of not marking her face.'

Patterson was still curious about her being tied down. 'What makes you say she was tied down to possibly stakes or rods in the ground?'

'It's just one explanation for some of the injuries. You see, there are also countless scratch marks on her back. The kind you would get if you were constantly moving, writhing, rubbing your back against rough, stony ground. I would say it's the most likely scenario.'

'Anything else?' asked Weaver.

'Yes,' Rob announced as if keeping some good news back until the end. 'On both her shoulders, I've found traces of paint. The river didn't wash everything away; it appears to be traces of yellow fluorescent paint. Very bright. I'll send some samples to the lab later. You could well be able to get a match of that paint to a supplier or store. Given the location of the paint on her upper back and shoulders, it's another indication she was held on her back, and this paint was on the ground beneath her. There isn't a huge amount, but it's definitely fluorescent yellow paint.'

'OK,' Patterson said, 'I guess that could be something to work on. You'll get the analysts' results to us ASAP, yes?'

'Of course,' Cooper said.

'One other thing, in your opinion, do you think this is likely to be the result of one attacker or more than one?' asked Weaver.

'Hard to say; that's another thing you'll have to work out for yourselves. Nevertheless, to overpower Cheryl, a fit young woman, tie her to the ground, one person could have managed it. Yet, now you mention it, it could well have been two people. I'll send the full report later.'

Weaver and Patterson had heard enough and made to leave. They thanked Cooper and then looked at Cheryl one last time as they made their way out the swing doors. Both men were thinking the same thing. Whoever murdered Cheryl was a very dangerous individual who had to be caught quickly. Not only for the sake of Cheryl but to make sure another innocent person didn't succumb to the same terrible fate as Cheryl Kerr.

Chapter 11

Questions

Patterson and Weaver arrived back at Partick station and entered via the main entrance. The reception area of the police station had recently been refurbished. The bright oak panelling and curved laminated counter were designed to make the station more 'customer focused'. The hard, red plastic chairs of old were discarded. In their place were three cushioned chairs in faux cream leather lined up against a side wall. A large reception sign was above the counter just in case any newcomers had any difficulty realising this was indeed the reception area. As Patterson and Weaver passed, a knock on the glass partition made both men turn. DS Jessop, often chosen for desk duty because of his customer-friendly manner, slid a glass panel to one side, 'The boss wants to see you chaps ASAP.' Jessop smiled as if enjoying the despairing looks on his colleagues' faces.

Although it was now a murder enquiry, Superintendent Dunard informed the two officers there would only be one investigative team. Cutbacks were given as the reason. Weaver would be kept on as SIO, with Patterson as his number two. Dunard hoped the two senior policemen working together would bring quicker results. Overall, the number of officers involved had actually been scaled down. However, there was still a good number of detectives assigned to the murder investigation. The core of the senior investigative team would be Patterson's main colleagues, DI Pettigrew, DS Simpson and DC McKinnon, and those who Weaver brought in, such as DI Davies, DS Brown and DC McLean.

An hour later, DCI Weaver stood in front of the incident board that was usually the property of Patterson. As Weaver updated the team about the autopsy's findings, it felt strange for Patterson not to be the SIO on a murder case.

'OK,' began Weaver, 'one of our first priorities is establishing where Cheryl was held. If we suppose Cheryl was abducted straight after leaving Kelvinbridge on late Saturday afternoon and was found in the early hours of Tuesday morning, we need to ask where was she held for around three days? If we find that location, we'll be a lot closer to finding the murderer. I suspect Cheryl was possibly taken to a remote location, perhaps forest, woodland, somewhere outside Glasgow and then brought back.'

'Brought back?' said Simpson. 'I get the murderer would take Cheryl somewhere remote, but why bring her back?'

'Because whoever did this wanted it to look like she fell into the river accidentally. That was why she was found fully clothed despite evidence showing she had been naked at some point. For instance, the pathologist said Cheryl had scratches on her back consistent with writhing on rough ground. The nature of these injuries alone meant Cheryl would have been naked. Plus, with the killer hoping we would somehow believe she had accidentally fallen in the Kelvin, this was why she was placed in the river near to where she disappeared.'

'Yet, what about those cuts and bruises all over her body? Not to mention the marks around her wrists and ankles? Surely the murderer would know we would quickly realise it wasn't an accident?'

'You would think so,' said Weaver, 'but perhaps it was wishful thinking. Perhaps he thought we would assume the bruising and broken bones would be attributed to her being swept downriver. Who knows. He probably hoped she would be swept all the way into the Clyde and not be found for some time.'

'So why not drop her into the Clyde, to begin with?'

'Again, who knows?' said Weaver. 'Perhaps, he was trying to make it look as realistic as possible.'

McKinnon spoke up. 'Can I just clarify that

you say the autopsy shows she was assaulted by an object thrust into her? Why do that? Why assault her with an object instead of raping her?'

Patterson spoke up. 'It's possible he was afraid of leaving DNA evidence. Or maybe this is a sign we could be looking for a woman. There could be many reasons why Cheryl was penetrated by an object and not raped.'

Weaver's thoughts were drifting in another direction. 'One thing we do need to check immediately is the records for all previous sexual assaults. I know some of you have already reviewed similar crimes for me in the Greater Glasgow area. We need to expand that, and I'll be assigning more officers to look into similar past crimes. This person has almost certainly done this type of crime before.'

Patterson added, 'It's also possible this person knew Cheryl would be coming out of Kelvinbridge subway station that afternoon.'

'Such as her flatmates?' Simpson asked.

'Such as her flatmates, yes,' replied Patterson.

'What about social media? She could have mentioned online that she was going away or when she would be coming back,' asked McKinnon.

'Apparently not. We've already gone over Cheryl's computer, and her public posts didn't mention she was going away.'

Weaver pointed to DS McKinnon and DS

Brown. 'You two, find out about all Cheryl's friends and family. Davies and McLean visit her tutors and fellow students at the university. Patterson is right. It's very possible that her killer knew Cheryl.'

'OK,' Weaver said, moving away from the incident board, 'We'll start properly tomorrow. Given it's six PM, what I suggest for today is we all go home, think things over and get a good night's rest so we can tackle this nice and fresh in the morning. Agreed?'

A lack of response was taken as agreement, and everyone gratefully began to make moves to leave.

Desk computers were switched off; files and papers were put in drawers. Jackets and coats were taken from the back of seats and put on shoulders while McKinnon went into the locker room and changed into his cycling gear. Patterson could see that all the officers were thinking over the case as they walked downstairs and made their way to their cars, which was a good sign. This was an experienced team of officers, and all going well, Patterson was confident Cheryl's murderer would be caught sooner rather than later.

Chapter 12

The Tunnel

It was just before seven in the morning, and Patterson sat at the kitchen table eating toast and marmalade. The date on the clock said it was the 4th of December. Soon be Christmas, Patterson thought, not for the first time. Stephanie moved around him, washing up last night's plates and tidying up. The radio was on a talk news show. Both knew Stephanie would change the station to a music station the minute Patterson was out the door.

'So, what's on the agenda for today then?' It was Stephanie asking the question, and, at first, Patterson didn't know how to respond since he wasn't quite sure what the agenda would be for that day.

'Well, I'll guess it's up to Weaver. I'll be taking my lead from him.'

'Must be strange having Weaver as SIO.'

'Aye, well, you could say that, but I'm not fussed; taking a back seat for a time might not be such a bad idea. What about yourself?'

'I'm going into town later,' Stephanie said. 'I have an Alcoholics Anonymous meeting at one-thirty, and then I'm meeting Jenny.'

'Oh aye?'

'Aye, just going to have a coffee and do some Christmas shopping.'

Patterson nodded. 'Where's the AA meeting today, then?'

'It's a place I haven't been to before - near the Mitchell Library. Off a side street somewhere. Afterwards, I'm meeting Jenny in a café we go to on Sauchiehall Street.'

'How is Jenny, by the way?'

'Fine - she's just started up this aerobics class. You know what she's like. Always starting up something, and she wants me to join it. Not sure I could handle it, though.'

'Right,' Patterson's reply was absent-minded, which gave Stephanie the impression that he wasn't even listening.

'Everything all right?'

'Eh? Aye, just thinking.'

'The Cheryl Kerr case?'

'Aye,'

'So what is it, then?'

'It's just that I was wondering why Cheryl Kerr was found where she was. If she was abducted and taken elsewhere, as Rafe thinks, why bring her back to where she was abducted and dumped in the river? Weaver thinks the murderer wanted it to look like she had fallen into the river, but I'm not so sure.'

'I thought you'd know better by now about trying to figure out the logic of a murderer.'

'I know, the thing is...you know, I saw her two flatmates on Monday; they have a shared flat in Bank St.'

'I know, you said. And?'

'Well, there was definitely something not right about them. Just their manner, like they were hiding something.'

'You really think they've got something to do with Cheryl's murder?'

'I don't know about that, but let's just say Cheryl wasn't taken elsewhere. Then perhaps she was held somewhere close to where she was found. If that was the case, then why not in her own flat? Or in her tenement, a cellar, the backcourt, somewhere like that?'

'Hasn't the place been searched already?'

'Aye, but they were just looking for Cheryl. Nothing suspicious was found.'

'There you go then. You need evidence before you can go around accusing people. Look at me, having to tell you your job!'

'I know, I know.'

Patterson rose from his chair, wiped some crumbs off his trousers, took one last sip of coffee and picked up his jacket.

'Better go. See you later, Steph.'

See you later.'

'Love you,' Patterson then added, giving her

a hug.

'Love you too,' Stephanie replied.

Patterson left home, got in his car, and drove towards Partick Police Station. Yet, the thoughts and questions about Cheryl came back to him. According to the pathologist, Stephanie had been suffering from hypothermia, which began before she entered the river, suggesting she was held outside. There were countless places she could have been held in or near the River Kelvin. Kelvingrove Park itself, for instance. The more he thought about that possibility, the more he was drawn to that idea. So much so that Patterson took a detour and drove towards Kelvingrove Park.

At first, Patterson had planned to park at Kelvinbridge Subway Station and walk down to where Cheryl was dragged out of the river. On the way there, however, Patterson changed his mind. He parked his car along Kelvin Way, a wide, tree-lined boulevard that ran alongside the park from University Avenue to the Kelvingrove Art Galleries and the west end of Sauchiehall St.

Before getting out of the car, Patterson put on his leather gloves, took a pair of polythene gloves, and the torch he kept in the glove compartment. Then he stood outside and surveyed his surroundings. The Kelvin Walkway was relatively quiet in terms of people, as it usually was apart from weekends. He could see a steady stream of vehicles heading up University

Avenue or down Gibson St. It was a cold day, cold enough for his breath to be visible but not as cold as it had been of late. Light blue skies above meant it could still be classed as a beautiful day too.

Patterson walked down and across the Prince of Wales bridge, one of the finest bridges to cross the River Kelvin, Patterson thought. How many times had he walked or run across this bridge as a kid as he went to play football in the gravel park or head along to play putting or go to the Art Galleries? He always felt at home here, probably because it *was* his home.

As a man in early middle age, his reason for crossing this bridge was far grimmer than in his childhood days. He stopped midway on the bridge and looked over the elegant speckled marble balustrade. The river was still fast-flowing, and he imagined Cheryl Kerr being swept down the river in the ice-cold waters and early morning darkness – gulping for air, the rush and roar of water, the panic, the fear, the awareness she was going to die.

Patterson walked to the end of the bridge, then turned left to walk along the path that followed the route of the river upstream. It was more secluded here, as the main walkway through the park was high to his right. As the trail dipped into a slight trough, Patterson constantly scanned the river's edge. He was looking to see if there was anywhere that Cheryl could have been hidden, perhaps in shrubbery or bushes. He knew if she was held near the river, it would more likely be where there was some dense woodland scattered by the river's path.

The quiet path that Patterson followed now began to rise up again. He looked onwards and saw a small animal scurrying across; a fieldmouse, Patterson thought. He continued walking, following the walkway where it dipped under the Gibson Street bridge. This was a secluded spot, Patterson thought as he descended further under the bridge. Now he could see Kelvinbridge subway station in the distance as he passed the old disused railway tunnel to his right.

Patterson stopped at the bottom of the path leading to the large subway station parking area. He looked at the tunnel again. Patterson knew that Weaver would have had the tunnel checked out. Besides, the entrance to the tunnel was blocked off by thick grey steel gates with spikes on top. The gates had a large lock for one key and a smaller lock for another. Patterson gave Weaver a call.

'Hey Rafe, how you doin', listen you know the old railway tunnel at Kelvinbridge?'

'Kind of. Which one?'

'The one that runs under Gibson Street, just down from the subway station.'

'Yeah, I know it; what about it?'

' You did have it checked out, didn't you?'

There was a silence on the other end of the line before Weaver answered.

'Yes, of course. At least, I think I did. I'm sure I did.'

'What do you mean you think you did?'

'I mean, I'm sure I did. Anyway, it was locked up securely when Cheryl was murdered.'

'I know, but you did have it checked out, didn't you?'

There was another silence, then a hesitation, 'Like I said, I'm sure I did, but if you want to check it out yourself, go ahead. As I said, the tunnel is always securely locked. There is no point –'

'OK, Rafe, it's probably nothing. Do you know who has access to the keys for the tunnel gate?'

'Can't think offhand, the park department maybe. Or the council.' Weaver's tone was still unsure.

'Listen, if he's there, put McKinnon on the line, will you?'

A moment later, Patterson heard McKinnon's voice.

'Brian, I want you to find out who has access to the old railway tunnels at Kelvinbridge. The tunnels are barred by locked gates. Find out who has the keys. If it's the council or parks department, or someone else. Find out ASAP, and then get someone down here with the keys for the tunnel gate that starts at Gibson Street. I'll be waiting until someone arrives, so make it as quick as possible.'

Patterson clicked off his phone and walked down to peer through the thick grey metal gates at the tunnel entrance but couldn't see far inside the tunnel darkness.

As he continued to wait for the official to arrive, Patterson further inspected the area around the tunnel entrance. On one side, stairs led up to Gibson Street. On the other was the sloping, winding path that Patterson had taken from the direction of Kelvingrove Park. It was a relatively quiet and secluded area. However, it was still passed by countless people who strolled or jogged alongside the river and through the park's natural splendour. Those with the fitness and appetite could even follow the path onwards towards Maryhill and for the eight miles or so further to Milngavie, a small town north of Glasgow.

The original tunnel entrance itself was about 15 feet high. Its sides had been narrowed by the placement of large, aesthetically pleasing rectangle blocks of stone. The smaller entrance was now a rectangular opening barred by the two grey steel gates. The outside walls leading to the tunnel had whiter patches where graffiti had recently been removed. The ground outside the tunnel was mostly dirt, frozen over, scattered with brown leaves, a few empty alcohol bottles, cans, and old newspapers.

Eventually, the official arrived, who, it turned out, was from the council. He looked at the detective with curiosity, prompting Patterson to show his ID. Patterson took off his leather gloves and put on his polythene ones. He then asked the council official for the keys. He was duly handed a large key for the main lock and a smaller key, which opened the second smaller lock. He told the official to stand back and not move or touch anything while he went inside. Patterson turned the two keys, and the tall gate opened with a long metallic yawn. Walking inside, the noise of the Gibson Street traffic became hushed, and soon, he could only hear the echo of his feet crunching on the frozen ground underneath. The tunnel had an eerie atmosphere, like an ancient, long-forgotten cave.

Patterson shone the torch around him but didn't see anything of interest. The ground was hard, rough and covered in small stones.

However, as Patterson walked on, he noticed an area of ground which stood out from its surroundings. Whereas the earth on the tunnel floor was generally rough and unkempt in most places, a patch of ground appeared to be smoothed down. It was the effect you would get if someone had been lying there. This impression was heightened by small mounds of dirt pushed out around this area. Walking over and scanning the area with the bright light of the torch, Patterson noticed a small hole in the ground. He then spotted another a couple of feet away. At first, they appeared to be from a very small animal burrowing its way into the earth. Yet, on further inspection, it was apparent these holes were man-made. Could the pathologist Rob Cooper have been spot-on about rods being pushed into the ground? Patterson scanned around further, and there were two other holes. The four holes made a rough rectangle, exactly as you would expect if someone had been pinned down on the ground with cords tied to rods or stakes.

For Patterson, the possibility it was here that Cheryl was held captive increased with every passing moment. If she was held here, no doubt she could hear the faint noise of life outside. Voices and cars. So near and yet here she would lie, freezing, starving, being beaten and sexually assaulted again and again. All in this abandoned tunnel yards from where she had last been seen alive. That brought forward another thought and question. If the tunnel had been searched, how come Weaver wasn't sure who had the keys? Patterson quickly realised the tunnel couldn't have been searched. Because this was almost certainly where Cheryl was held from Saturday afternoon until Tuesday morning, and if the tunnel had been searched, Cheryl would have been found.

Patterson had seen enough and made to exit the tunnel. However, one thing more made him pause a moment longer. Crouching down and from the light of the torch, Patterson could just about make out faint traces of paint on the ground. Yellow fluorescent paint. Standing up, he shone his torch into the distance of the dark tunnel. Two marker poles could be seen, each painted with the same yellow fluorescent paint. Patterson was now in no doubt. This abandoned tunnel was where Cheryl Kerr had been abducted, beaten, sexually assaulted and, in all but name, murdered. He not only knew this was a significant turning point in the enquiry, but for someone involved in the search for Cheryl, there would be absolute hell to pay.

Chapter 13

A New Lead

A substantial area around the tunnel was immediately cordoned off, from Kelvinbridge subway station down to the Stewart Memorial Fountain on the other side of Kelvingrove Park. The increased activity and word spreading around soon resulted in the press being drawn towards the crime scene.

Officers were under strict instructions not to say anything to anyone, yet inevitably, someone blabbed. So it soon became common knowledge that it was in this tunnel where Cheryl Kerr had been held, only 500 metres from where she disappeared.

To all who learned this fact, it seemed incredible that the police hadn't found her. This was police incompetence taken to the next level, and the media, and the general public, were immediately after blood.

How could this have happened? Surely, even though the tunnel entrance was closed by steel gates, it was beyond belief that this natural hiding place yards from where Cheryl disappeared could have been left unsearched. The next question was who could be responsible for this major error.

Initially, the focus landed on two people. The head of the investigation, DCI Weaver and Superintendent Dunard. With those two in contention, there would only be one winner, or rather one loser…

DCI Weaver.

As Patterson arrived at Partick Police Station the next morning, a large press presence was camped outside the entrance. It was no surprise either that as soon as Patterson entered the building, he was informed that Dunard wanted to see him immediately. What *was* more of a surprise for Patterson was what Dunard said to him as soon as he entered his superior's office.

'You're now the SIO for Cheryl Kerr's murder investigation.'

'What about DCI Weaver?'

'DCI Weaver is on gardening leave pending further enquiries.'

This surprised Patterson since he had assumed Weaver was untouchable no matter what the golden boy did. Apparently not.

As if to back up his announcement, Dunard had a selection of morning papers on his desk. They each had a headline based on the statement, 'The police really messed up this time,' without using those exact words. There were some photos of Weaver, but many more were of Dunard. The previous afternoon, he stood on the station steps and issued a heartfelt apology on 'behalf of his officers and the entire police force.'

It was clear that, since then, to save his own skin, Dunard decided he needed a sacrificial lamb, and Weaver had the honour of being that lamb.

As for Patterson, he had mixed feelings about becoming the SIO in such a high-profile case. On the one hand, he knew all the intense media scrutiny this case had already generated would now be thrown in his direction. This was something he could well do without. On the other hand, finding the murderer of Cheryl Kerr was precisely why he became a police officer. To bring evil persons to justice.

Patterson sat down, a thousand thoughts running through his mind. Dunard looked groomed for the additional media scrutiny, pristine. His uniform was immaculate, as was his overall appearance. For someone in his late fifties, his short, dark hair was suspiciously almost as black as his uniform. Patterson also detected an expensive eau de cologne in the air.

'You say Inspector Weaver is being suspended?'

'Let's not prejudge the situation,' Dunard answered, 'Inspector Weaver is on gardening leave whilst a full independent enquiry takes place, *then* he'll be suspended. In all likelihood, Cheryl Kerr could still be alive if that tunnel had been searched.'

Patterson wanted to disagree but found, in all honesty, he couldn't.

'Of course,' continued Dunard, 'I don't want to throw Weaver under the bus; however, there is no way he could continue in his present position after what has happened.'

Patterson thought he should be enjoying this moment when his perfect cousin was found to be far from perfect, yet, to his surprise, he felt more sympathy than pleasure. 'So, just to be clear, you're saying I'm SIO on this case.'

'That's what I'm saying. As of now, 8:32 am on Friday the 5th of December, you're SIO, and under no circumstances can we afford to make any more mistakes. Absolutely none. The best way to improve things is by finding out who murdered Cheryl Kerr ASAP. Preferably by Christmas.'

'Preferably by Christmas? You're not serious?'

'Why aren't I serious?'

'Because it doesn't work like that.'

'Nevertheless, I want you to find this murderer as soon as. We now know where Cheryl was held; that should give you a good enough lead.'

Patterson looked down at his hands and saw they were clenched into small fists. The desire to avoid excess pressure after his return from holiday a few days ago now seemed a lifetime away.

'Anything you need, just let me know, and don't let me down like Weaver has.' Dunard added.

'I'll do my best, sir.' Patterson said, now folding his arms and crossing his legs. 'Well, I best get started then,' Patterson said as he rose out of his chair.

'Remember Mike, we must catch this one sooner rather than later. We're all depending on you.'

Patterson turned to leave and felt that knot of anxiety in his stomach tighten a little more.

'No pressure then,' Patterson said quietly as he walked out the door.

Chapter 14

The Understudy

From Dunard's office, Patterson walked down the stairs and into the briefing room to see it was just as busy as it had been for Weaver's earlier briefings that week. Only this time, there was a look of surprise from his colleagues as Patterson stopped in front of the incident board.

'OK, everyone, 'Patterson started, 'Now I know some of you will probably have heard the news, but for those who aren't in the loop, DCI Weaver will be taking a short break from this investigation.' Patterson felt as if he was announcing that the understudy would now be playing the lead as the big-name star was suddenly indisposed. There were indeed some murmurs of discontent from the audience.

'It means, from this point onwards, I am the senior investigating officer for the Cheryl Kerr murder investigation.'

More murmurs were heard, and Patterson

felt he had to explain further.

'There will be an independent enquiry into the search for Cheryl Kerr's body. While that is ongoing, DCI Weaver is on gardening leave.'

The Weaver fan club was getting restless, prompting Patterson to keep talking.

'I understand some of you will be disappointed with this news, but I don't want Weaver's absence to distract from the very important job we still have to carry out. We have a murderer to —'

The small, blonde figure of DS Linda Dawson interrupted him. 'Sir, when you say DCI Weaver is on gardening leave, you mean he's been suspended?'

There were further noises of discontent, and Patterson knew if he wasn't careful, he could have a full-scale, albeit small-scale, rebellion on his hands.

'DCI Weaver has not been suspended. As I said, pending an independent investigation, he is on gardening leave.' This raised a couple of sarcastic chuckles and officers talking amongst themselves. Patterson now felt the need to raise his voice.

'OK, enough! Listen, If anyone isn't happy, you can go now.' There was silence in the room, and to Patterson's relief, no one walked out.

Nevertheless, Patterson was still slightly flustered by the initial disruptive hiccup and tried his best to hide his inner feelings of deep unease. He did this by pausing to look at the incident board for a few moments. He wasn't used to raising his voice and could feel a bead of sweat running down his back. An uneasy silence now filled the air. The slight disobedience he felt towards himself also made him quite angry. Even if, in principle, Patterson couldn't give a fuck about being liked, knowingly being disliked never did his nerves any good.

And besides, he knew they would never have dared act this way with Weaver.

'OK,' Patterson cautiously continued, 'let's go over what we know with our new information about where she was held taken into account.'

With some reservations, the room slowly but surely continued to let the understudy show what he could do. Nevertheless, even while talking more, the anxiety within Patterson wouldn't go completely.

'Now, on Saturday the 29th of November, shortly after leaving Kelvinbridge subway station, at 4:42 pm, we now know Cheryl Kerr was taken to the disused railway tunnel, approximately 500 metres away.'

'When you say she was taken there, how do you mean exactly?' asked DI Davies.

'Presumably, her assailant had a knife or other weapon against Cheryl. For now, we should also presume the assailant is a man since the nature of Cheryl's murder, namely the force needed, leads us to that conclusion. So perhaps this man simply threatened to kill Cheryl if she didn't do as she was told. It's pretty dark around that time; street lighting is quite distant, and the car park lighting is poor. Two people walking close together in the evening half-darkness could have easily been mistaken for a loving couple. It would have taken less than five minutes to get from the subway exit to the tunnel entrance. Nevertheless, we still need to conduct door-to-door enquiries again, especially the continued no-answers, to ensure no one saw or heard anything suspicious around the tunnel. Baker, Galbraith and O'Connor, that's your duties for today. Check the whole area, including the tenements on Gibson St. I also want DS Harris, Lane and Jackson to enquire in every shop, pub and other business in the area. Find out if anyone saw or heard anything in the days and even weeks leading up to the 29th of November. No matter how trivial, I want you to note everything. We'll be putting out public appeals later, and I'll set up an incident cabin near the tunnel.'

Patterson surveyed the room with some satisfaction as he noticed his once disruptive pupils were now listening intently.

'So, on Saturday, outside the subway station, Cheryl's murderer could have waited some time for any suitable victim to appear. At the moment, a suitable victim appears to be any young female.'

Patterson's anxiety was all but gone as he became immersed in the case details and the questions that arose from those details.

Mckinnon spoke. 'It's possible he wasn't waiting at the station. He could have followed Cheryl from St Enoch and got off at Kelvinbridge with her.'

'Good point Brian. Get someone else to help to check up on that. I'm sure the CCTV from the subway has been studied already, but double-check in case we have missed anything.'

'Even in the darkness, the murderer is still taking a risk in leading Cheryl to the tunnel,' Pettigrew said.

'Taking risks could have been part of the thrill for him, said Patterson. 'The fact remains he somehow got her into the tunnel. Now, once in the tunnel –'

'Isn't this tunnel usually closed off?' asked DC Fullerton

'It is. This tunnel is locked by steel gates. The only way to enter is with two keys for the two locks, one large and one small. So unless the gates were already open, someone must have had those keys. Brian, I want a list of everyone at the council who had access to those keys. Everyone who could have possibly had a set of keys or a copy of the original keys cut. To begin with, we need to see if anyone with previous has managed to wrangle his way into getting a job with the council. If so, we need to bring them in immediately for questioning.

'It's possible the gates were left open, and presumably, the murderer knew that,' asked Simpson

'It's possible. This doesn't appear to be a spur-of-the-moment killing. If the gates were already open, the murderer was indeed aware of that. Now, let's get to when Cheryl was inside the tunnel. Cheryl was stripped naked and pinned to the ground —'

'Pinned to the ground, how, sir?' asked DC McGinn.

'Simpson?'

'the indications are that Cheryl was held down with ties attached to small metal rods pushed into the ground. Holes found in the tunnel are consistent with that theory. Cheryl was positioned, naked, on her back with arms and legs spread apart.' Patterson felt completely calm again, so much so that he wasn't even aware he was calm again. He took a drink of water from a paper cup before continuing.

'After being abducted, Cheryl was repeatedly beaten and sexually assaulted over the next three days, basically tortured. It should also be noted that this was carried out in sub-zero temperatures. The pathologist said Cheryl had suffered severe hypothermia. My initial thoughts are that after holding her in the tunnel over those three days, sometime in the early hours of Tuesday morning, the 2nd of December, preliminary put between 3 am and 5 am, Cheryl was carried from the tunnel and dropped into the River Kelvin. Remember, Cheryl was still alive when she hit the water. Her official cause of death is drowning. Are we all clear on everything so far?'

No one said anything, so Patterson continued. 'So, as we now know, Cheryl was held right under our noses. That means we're looking for someone incredibly confident, who most likely gets a buzz from taking chances. Another question we should ask is, did our killer know Cheryl, or was she really just in the wrong place at the wrong time?'

'Claire, do you have more you can tell us?'

'Just that forensics have found residue of tape placed across Cheryl's mouth and eyes. It appears to be silver-coloured thick industrial tape.'

'Which leads us to our next line of enquiry. We should soon have an idea of the types of rods pushed into the ground in addition to the industrial tape used to gag Cheryl. These two items alone could have been bought from a DIY store. I want some officers to check out every DIY store and supplier of these types of rods once we know more about them.'

Patterson thought for a moment. 'DI Davies, you checked out her friends at the

University?'

'Yes, by all accounts, she was well-liked. No enemies, a hardworking and conscientious student according to her tutors.'

'OK, we'll still check out the university to ensure we haven't missed anything or anyone. What else can I tell you? Yes, in case you don't know, the other end of the tunnel is completely blocked off. So we know our man could only have entered the tunnel from the entrance at Kelvinbridge. OK, let's get on with it.'

With that, everyone rose, and the briefing ended, and the understudy, relatively happy with his performance, returned to his office.

Chapter 15

Breakthrough

Later in the afternoon, Patterson was in his office when McKinnon entered and informed him the keys to the tunnel were always kept securely locked away at the Glasgow council offices in Easterhouse.

'Why Easterhouse?'

'That's where the maintenance department is. They keep all keys needed for maintenance jobs in Easterhouse.'

'And no one has access to them except for maintenance work?'

'Nope. The keys must be signed in or out and only after management authorisation, which would only ever be in the case of maintenance work being carried out.'

'I don't suppose there had been any maintenance work happening recently?'

'Then you'd suppose wrong. Council workers were carrying out work at the tunnel in the week leading up to Cheryl's abduction and murder.'

'Well, well, isn't that a coincidence?'

'Isn't it just.'

'How many workers were at the tunnel?'

'Four. I've got a list of names here. They usually work as a four-man team right across the city doing odd jobs, clearing up litter, painting and suchlike.'

'Run their names by me.'

'Gerry McBride, Calvin Roberston, Andy McGregor and Tommy Beaton.'

None of the names rang any bells for Patterson. 'Are any known to us?'

'Three have previous. Calvin Roberston is the odd one out. As for the others, one of them was done for stealing cars when he was younger. Joyriding, nothing else.'

'Who's that?'

'Andy McGregor.'

'And the other two?'

'Gerry McBride was convicted for being part of a three-team gang that did a couple of robberies.'

'That's interesting.'

'Don't get your hopes up. Bunch of amateurs, by all accounts, did a couple of newsagents about twenty years ago and then got caught. End of. Seemed to have learnt their lesson. No trouble since.'

'And the other one?'

'Tommy Beaton. Sexual assault.'

Bingo. In Patterson's experience, one coincidence was usually one too many, and more than one coincidence was never coincidence. Patterson tried to keep his excitement in check as McKinnon continued.

'He served four years of an eight-year sentence. From 2001 to 2005. No trouble since.'

'OK, looks like we're going to be interviewing Mr Beaton tonight.'

'What about the others?'

'Let's just concentrate on Beaton for now. I'll get Pettigrew and Simpson to round up the others tomorrow. Send a team round and bring Beaton in. Let me know when he's here.'

'Will do.'

As Patterson sat back in his chair, he didn't want to get his hopes up. Yet, he intuitively felt the investigation had just taken a major leap forward.

Chapter 16

The Interview of Tommy Beaton

As Tommy Beaton was led into the interview room and as Patterson studied him through a monitor, he was glad he didn't feel as rough as Tommy Beaton looked. Tommy was in his mid-twenties, of average build, average height and average appearance. You could be his best friend and still not pick him out of a line-up. Tommy was also visibly very nervous as he sat waiting for Patterson to arrive. That could have been for a multitude of reasons. Whatever the main reason was, Patterson let him stew a bit longer.

Patterson wanted to interview Tommy under the guise of him being a possible witness to seeing something suspicious at the tunnel, which was partly true. The last thing he wanted was Tommy shouting for a lawyer, which would make for a very long night. When Patterson finally entered the room, he smiled a welcome Tommy was unwilling to reciprocate.

'Tommy, glad you could make it. I just—'

'What huv ye brought me in here fur? I huvnae done anything.'

'No one has said you have, Tommy; I'll explain exactly why you—'

'This is no real, by the way, noising me up like this. I'm gonnae miss the final of I'm a Celebrity cos of yous.'

'If you don't drop the attitude, you'll be missing Strictly tomorrow night n' all. Just calm down; all we want is to ask you a few questions.'

'Aye, right. Just cos I gave a bird a slap a few year back. It's no real man.'

'A slap? You broke three of her ribs and an arm. Not to mention the sexual assault.'

'She wiz asking fur it.'

'See, that's the kind of statement that doesn't exactly make me warm to you.'

'It's true, but. Besides, I did my time. If you're trying to stitch us up for—'

'Just listen for a minute...'

Tommy didn't reply but sat looking off to one side, his arms defiantly folded.

'You were part of a team of council workers carrying out maintenance work at a tunnel in Kelvinbridge.'

Tommy didn't change his pose.

'Shortly afterwards, a young woman was held captive in that tunnel before being murdered.'

'What's that to dae wi' me?'

'When you were at the tunnel, did you see or hear anything suspicious while you were there?'

'Suspicious? How do you mean suspicious, and how come yer no' asking the other workers these questions?'

'Who says we aren't? Don't assume you're getting special treatment. As I said, all we want to know is if you saw or heard anything when you were there that made you think, I dunno, that's odd or if anyone was hanging around, anything.'

Tommy looked up at Patterson as if he was still trying to suss him out. 'Seriously, that's all you want to know?'

'Yes. So?'

Tommy shrugged. 'Nothing unusual happened, I don't think. We did the work, and then we went hame.'

'No one came up to you, say to ask the time, anything at all? It could be the slightest thing.'

'A lot of the time, we were inside the tunnel. We had to paint these poles wi' this special paint. Marker poles inside the tunnel. It was a fairly easy job, but nae one bothered us or anything.'

'What about your co-workers? Did you see any of them talk to anyone?'

'Naw, don't think so. How? Do ye suspect one of them?'

'We don't suspect anyone, Tommy. You worked at the tunnel the week before a woman got murdered there. We'd be failing in our duty if we didn't ask you these questions. So stop being paranoid.'

'Who's paranoid? Ah'm no paranoid.'

'Pleased to hear it. The name of the woman who was murdered was Cheryl Kerr?'

'So?'

'Patterson brought out a photo of Cheryl, which he placed in from of Tommy.'

'Have you ever seen her before?'

'Who's this?'

'Cheryl Kerr. The woman who was murdered.'

'Naw.'

'You don't recognise her? You are absolutely sure you don't know her?'

Tommy slowly shook his head. 'What was her name again?'

Patterson refused the temptation to sigh as

he didn't want to give Tommy the satisfaction of knowing he was pissing Patterson off. 'Cheryl Kerr. She was beaten, tortured, sexually assaulted and murdered. Rather matches your hobbies.'

'Ho, I thought you said you didnae suspect anyone?'

'OK, tell me about the keys.'

'What keys?'

'The keys that opened the tunnel gates. Who had these keys?'

'The gaffer, Gerry McBride.'

'So you never had access to those keys yourself?'

'Why would I? The gaffer had them. We'd arrive at the tunnel and have to wait till Gerry came and opened the gates. Think he picked them up from somewhere or something.'

'So only Gerry had access to those keys? What do you think of Gerry?'

'How do ye mean?'

'Well, is he a good gaffer? Do you get on all right?'

'Aye, ye could say that. He gets me to do some shitty jobs sometimes, but ah don't mind. Maist of the time, he just lets us get on with it.'

'Would you say he's trustworthy?'

Tommy shrugged. 'Dunno, as much as anyone is.'

'You're quite certain you never had access to the keys that opened the tunnel gates?'

'Naw, ah told ye.'

'What about the other two? Calvin Robertson and Andy McGregor. What are your thoughts on them?'

'Dunno, Andy can be a bit of a bawbag at times, but they're all right.'

'Do you think any of your co-workers could have anything to do with this murder?'

'Are you fur real? Naw, course not. Fuck sake.'

'Where were you on Saturday the 29th and Sunday the 30th of November?

'In ma hoose.'

'The whole time?'

'Aye,'

'The whole weekend? You never went anywhere? Not once?'

'Naw, I never go out much at weekends. I just stayed in, watched TV, and played games on my computer.'

'Can anyone verify that?'

'Verify? Ah, live on ma tod. Listen, is this gonnae take much longer?'

'Did you not order a takeaway? Open the door to the postman? Talk to a neighbour? It could make all the difference for you.'

'Naw, ah didnae talk tae a neighbour or the postman or get a takeaway. Anything else?'

Patterson thought for a moment. Hearing what the other workers said before proceeding would be the better bet. Besides, it was enough for the moment that Tommy knew he was on Patterson's radar.

'OK, Tommy, that's all for now. I'll let you go and watch your TV programme. Trust me, though; we'll be back in touch. Let us know if you can find someone to vouch for where you were that weekend. Plus, if you do remember anything that happened while you were at the tunnel, let us know ASAP.'

Patterson then looked directly at Tommy. 'And if I find out you had anything to do with this murder, I'll make sure you're put away for a very, very long time. Understand?'

Tommy stood up. 'And I'll tell you again. I had nothing to do with that lassie's murder.' Tommy turned, and Patterson led him out of the room.

Patterson was frustrated by the interview,

but he did learn one important fact.

Tommy Beaton was lying.

Chapter 17

Meeting The Gang

The next morning, Pettigrew phoned the council to double-check they had the right addresses for the other three council workers. To her surprise, she was told that rather than finding them at home, all three employees were working that Saturday morning at a site in Possilpark. So, with Simpson by her side on Saturday morning, she drove out of the police station. The first part of the journey was driven in silence.

Dumbarton Road was busy, as it usually was at weekends. It had a mix of various shops that were more practical than aesthetic. Value attracted customers rather than beauty. One example of this was the significant number of charity shops. In addition, you would also find a splattering of pubs, bookmakers, cafes, furniture shops, bakers, opticians, banks and newsagents; the everyday premises that could be located on any main thoroughfare in Glasgow.

Simpson finally broke the silence.

'So, how do you think our boss has been since he returned from holiday?'

Pettigrew looked across at Simpson as if she had just woken up.

'How do you mean?'

'I mean, you know how Patterson was when he left after the last case as well as I do. Do you think he's less stressed, more relaxed?'

'Not sure relaxed is the right word. He does seem more...Well, he's not as bad as before, let's put it that way. Less anxious, yes, I think. The holiday seems to have done him some good.'

'Definitely. Let's hope it lasts. For a time, I wondered if he would be back at all.'

'You and me both,' Pettigrew said as the car turned left at Partick Cross and into Byres Road. The bottom half of Byres Road always appeared poorer than the top half. As if the road was always forgetting to tuck its shirt in.

'Bit of a do with Weaver getting bumped, weren't it?' Simpson said. 'I know Patterson doesn't like him for some reason, but I think even he was surprised at what happened.'

'You think?' Pettigrew asked. 'You have to admit it was a bad mistake. Don't see how Dunard could have made any other decision, to be honest.' She looked out once more at life going on in Byres Road.

Byres Road was very much the real and symbolic heart of Glasgow's West End. It was often described as upmarket, which, in reality, just meant it had more than one patisserie. It was a place very much influenced by the students of Glasgow University who would wander down University Avenue during the day for something to eat or at night for something to drink. Ahead of the curve, it attracted trendier shops, the out-there independents that wanted to open up in the city but not in the city centre.

'Hey, what is it with Patterson and Weaver anyway? I don't know why Patterson has a problem with him. Weaver seems an alright bloke to me.'

'I know. I did once ask him why he didn't like Weaver, and he said,' He's the type of guy who wears his mobile in a holster.'

'What the hell does that mean?'

'Search me. He's a queer old bird sometimes, is our DCI Patterson.'

Simpson gave a small laugh. Soon they were crossing Maryhill Road and heading towards the depths of Possilpark. Possilpark could be described as a more run-down part of Maryhill. Considering Maryhill was one of the most deprived areas in the UK, that was quite an achievement. However, in the daytime, before the wolves came out, it was a pleasant enough area. It had wide roads dominated by well-kept council houses for the most part.

Pettigrew was informed that the employees were working on a playground off Balmore Road at Ashgill Road. Simpson soon noticed the workmen at the play area and parked across the street. The two officers walked across to the playpark.

The workmen, most wearing bright orange waistcoats, were busy carrying out their duties. Both officers noticed there were seven workers and not four. Two workers painted railings while another stood beside a silver corrugated iron shed. Two men dug up and levelled off a piece of ground while another two took the soil into a skip by running up a wooden plank with a wheelbarrow. It was heavy work, and these men were obviously fit. One man was standing apart from the rest, doing nothing. He was either a skiver, the gaffer or both.

Pettigrew and Simpson walked up to him. He looked back suspiciously at the couple he immediately marked down as coppers. Pettigrew wore her best-disarming smile as she tried to break down the man's clear wariness of the approaching pair. 'Hello. I'm DI Pettigrew, and this is DS Simpson, Partick CID.' She showed her warrant card. 'We're looking to speak to the workers who were at Kelvinbridge a couple of weeks back, the disused railway tunnel? I was told they are working here.'

'That's right. I'm one of them. Is this aboot the murder that happened?'

'Yes,' answered Pettigrew. 'We'd like to see if you and the others noticed anything suspicious while you were there. Who are the other workers who were at the tunnel?'

'Well, there was that guy there with the wheelbarrow, Calvin Robertson,' he pointed to a fit-looking mixed-race man in his mid-twenties. Andy McGregor was there. Where's Andy, for fuck sake? Oh, aye, there he is, next to the hut, the skanky cunt with the shovel. Tommy Beaton wiz there n'all, but he's no turned up this morning.'

'That's all right, we've already spoken to Tommy. And you are?'

'Gerry. Gerry McBride. I'm the foreman.'

'So you three were at the tunnel along with Tommy Beaton?' Simpson asked for clarification.

'That's what I said.'

'OK, well. I'm afraid you'll all have to come down to the station with us.'

'Seriously? When?'

'Now.'

'Now? Nae chance. Can we no just talk here?'

'Fraid not. We have to make it formal. It shouldn't take that long,' said Pettigrew.

In that case, you have tae talk tae ma boss first. We're here till two.'

'Not anymore. We've already spoken to your boss. If you give her a call, She'll confirm you're finishing early. The rest of the workers can go home. We can give you a lift to the station, or you can come in your own vehicles.'

'I've the works van; I'll drive the others

down. First, I best check with my boss and make sure she agrees.'

After making the phone call, a short time later, all three workers were at Partick Station.

Chapter 18

More Interviews

With Patterson going to meet Cheryl's boyfriend Ryan at Central Station, the three council employees were interviewed simultaneously by Pettigrew, Simpson and McKinnon.

Calvin Robertson was led into interview room one by McKinnon. Calvin was in his early twenties and appeared confident and intelligent. McKinnon began by asking what tasks the employees had carried out at the tunnel. He was told that it was a regular job. They had to clean up some graffiti, level some ground off and clear up rubbish in and around the tunnel entrance. The only slightly unusual task was painting some marker poles with fluorescent yellow paint. Calvin said he didn't see or hear anything out of the ordinary as far as he could remember. They started work at eight each morning and finished at four, except for the Friday when they finished at two. To find out more about Tommy

Beaton, Calvin was asked his thoughts on all three of his co-workers. They were a good laugh, said Calvin. Tommy was a bit quiet but a good co-worker.

Andy McGregor, unshaven and slightly pungent, was interviewed by Simpson in interview room two. He confirmed the team began work on Monday, the 24th of November, at 8am and finished on Friday, the 28th, at around 2pm. They didn't work on Saturday morning. Andy didn't see or hear anything of interest and didn't see any of the others acting out of the ordinary. Yes, Andy confirmed on Friday they ensured the gates were locked. He distinctly remembered the foreman, Gerry McBride, locking the gates as the other three looked on. Him and Calvin were dying to get to the pub. As for his co-workers, they were a good bunch. At times, Tommy Beaton could be a bit serious, but Andy liked him.

It was Pettigrew's task to interview the foreman Gerry McBride in interview room three. McBride was in his early forties and gave the impression of being world-weary and cynical. Pettigrew was particularly interested in who was the keyholder, and Gerry confirmed it was himself. Each day, he would travel to Easterhouse, pick up the keys around half seven and then return them to the council offices, usually between four and five. This was done without fail every night. Yes, it was an inconvenience, but that was why he 'got paid the big bucks'. On Friday, he locked the gates as usual with both keys, and he clearly remembered pulling at the gates to ensure they were shut. His thoughts on Tommy Beaton? He was a good worker, said Gerry. You could always trust him to get on with the work and get any job done.

So all three interviews concluded, and the consensus among the officers, before alibis were checked, was that the three workers were truthful enough. If anyone had become more of a suspect because of these three interviews, it was Tommy Beaton.

Chapter 19

Meeting Ryan Maxwell

As the interviews of the three workers were taking place, Patterson waited on the concourse at Glasgow Central for the train from Sheffield via Manchester to arrive. It had been arranged for Cheryl Kerr's boyfriend, Ryan Maxwell, to travel up to Glasgow mainly to visit the scene where Cheryl died and pay his respects.

Partick police had conducted their own background checks on Ryan Maxwell. Ryan was only thirty-three but had been married twice already. He was also quite a few years older than Cheryl and had only known her for around eight months. Apparently, the visit to Sheffield by Cheryl was the first time Ryan and Cheryl had met in person. However, like a father judging a prospective son-in-law, Patterson concluded Ryan was respectable enough. Importantly, he had never been in trouble with the police and even won a Duke of Edinburgh award in his teens.

On this Saturday morning, Glasgow Central was its bright and breezy self. It resembled countless major railway stations worldwide though it had an elegance and charm many others didn't have. It was rendered more generic on days like today by crowds looking up at the arrivals and departures boards and the two large TV screens that played news and adverts in subtitled silence. Commuters and non-commuters sat around the station on benches. Others walked through the station as a shortcut across town or popped into one of the numerous shops and food outlets dotted around the edge of the concourse.

Looking up at the departure board, Patterson could see the Manchester train was due to arrive on time. Sure enough, just after 11:40 am, a steady stream of people started to unfurl from the train onto the concourse from the direction of platform three.

Patterson had been given a photo of Maxwell, so he knew who to look out for. However, to be sure they found each other, Patterson gave a description of himself. That description said that Patterson was tall, slim and in his late forties. He had short grey hair and wore silver-rimmed spectacles. On early Saturday morning, he sent the additional information that he would be wearing a white shirt and blue tie along with a green V- neck jumper and grey corduroy trousers. Style was never one of Patterson's strong points.

As the train emptied its human cargo into Scotland's largest city, Patterson scoured the passengers intently for a Ryan Maxwell lookalike.

Some arrivals were speed walkers, others were dawdlers. None of the speed walkers looked like Ryan, but a later dawdler included a likely Ryan Maxwell candidate. He emerged with other backmarkers, taking the tourist route from the platform to the concourse. He was carrying a large red leather holdall over his shoulder.

Patterson's first impressions of Ryan Maxwell were of a youthful, good-looking man with a tired look. He was smartly dressed in a tan leather jacket and white open-necked shirt. He wore expensive-looking jeans that, on closer inspection, were ripped. He had thick black hair, some of which casually drooped over his forehead, which like the rips in his jeans, were either by accident or design. Patterson considered Ryan an ex-boyband member who had lived fast and now spent his life with a permanent hangover.

The description Patterson gave of himself must have worked because, on looking across in Patterson's direction, Ryan slowly raised a hand as if acknowledging the solitary fan who recognised him from days gone by.

Patterson, in turn, walked towards Ryan and held out his hand. 'Ryan? I'm Inspector

Patterson, Mike. Welcome to Glasgow. Sorry, it isn't in happier circumstances.'

Ryan gave a half-smile in return. 'Ta. Wish it were different bloody circumstances, ah tell ya. What's 'appening now then?' To Patterson's untrained ear, Ryan's accent was simply Yorkshire rather than specifically Sheffield. It even reminded him, to some degree, of Simpson's Manchester accent.

'I thought, first of all, we could visit the scene of Cheryl's death, and then I could drive you to your hotel if you like.'

'Aye, let's get t'it over with.'

Having got the green light, Patterson pointed to the back of the station where his metallic blue Renault Megane was parked. Being able to park within the station, right next to the high-numbered platforms, was one of the perks of being on the force. After putting the holdall in the boot, they drove out of the station via a short tunnel which ran under the Central Hotel and led out into Hope Street. Patterson then turned north towards Charing Cross.

As they drove up Hope Street, Ryan looked out the window at the blocks of buildings and busy streets of Glasgow city centre.

'Your first time in Glasgow?' Patterson asked.

Ryan continued to look out the side window as if lost in thought. 'Aye, tis that. Didn't think it would bloody well be to see where my fiancé was done in. I would av' come up earlier, but the bastards wouldn't give me time off work. At least they've let me av' a long weekend.'

Patterson glanced over at him. 'Fiancé? You were engaged to be married? I didn't know that.' Was that the news Cheryl was going to tell her flatmates?

'Aye, well, it wasn't certain like, but we'd talked about it. She was my soulmate was Cheryl.' Even from a side angle, Patterson could see moisture hovering in Ryan's eyes.

'I guess it must have been quite a shock when you heard she had gone missing.' As soon as he asked it, Patterson knew his question was stupid – of course, it would have been a shock - but he was woeful at small talk at the best of times.

'Aye, you could say that. At first, I wasn't that worried, to be honest. I just thought she must ave' gone t' a friend's or summit and not told anyone. Thought she would turn up. Guess you lot did too. Then Coppers come t' door looking grim as 'ell. That was when I knew she'd been found, and it wern't good news.'

'You'll have heard about her being held in the tunnel and everything else?'

'Aye, someone from local nick filled me in. Bastard. I 'ope you catch the bugger soon, and he gets what's coming to 'im.'

Patterson wanted to bring up the error in not finding Cheryl sooner and get it out of the way. 'You know as well about the tunnel—it was a place that should have been searched straight away.'

'Yeah, I 'erd. Listen, I don't blame yer. I know you're doing yer job as best you can. These things 'appen.'

Patterson thought that this was very gracious of Ryan. 'Just to say, we all feel terrible about what has happened. In fact, I don't know if you know, but the lead officer in the case has been suspended pending an enquiry. I'm the senior investigating officer now. I can assure you we'll do everything possible to catch Cheryl's murderer.'

Maxwell turned round for the first time to look at Patterson.

'Have you already an idea who did it, like?'

'No, not yet, but as I say, we're confident we'll catch whoever is responsible. I mean, we have some idiots on the force like anywhere else. My superior, for one. Best keep that to yourself. No, but apart from the deadwood and the imbeciles, we're a good team. We sometimes make mistakes but generally know what we're doing.'

Patterson turned the car onto a slip road that led up to Charing Cross.

'By eck, It's busy 'ere int'it,' Ryan said, looking at the crowds walking along Sauchiehall Street. Ryan's speech almost seemed like a caricature of Yorkshire dialect to Patterson.

People really did speak like that, then?

'Glasgow can be busy at times. I guess it's a bit like Sheffield.'

'Aye, a bit.'

'What do you do for a living?'

'I'm a plasterer.'

'Did you not want to drive up then?'

'Oh, I can't drive. Always been meaning to pass my test but never av.'

'Right.'

Patterson's car crossed the maze of Charing Cross and turned left up Woodlands Road.

'It's not far now,' Patterson said as he took a right turn and parked in a side street near the tunnel.

They got out of the car and walked to the location of Cheryl's murder. The area around the tunnel entrance was still sealed off with blue and white police tape, which fluttered in the cold wind. Bunches of flowers lay propped up against a wall near the entrance.

'So Ryan, this is where Cheryl was held captive. We can't go inside the tunnel since they're still doing some work.' Patterson then pointed along to the subway station a few hundred metres away. 'Over there, that's Kelvinbridge subway station. That's where Cheryl arrived after travelling up from seeing you to Glasgow Central. We believe she would normally have walked along here and gone up those stairs and onto her flat, which isn't far.'

Ryan wiped away tears that were now falling freely from his eyes. 'I still bloody can't believe it,' Maxwell said as he tried to catch his breath. 'Cheryl. My Cheryl. I really can't believe it.' Then, Ryan straightened up suddenly as if a thought had come to him. 'Bloody 'ell. Forgot to bring some flowers. 'Ang on. Need to go to flower shop.'

Before Patterson could react, Ryan walked across and then bounded up the stairs, which led to Gibson Street. Patterson looked up towards Gibson Street Bridge and saw part of Ryan's brown leather jacket walking fast along the above road. A few minutes later, Ryan came back with a bunch of chrysanthemums.

'Sorry,' said Ryan breathlessly when he returned. 'Should av' thought of that beforehand.' He held the bunch of Chrysanthemums as he looked towards the tunnel entrance, ready to place them next to the others.

Patterson thought this was an opportune time to make himself scarce. 'Anyway, I'll give you a moment to yourself, Ryan; I'm just going to walk towards the subway station. I'll be back in a few minutes.'

Ryan didn't react but moved towards the pile of flowers beside the tunnel entrance and then bent down to place his own beside them. He then stayed kneeling down, reading some of the messages on the flowers as Patterson subtly walked away and back up the path towards the subway station.

As Patterson walked along the path alongside the river, he looked over the thick old wall where it was presumed Cheryl had been lifted and tipped over into the river. It's doubtful if anyone would have even heard a splash against the river's flowing waters, especially in the early hours.

The sound of the river now, which was still fast-flowing, was quite soothing to Patterson's ear. The whole area was quite peaceful. Many places like this were to be found in the middle of Glasgow. Unexpected areas of natural green and quiet were around every corner. Patterson looked back at where Ryan stood in front of the tunnel. He was surprised to see a man talking to him. The man had his back to Patterson but then walked a couple of paces away from Ryan and appeared to take photographs of him from different angles. Patterson walked quickly back towards Ryan. However, the man who had taken the photos had himself seen Patterson returning and walked away rapidly, got into a car, and drove off.

'Who was that?' Patterson asked as he finally reached Ryan.

'Dunno, Just some bloke. Asked if I was a relative or friend of Cheryl. Said he wanted to take some pictures.'

Patterson watched as the man drove away.

He couldn't see the licence plate but could make out the car was a silver hatchback, probably a Volvo. He then turned to Ryan, 'You didn't wonder why he wanted a photo of you?'

'A bit. I guess you have some weird people in this town. Maybe he knew about Cheryl or something.'

Patterson looked at Ryan. 'You alright?'

'Yeah, ta. Bugger it, best get going. Still can't believe my Cheryl is gone.' He looked one more time at the tunnel before turning away. 'Might as well get to me 'otel.'

'Aye,' Patterson agreed. 'Where you staying?'

'The Marriott.'

'The Marriott?' Patterson was surprised. Strathclyde police paid for Ryan's accommodation, but the Marriott was not the usual choice. Still, Patterson drove and dropped off Ryan at the Marriott. However, while driving back to Partick Police Station, something was troubling Patterson. Although he couldn't put his finger on exactly why, he found there was something not quite right about Ryan.

Chapter 20

Questions

Patterson returned to Partick Station and immediately queried Simpson, McKinnon and Pettigrew regarding the interview of the tunnel workers.
'Did you find out anything interesting?'

'Fraid not,' Simpson answered while looking across at Pettigrew and McKinnon for confirmation.

'They parrotted what Tommy Beaton said to some extent. None of the workers noticed anything or anyone unusual when they were working at the tunnel. It was a routine job, by all accounts. They secured the entrance, cleared some graffiti, painted fluorescent markers, cleared rubbish, and what have you. They did that over five days, Monday to Friday. Each day they started at eight, finished at four, apart from Friday, when they finished at two.'

Patterson looked towards Pettigrew. 'What

about the workers themselves, anything or anyone worth noting?'

'I would say they came across as everyday guys.' Pettigrew answered. 'Nothing out of the ordinary. I interviewed the foreman, Gerry McBride. He seemed all right. As I say, they all came across as your everyday council workers; nothing unusual about them.'

'What about the keyholder? Was that Gerry McBride, as Tommy Beaton said?'

'Yeah,' replied Pettigrew. 'Gerry said he took the keys back to the office each night without fail and picked them up the next morning.'

'OK. Brian, I still want you to visit the council offices on Monday. Talk with whoever the foreman handed the keys to and double-check McBride did hand them in every night as he said.'

'Will do,' McKinnon said as he returned to his desk.

'How did the meeting with Cheryl's boyfriend go?' Simpson asked.

'Fine,' Patterson replied. Seems a nice enough lad. I took him to the tunnel. He was upset, of course.' Patterson seemed to ponder something.

'Something wrong?' Pettigrew asked.

'No, it's just that a slightly strange thing

happened at the tunnel. When I gave Ryan a moment to himself to lay flowers, some character came up to talk to him.'

'How do you mean some character?' Pettigrew asked.

'A man in his late thirties, I'd say; I didn't recognise him. He took a couple of photos of Ryan, but as soon as he saw me, he scarpered.'

'Sounds like a journalist,' said McKinnon

'Aye, that's what I thought, ' said Patterson. 'I asked Ryan about him, and he said he asked Ryan if he was there because of the murder.'

'Did something else happen?' asked Pettigrew sensing her boss was troubled by something else.

'Not exactly. If anything, it was just Ryan himself.'

'What about him?'

'I dunno. Can't put my finger on it.' Patterson turned to McKinnon. 'He has been thoroughly checked out, hasn't he?'

'Of course, he has,' McKinnon said, 'Besides, need I remind you he was in Sheffield when the murder occurred.'

'Aye...you know Ryan has been married twice already.'

'What's that got to do with anything?' said

Pettigrew.

'Nothing, except he is only thirty-three. He was saying today that Cheryl and himself were talking about marriage. That would make three marriages before he hit his mid-thirties.'

'That's the way of the world, nowadays,' said Simpson.'

'Aye, I guess so. Anyway, it doesn't matter.'

Later, back in his office, Patterson cleared up the last few remaining bits of paperwork of the day, and there was a knock on the door. Without looking up, he muttered, 'Come in'.

Only after Patterson heard the door close did he look up to see Emma Booth standing before him. Patterson stiffened. Emma Booth had been the family liaison officer on the last case Patterson had worked on before he took his extended break. During the case that had become known as the Drainpipe Killer Murders, Patterson felt Booth had become too close to him emotionally. He even began to suspect that Booth had formed some kind of fixation on him.

Although nothing had happened, he also knew he hadn't deterred her as much as he could have. Perhaps he could have blamed the whole situation on the pressure of the case; maybe it had been the situation with Stephanie, whose drinking had become even more troublesome a few months back. Perhaps, he had simply been flattered by the attentions of this much younger, attractive woman. He was only glad his relationship with Booth hadn't become anything more than it did.

Nevertheless, his strong moral side had taken a dent to its pride. He hadn't seen Booth since he had gone on holiday and dreaded seeing her again.

'Emma,' Patterson finally said after his initial surprise, 'How are you?'

'Fine, thanks, sir,' Booth said, smiling. 'I just thought I'd pop in and say hello.'

'Of course, of course, take a seat. Weaver told me you were back. So, how is everything? You were off for a time, is that right? Are you all right now? Health-wise, I mean.' Patterson knew he was talking too fast and was asking too many questions, but he couldn't stop himself.

'Fine, sir, it was just a bug I picked up, nothing serious. I just had to spend some time away.'

'Of course, of course.' Why was he repeating 'of course' all the time? For a moment, Patterson thought about mentioning Julie Henshaw and the car accident. Then the crazy thought that Booth could have been responsible for that car accident crossed his mind and made him hesitate. Was it crazy? Did he really think Booth could have been responsible so she could return to work with Patterson as soon as? Too late. The thought was there. Change the subject.

'So, how are the parents of Cheryl coping?'

'As expected. Devastated, but you know, coping in a way.'

Patterson was still taken by surprise at the appearance of Booth. Not by her acting strange but by her acting perfectly normal. Had Patterson misjudged the situation? Blown it up out of all proportion? It seemed that way, and Patterson began to relax a little more. Patterson wanted everything to continue as normal as normal could be. He wanted to be friendly, and yet, not too friendly. He wanted to speak to his fellow officer as a professional colleague without being too distant. It was all a bit of a difficult task, but Booth didn't appear to notice.

'To be honest, I haven't found out much of interest about Cheryl,' Booth said. 'Cheryl hadn't spoken about any issues or anyone causing her problems. Although, I got the impression that she hadn't mentioned Ryan Maxwell much to her parents. For instance, they only learned Cheryl was down in Sheffield through us. As far as her parents were concerned, it appears Ryan was a secret.'

Patterson thought about this. It wasn't unusual for daughters to keep certain boyfriends hidden. Then again, according to Ryan, the couple were talking about marriage. 'I met Ryan Maxwell this afternoon, as a matter of fact. He's a bit older than Cheryl; maybe that's why.'

'Possibly,' said Booth.

'Plus, Ryan's been married twice already, and I gather the parents of Cheryl are quite respectable.'

'Well,' said Booth, 'as I say, the parents vaguely knew there was someone in Cheryl's life, but that's all. Make of that what you will. Besides that, Cheryl was a typical young woman with her whole life ahead of her. A bright student, loving daughter, and well-liked by everyone by all accounts.'

Patterson nodded. It was a cliché, but for the umpteenth time, he noticed it was often the nicest people in the world who died young. As if God did take up the option of importing the best of humankind when deciding who should move upstairs.

'And how's yourself, Emma?' Patterson asked, trying to keep the meeting with Booth informal.

'Oh, can't complain, and you? I heard you went on holiday with your wife.'

'Yes,' said Patterson. 'We went to the Maldives.'

'Oooh, the Maldives, eh? Sounds nice.'

Sounds Nice. Why does everyone have the same reply whenever Patterson mentions the Maldives? 'Yes, it was nice, good to get away.'

'I'll bet,' said Booth.

'So, how are you getting on with Weaver? Everything going all right?'

'Yes, he seems very capable.'

'He is. We've worked together on many a case over the years.' Patterson looked at his fellow officer. She seemed a lot different than he remembered her. Calmer. There was none of that 'sexual tension' he thought he had sensed before with her. He was pleased this meeting, this reacquaintance had gone so well, but he knew he had to get on with his work before heading home. 'Well, thanks for popping in, Emma. Keep me up to date with everything.'

Booth rose from the seat. 'I'll do that, sir. It's nice to see you again.'

As Booth went towards the door, Patterson couldn't help but smile to himself. He had been so apprehensive about seeing Booth again. Yet, he now realised he had built up everything in his mind. He had started to imagine Booth as some kind of Glenn Close psychopath. It was ridiculous, and meeting Booth again, he realised his concerns had been completely unfounded. As he watched Booth go out the door, he felt a weight had been lifted off his shoulders.

Just as Emma was leaving, she turned back and looked at Patterson again.

'Oh, by the way, sir. I know you still want me.' Booth smiled, winked, turned, and closed the door behind her.

Smiling, Patterson watched through the glass partition as his fellow officer walked away. Eventually, he lowered his head and looked down at the papers on his desk, still with that frozen smile on his face.

Chapter 21

Lucas Ryba

It was just after five PM, and Lucas Ryba wasn't happy. It wasn't just that he hadn't had a good day; it was more than that. For one thing, Lucas was homesick for his native Poland. For another thing, he hated his job at the bottling plant.

For five days a week, and often on an additional Saturday like today, Lucas would stand next to a long metal table in a large, freezing-cold open shed where he would unscrew bottles of whisky and pour the liquid into a huge vat. For eight hours a day, four in the morning and four in the afternoon, separated by an unpaid half hour for lunch, that's all he did. Other workers stood around him, two lines on either side of the long battered table, doing exactly the same thing he did. Almost all the workers were from Eastern Europe and earning minimum wage. He didn't really want to work the additional Saturday either, but felt obliged when they asked and, besides, the extra money would come in handy too.

Minimum wage was a bonus, but it really was freezing in that shed and monotonous, soul-destroying work. Once Lucas emptied the whisky out of the bottles, he would chuck the empties into a large metal bin. Once the container was filled, it was wheeled away for recycling. Lucas never asked why he was doing what he was doing since he wasn't that interested in why he was doing what he was doing. He assumed it was because something was wrong with the labelling, the bottles themselves, or the whisky. Maybe they were making a new whisky with the old whisky or something like that. Lucas didn't know, and even if he had wanted to know, there was no one to ask.

Back in Krakow, he was an assistant medic working as part of an ambulance crew. The fact was he got paid more for emptying whisky out of bottles. At the same time, he missed having a job where he actually helped people. Every day now, Lucas weighed the pros and cons of working for more money in a foreign country against having a job that gave him emotional satisfaction in his home country. Every day, the latter option became more and more attractive.

So it was that Saturday afternoon, just after five, he left the factory off Helen Street in Govan. He walked up towards Golspie Street, lost in thought. Yet, this particular day was an especially important day for Lucas. He decided once and for all to return to his true home, Poland.

Lucas made his way across Golspie Street amidst the traffic of cars, buses and pedestrians. Streets once filled with tenements were now wide open spaces, the tenements long since gone. It was freezing cold, and Lucas shivered as he tried to get some warmth into his bones.

With tired, aching legs, he wandered towards Govan Cross. The bright lights of Govan, the starlit attractions of the shopping centre, job centre, small shops and longstanding pubs lit up the otherwise darkened streets. Most of all, Govan subway station stood like a magic portal that could transport citizens across the city in no time at all. However, its architecture was unremarkable. Dirty, different-sized blocks of grey brick and cladding clumped together like a lego building constructed by a bored four-year-old. Yet, Lucas loved this station because it would take him to a bus stop outside Bridge Street station in under ten minutes. From there, a final bus ride took him further south to his shared accommodation in Govanhill. The bright S above Govan station welcomed him forward. As he entered the subway station, Lucas was happier than he had been for weeks. The thought of going home cheered him no end, and he pushed through the silver turnstile as he heard the rumble and the toot of a train entering the station down below. He was finally going home, he thought, finally, thank God.

Lucas Ryba had no idea he would never make it home. Not to his native Poland or even to his shared flat in Govanhill.

Chapter 22

Old Railways

It had been a long day, and after meeting Ryan, not to mention Booth, Patterson was looking forward to getting home and spending a nice quiet Saturday night with Stephanie. He thought about the abandoned railway tunnel itself. Could that have any significance to the murder of Cheryl Kerr? This was why, later, on the way home from the police station, Patterson stopped at Partick Library and picked up a couple of books on Glasgow's railway past. Later that night, having had a lovely meal Stephanie had cooked for him, Patterson now sat on the settee contentedly looking through one of the books.

From what he was reading, Patterson looked up to see Stephanie enter the room and randomly move some ornaments around the sideboard.

'You all right?' Patterson asked her.

'Aye, fine, why?'

'No, nothing, you're not –'

'Not what?'

'Not worrying about the kids coming up, are you?'

'Och no!' Stephanie said a little too loudly, and he immediately knew his wife was worrying about the kids coming up.

'What's the book you're reading?' Stephanie asked, obviously trying to change the subject.

'It's about the old railways in Glasgow, you know, the old steam trains from years back.'

'Didn't think you were into that kind of thing,' Stephanie said.

'I'm not; it's because of the old railway tunnel where Cheryl Kerr was found. It got me thinking about the old steam trains. Did I tell you I used to play in these tunnels when I was a kid? We used to walk through them. The tunnels are very long and dark, and you should see the old abandoned station at the Botanic Gardens; it's quite something. I think they were going to turn it into a café at one point. Aye, there were old steam railways right across the city at one time. Listen to this –'

'Mike, I don't want to be rude, but I'm really not that interested. I —'

'I know, but listen, it says here the tunnels at Kelvinbridge were part of the Glasgow Central Railway, which first opened in 1896. The line ran from Newton, that's just past Cambuslang, all the way to Maryhill Central. Maryhill had a huge station at one time. It's where the shopping centre is now. Kelvinbridge station was a fair size too. That whole car park outside the subway was once part of the railway. In fact, the station building still stands.'

'Does it? Well, I haven't seen it,' Stephanie said dismissively.

'It's on the corner, just down from the actual bridge over the Kelvin. Here look.'

Patterson leaned over and showed Stephanie the photo of the station in the book. 'There. You must have seen it at some time.'

'Possibly.'

'See, I told you you'd be interested.'

'I didn't say I was interested; I just said I possibly have seen that building. Move over.' Stephanie picked up the remote, switched on the telly, and sat beside her husband. 'Listen, Strictly will be starting any minute, so if you don't mind...'

'I know, I'll keep quiet.' But then Patterson read on. 'The railway was closed around 1964, but some of it is still in use today.'

'Is it?' said Stephanie, absent-mindedly looking at the TV screen and switching channels.

'Aye, you know that electric line that goes past the Exhibition Centre? It's called the Argyle line now. Goes from Rutherglen to Partick, I think. Well, that was part of the Glasgow Central Railway.'

'Really,' Stephanie said in a bored voice. Patterson should have known how much

Stephanie liked her peace and quiet to watch Strictly Come Dancing. Patterson could talk about anything at any other time, but during Strictly, Stephanie, as good as had a Do Not Disturb sign hanging from her forehead.

However, Patterson was so fascinated by what he was reading he didn't heed the warning signs that he was getting on Stephanie's nerves.

'And listen to this –'

'Mike, will you please shut up!'

The full voice bellow took Patterson by surprise. Even when annoyed, it wasn't in Stephanie's nature to shout, at least when sober.

'Sorry. Didn't realise.'

Stephanie sighed. 'No, I'm sorry,' She had tears in her eyes. 'If you must know. It's just –'

'Just what?'

'I have been thinking about Aisling and Callum coming up. God, Mike, there's so much to do; I'm worried I won't get it all done.'

'Get what done? There's nothing to do. It'll be fine, I promise you. You shouldn't get yourself in such a tizz about it.'

To Mike's surprise, Stephanie started crying, letting the tears escape her eyes. Mike moved closer and put his arms around her. 'Honest love, it'll be fine. They're just here for a few days, and it'll be good to see them.'

'I know it will, but you know what happened last time,' said Stephanie, 'what if?'

'What?'

Stephanie gulped back more tears, trying to catch her breath, to not cry more. 'God, Mike, I don't want to start drinking again! I really don't, but I'm scared. I just want everything to be just right. I don't want –'

Patterson bent down and put his arm around his wife. 'Just don't worry about it. You've done really well so far. You should have more faith in yourself. Honest, trust me, everything will be fine.'

'You keep saying that! Sorry, I just can't help feeling – the thing is, I want a drink. I mean, I really want a drink. These past few days. You have no idea. No idea how hard it is.'

'I know, Steph, I know. Is there no one you can call? Someone from one of your groups?'

'I could but –'

'But what?'

'Och, just let me watch Strictly for now.'

Patterson kissed her gently on the cheek. The familiar Strictly Come Dancing theme music started.

'Love you,' Stephanie said quietly, wiping her eyes.

'Love you too,' Patterson replied.

'Now get out of the way and let me watch my programme.'

Patterson got off the couch, took his book, and headed upstairs to the bedroom.

Chapter 23

Traffic

It was Monday, the 8th of December, and Patterson sat in the early morning traffic, heading through Anniesland on his way back to Partick Police Station to start another week at work. He had spent most of Sunday at home and enjoyed the rare time away from the station and the pressures of work. Now though, it was back to the grind, and the traffic was horrendous. He was so close to the police station too. Five minutes at most if the roads were clear.

As he waited for the traffic to move, he thought about his Saturday meeting with Ryan again. What was it about him? Did it even matter?

Patterson looked at the cars around him, and from out of nowhere, pinpricks of anxiety started to tickle his skin. He felt trapped. If he needed to escape from the car in a hurry, he couldn't. The vehicle on the driver's side was too close. He would somehow have to clamber out of the car's passenger side. Could he make it in time? Patterson knew he was being irrational, yet irrational was anxiety's mood of choice.

Occasionally, cyclists would go speeding past the car's left side. Canny buggers avoiding the suffocating hell of being stuck in early morning traffic thought Patterson. He looked in his left-side rearview mirror, and yet another cyclist was approaching, then Patterson thought he recognised who it was. McKinnon? Yes, that was McKinnon, all right. In full cycling gear, no less. Patterson thought of tooting his horn or giving some other acknowledgement. However, by the time Patterson thought about it, his detective constable had already sped past.

The traffic was still not moving. As a result, Patterson didn't either, and he felt his breathing become a little more laboured no matter how hard he tried to ignore it. It was often the thought of having a panic attack that accelerated a panic attack. That was how Patterson was feeling at that moment. As such, he knew he had to think of something else apart from having an anxiety attack to stop the anxiety attack. So, while only moments earlier he had tried to dismiss any thoughts about Ryan, now he tried to fully concentrate on those thoughts.

Ryan Maxwell. There was definitely something not right about him. Married twice yet planning to marry a third time at the age of thirty-three? To a woman who was quite a bit younger and, by all accounts, someone he didn't know that well?

Patterson still felt as if he couldn't quite breathe properly. The diversion tactics weren't working. Anxiety was far stronger than the thoughts about Ryan Maxwell. Every minute seemed like an hour. McKinnon would arrive at the station soon while Patterson was still stuck in this traffic jam. It was hell. The sweat dripped down his back despite the cold day seeping into his car. He felt light-headed, dizzy, and sick. He needed to —

That's it! All of a sudden, it came to him. Like the proverbial lightbulb flashing above his head, Patterson knew what it was about Ryan Maxwell that bothered him so much. Of course! Patterson still felt ill at ease, but the anxiety had almost been instantly booted out of his system.

He reached over to the car phone and tapped the speed dial number. It automatically went to loudspeaker, and Simpson's sleepy Mancunian tones could be heard saying hello.

'Simpson, is McKinnon there yet?'

'No, why?'

'Never mind why. Do you know anything about the background checks he did on Ryan Maxwell?

'Sir, you're not still thinking Ryan had anything to do with Cheryl's murder?'

'Do you know something, Jack? You're a right pain in the arse sometimes.' Simpson could sense the real annoyance in his superior's voice and knew not to push his luck.

'Sorry, sir. McKinnon hasn't said anything other than Ryan's completely clean, as far as I know. You heard him say so yesterday. No record at —'

'Listen, as soon as McKinnon arrives, put him on; he should be there any minute.'

Patterson heard McKinnon shout 'Morning all' and Simpson calling him over.

After a short silence, Patterson heard McKinnon's laboured voice.

'Brian?'

'Sir?'

'You checked into the background of Ryan Maxwell, didn't you?'

'I did. Nothing of interest, no criminal record if that's what you're wondering.'

'Do you know if he has a driving licence?'

'A driving licence? Em, yeah, I think so, if I remember correctly. Hang on, I'll just get his details up on screen.' There was another short pause as McKinnon walked over to his desk with the phone.

'Yes, Ryan has a licence. In fact, he worked as a taxi driver not so long ago; he currently drives a red BMW no less.'

Patterson watched the traffic around him finally start to move. 'OK. One other thing, do you know when Ryan is due to go back to Sheffield?' A car horn peeped from behind at a still-immobile Patterson.

'I think he's due to go back this morning. Hang on...'

Patterson put his car into first and edged forward. There was once again a silence before McKinnon came back on the phone. 'Yeah, he's booked on the 9:05 this morning to London. He changes at York for Sheffield. So, by my reckoning, it leaves in approximately twenty-two minutes.'

'Right. I want you to get on to Central and get them to stop that train from leaving. Tell them, under no circumstances must it leave the station. You got that?'

'But sir.'

'No buts, you got that?'

'I've got that, but why?'

'For God's sake, stop asking questions and just do as you're told. I'm making my way to Central now; put Simpson back on.'

McKinnon put his hand over the mouthpiece and whispered to Simpson, 'He's completely lost it now.'

Simpson came back on with a question. 'Sir, are you all right?'

'Yes, of course, I'm bloody all right. I'm on my way to Central Station to pick up Ryan Maxwell. In the meantime, I want you to help McKinnon get everything we can on him. Every statement he has given, every fact of his life we know. Every last detail.'

'Right, sir. Can I ask why?'

Patterson sighed at being asked another question but decided to answer this time. 'Because I think Ryan Maxwell may have murdered Cheryl Kerr, that's why!'

Patterson clicked off the phone and switched on the blue flashing LED lights in his car's grille. Turning on the siren, the vehicles in front slowly started to move aside. Patterson knew that if Ryan got on that train, it could be an age before they got him back to Glasgow, if at all. Patterson should have realised sooner. At the very least, as Patterson continued to edge forward, the impending panic attack from moments before was long since gone.

Chapter 24

A Confession

With the heavy rush hour traffic and twenty minutes until the train was due to leave, Patterson knew there was little chance he could reach Glasgow Central on time.

However, he made good progress as his car turned onto Great Western Road. Patterson's good progress didn't last long. Even with its blue lights and siren, the vehicle again became bogged down in early morning traffic. He called the Partick Station again.

'What's happening,' asked Patterson impatiently.

'We can't get through to Central,' replied Simpson.

'What do you mean you can't get through?'

'Just that. The number is either engaged, or no one answers when it rings.'

'Have they not got an emergency number?'

'Not that we can find.'

'For pity's sake. What about a uniform in the area? Phone Baird Street and see if they have anyone in the vicinity. Failing that, phone the flippin' newsagent at Central and get them to stop the train. I don't want that train leaving the station!' Patterson clicked off his phone before Simpson could respond and looked at the clock. The train was due to leave in 16 minutes.

Patterson managed to pick up speed again, and, in no time, he had raced through to the top of Hope Street in the city centre. He glanced at the clock once more. There were now only 11 minutes till the train was due to leave. Hope Street was very busy with traffic.

His lights and siren did help to cut through the cars, buses and taxis. However, halfway down Hope Street, the traffic couldn't move out of his way even if it wanted to. Patterson decided it would be quicker on foot. He took a sharp right, parked in a side lane and exited the car. He glanced at his watch again. He had 5 minutes. He then ran down the alleyway, turned right, and started running down Hope St, dodging the early morning workers as best he could. Patterson's fitness wasn't that bad for someone in their late forties, and he was soon near the station. He looked at his watch. There were 2 minutes until the train left.

Patterson turned right into Gordon Street and ran across the road, where he entered the main station entrance. He looked at his watch again. 9:05. The train was due to leave now. As he made his way to stand in front of the main departure boards, he heard a whistle, but it could have been for any train. He couldn't determine what platform the Sheffield train was leaving from until he remembered it was the London train, which was usually Platform 1.

Just about out of hope and severely out of breath, Patterson ran up to the gate at platform 1 and saw a train was still there. He asked the guard what the train was.

'It's the Euston train. You better hurry up; not sure why it's been delayed, but it should be leaving at any minute.'

Patterson then noticed a couple of uniformed policemen standing further up the platform. Patterson made his way towards the first of them.

'Inspector Patterson?' The first PC asked.

Patterson acknowledged it was him.

'We were told to make sure the train didn't leave as you requested.'

'Thanks,' said Patterson, 'good job.' Patterson bent over, coughing and trying to catch his breath. Standing up again, he was sweating and could hardly speak. 'Come with me,' he managed to utter to the officer.

Still breathing heavily, Patterson pressed an illuminated yellow button to open the train's first carriage door. He walked up the train, listening to a hum of conversation, scanning the passengers as curious travellers looked back at him. The train had nine carriages, but Patterson didn't have to search for long. Ryan Maxwell was sitting in the third carriage. Ryan looked up at Patterson in surprise.

'Inspector, you, all right?'

'I'm fine, Ryan. Absolutely fine.' Patterson smiled. 'You'll have to accompany me back to the station. We have something to discuss.'

'Oh, you saw the papers then?' said Ryan.

*

Ryan sat next to the duty solicitor opposite Patterson in interview room two. Ryan didn't seem nervous as much as having one hell of a hangover, and he took constant sips of water from a polystyrene cup.

Once the procedural formalities of the interview were taken care of, Patterson began.

'The reason I'm interviewing you today, Ryan, is to clarify some of the details surrounding the death of Cheryl Kerr, who disappeared last month on the 29th of November and was found murdered on the 2nd of December. First, I'd like to clarify your relationship with Cheryl. You were her boyfriend, is that correct?'

Ryan looked back at Patterson with a mix of annoyance and contempt.

'Yeah, you know that. I was Cheryl's boyfriend.'

'It's for the benefit of the tape, Ryan. So you were in a relationship with Cheryl Kerr.'

'Yeah, we were in a relationship. I mean, we lived in different towns like, but yeah.'

'Can you confirm when was the last time you saw Cheryl?'

Ryan continued to look at Patterson as if he was not the brightest cop in the station.

'When she left for Glasgow. At Sheffield train station.'

'What date was that?

'Well, it were the Saturday. The same day she went missing, the twenty-ninth of November.'

'So when Cheryl left Sheffield on the morning of the twenty-ninth of November, the day she went missing, you're saying that was the last time you saw her. At Sheffield train station around 10:30 am?'

'That's right. Why are you repeating what I'm saying all the time? You know, I do have a job to go to back in Sheffield. How long are we going to be here?'

'We'll be here as long as it takes. I just want to be clear with everything said, for the record. It's for your benefit as much as ours. As you mention employment, is it true you've worked as a taxi driver in the past?'

'Aye, 'ave done; what the 'ell 'as that got to do wi' anything?'

'I assume you need a driving licence to be a

taxi driver.'

'Yeah, course you do.'

'Only, when I picked you up at Glasgow Central on Saturday, you said you didn't know how to drive and hadn't a driving licence. You said that was why you were getting the train that day.'

'Did Ah? Can't say, Ah remember. Maybe you 'erd wrong.'

'No, I didn't hear wrong. That's what you said. Why did you lie about having a driving licence?'

'I didn't lie. I just probably mis'erd your question, that's all.'

'You did lie, and I'll tell you why I think you lied about having a driving licence. You made out you couldn't drive because you didn't want me to know you drove up to Glasgow the day Cheryl went missing. That was also why you took the train on this trip.'

Ryan laughed. 'Listen, Inspector, whatever your name is, you better be careful with what you're saying 'ere.' He then looked across at the duty solicitor who spoke.

'You do need to be careful of what you're suggesting, Chief Inspector. If you accuse my client of anything, you better have reason to do so.'

'I'm just trying to establish if your client has a driving licence. It's perfectly simple.'

'Yeah, I have a driving licence, so what?'

'I'll get to the point. After you said goodbye to Cheryl at Sheffield train station, what did you do?'

'Went 'ome 'ad a kip.'

'That isn't true, though, is it? You see, we have CCTV of your car heading north towards Glasgow shortly after you waved goodbye to Cheryl at Sheffield train station. How do you account for that?'

'You're crackers,'

'Do you deny you arrived in Glasgow later that day?'

'You know summit, you're an absolute fruit loop. Are all the coppers up ere' friggin nutters like you?'

'As I said,' Patterson repeated, 'We already have CCTV of your car driving up to Glasgow. Apart from the licence plate, it's quite a distinctive car. A red BMW.'

'Hang on, Ryan.' The duty solicitor whispered into Ryan's ear.

'You're bluffing,' Ryan then said.

'We'll also soon have CCTV of you in Glasgow. The fact is, we know you were in Glasgow when Cheryl was murdered.'

Ryan just looked at his duty solicitor, who now kept quiet.

'Just tell us what happened, Ryan. Was Cheryl annoyed at you arriving unannounced? Did something not go according to plan? Did something get out of hand? Did –'

Suddenly Ryan rose out of his chair and went for Patterson.‘Shut it. How fucking dare you! –’

The uniformed officer in the room came forward and placed a hand on Ryan’s shoulder, pushing him back down on the chair. Maxwell suddenly slumped forward, laying his head face down on the table. His body started to move up and down as he started sobbing.

'Listen, I’m trying to help you here, Ryan. Just tell us the truth. Explain what happened. Did you murder Cheryl? This is your chance to explain –'

Ryan raised his head from the table, his face half-covered in snot. The duty solicitor handed him a hankie, and Maxwell wiped his face before speaking.

'I didn't kill Cheryl. I swear I didn't kill her. I loved her. I loved her!' He looked directly at Patterson. Yes, I was in Glasgow –’

The duty solicitor interrupted Ryan, much to Patterson’s annoyance. ‘Ryan, I advise you not to say anything further –’

‘No, I want to get it off me chest. Honest to God, I didn't kill her. I swear I didn’t. I didn’t even know anything about her going missing at the time.’

Ryan put his head in his hands and asked for another cup of water. Patterson nodded towards the uniformed officer, who went outside before returning shortly afterwards with the drink. Ryan took a gulp before repeating what he had already said numerous times. 'I didn't kill Cheryl. That's the truth.'

'So, then tell me; the truth this time. Let's start again; where were you, late Saturday afternoon, when Cheryl went missing?'

'Glasgow, but I didn't kill her Ahm tellin' ya!'

'OK, so let's take it back to the beginning. On Saturday morning, you were in Sheffield when Cheryl caught the train back to Glasgow. The train left at 10:30am. We agree on that. We have you on CCTV waving her off. Then what did you do?'

'Well, I waved her off like, and then I went back to me car in the car park. I was just going to go home, but I was well upset about Cheryl leaving. Having to wait to see her again. Then I thought, sod it, what the 'ell am I staying ere' for? Why don't I just go to Glasgow there and then? It was a crazy thought, but why not? I sat in the car, thinking about it and the more I thought about it, the more I wanted to do it. So I did. I said sod it! Let's just do it. I drove towards motorway and headed north.'

'You didn't tell Cheryl about this?'

'No, I thought it would be a surprise for 'er. Thought I'd turn up at her flat later that night and she'd be really pleased. I guessed I would arrive in Glasgow about a couple of hours after she arrived. Then while I was driving up, Cheryl texted me to say her train was stuck in snow somewhere near the border. It started snowing heavily as I was driving up, but the motorway was still all right, still clear. So time went on, and then Cheryl texted again to say she was still stuck on the train.'

'She didn't phone you?'

'No, just texts. Anyway, with Cheryl being stuck on the train, I realised I would arrive in Glasgow before she did. Then I thought I could meet her at the station as she got off the train! It was perfect. I could just imagine her face as she came off the platform and saw me waiting for her. She would be right gobsmacked!' Ryan became slightly tearful before continuing. 'Anyway, so that's what I did. At least, that was me plan. Once I reached Glasgow, I 'eaded towards the Central Railway Station.'

'You'd never been to Glasgow before?'

'No, never.'

'Was it not hard finding your way around the city.'

'A little, I guess, like I know the station were in the centre of town somewhere, and once I got in't centre, there were signs n' that. But course, it wasn't easy finding me way round. Plus, you've got a bloody one-way system and everything. Also, trying to find a place to park wasn't easy.'

'So, where did you park?'

'There were a multi-storey up this lane somewhere. Quite near station. Anyway, it were busy, but I managed to get a space –'

'You know exactly where this parking is?'

'Dunno.'

Patterson had an idea of where he was talking about in any case. There weren't that many multi-storey car parks near Central Station. 'OK, go on.'

'So I parked in this car park and then walked round t' station. It were freezing cold, pavements were like slush and snow, and the town centre was busy as 'ell. Anyway, I got to station and stood on concourse, and Cheryl's train still hadn't arrived. Which was brilliant, but I looked up at the boards, and it still didn't give a time when Cheryl's train was due. It just said delayed. So like, I'm standing there, freezing my bollocks off, and I said, sod this, I'm away for a beer while I'm waiting. So I went across road to this pub. Really nice it was and warm and –'

'You remember the name of this pub?'

'Nah, but it was right opposite the main entrance to station, though. Think it were green outside if I remember. '

Again Patterson had a good idea of where he was talking about. 'So you went to this pub for a beer and then returned to the station?'

'Well, thing is see, I had a pint and got talkin' to this bloke. Dead interesting he was. A right laff. He bought me a pint, and then I bought him one. Well, by the time I head back to the station, Cheryl's train's already arrived, and I've bloody missed her! All that way driving up 'ere, and then I miss her. I felt a right pillock.'

'So what then?'

'Well, then I thought I could go to Cheryl's flat, but by then, I already had another couple of pints and thought I can't see her in this state; plus, how do I get there? Can't drive me car. Course, I could get a taxi, but then I thought, sod it, let's just go for drink, so I headed back to the pub.'

The impression Ryan was giving of himself was not a good one. This was someone who had a habit of saying sod it and just doing what he wanted to do, regardless of the consequences. Was that also a factor in how Cheryl died?

'OK, Ryan, let's just recap for a moment,' said Patterson. 'So you're saying you drove up to Glasgow intending to see, to surprise, Cheryl. You've gone to Central Station to meet her, but while you're waiting, you've gone to the pub, had a drink, returned to the station and then missed her. So, you then decide to head back to the pub instead of going to Cheryl's flat. Is that where we're at?'

'I'm not proud of meself, but that's about the gist of it, aye. See, ah, know I were a bloody idiot, but it was my first time in Glasgow. I'd heard about how your pubs were crackin' like, and they were as it 'appens, so I decided to stay out. Thought I could see Cheryl the next day.'

'Did Cheryl not text or call you during this

time?'

'No, she didn't text at all, which I did think was strange. But then, to be honest, I was just drinking a lot, and I had no idea what had happened or might have happened to Cheryl by then. You know, now, I keep thinking to meself, if only I had stayed in the station and waited for Cheryl, she would still be alive today.' Ryan started to cry quietly but just as quickly stopped.

'What did you do that night, then?'

'I got bloody pissed out me 'ead that's what. Got completely drunk and then stayed in a hotel somewhere. Like I say, I'm not proud of meself, but that's what I did.'

'You know what hotel?'

'It overlooked a river; that's all I remember. Bloody expensive, too, I tell yer. Rip off.'

All this information about the hotel, taxi, parking and pubs would be vital in seeing if there was any truth in what Ryan was saying or in proving he was making this whole elaborate story up.

'You say you slept overnight at the hotel. What did you do the next day?'

'Well, I saw there were no texts from Cheryl, which was still strange, but I assumed she must have crashed out after her journey home. Then I noticed a text from me mam. It said my grandad was ill. They thought he'd had a stroke and he was rushed to hospital. So I thought I better drive back home as soon as. But of course, I still wanted to see Cheryl. I didn't know what t do. In the end, I thought, sod it. I can explain everything to Cheryl later. In fact, I could even drive back down to Sheffield, and she'd be none the wiser I'd ever been in Glasgow. So that's what I did. Found the parking place. Found me car and paid the excess fee and stuff. Then drove all the way back down to Sheffield that morning. Like I said, I thought Cheryl would be none the wiser. All the while, I had no idea about anything that might have happened to her. I swear.'

Patterson thought a little more before continuing. In some ways, it could be a plausible story, but in other ways, it was complete bullshit. Patterson knew the best liars were often the most desperate. Plus, something else didn't add up about Ryan and his story. Something else that had been bothering Patterson since he had met him on Saturday.

'Ryan, you say you had never been to Glasgow before. But that's not true, is it?'

'How do you mean it isn't true?'

'You see since I met you on Saturday, something else was bugging me, and I couldn't think what it was. Then it came to me. When I was with you that day at the tunnel, you remember when you said you needed to get some flowers?'

'Yeah?'

'The thing is, you didn't even bother to ask me where a flower shop was. You immediately rushed off as if you knew precisely where to go. Sure enough, you went in the right direction and went straight to Gibson Street, where there was indeed a flower shop. How could you have possibly known where Gibson St was, let alone know there was a flower shop there? In fact, I had the distinct impression you knew the area around where Cheryl lived fairly well. So, you have been to Glasgow before, haven't you?'

'I can see why you would think that, but I can explain.'

The duty solicitor still remained quiet, apparently having given up the fight.

'Then explain,' said Patterson.

'See, I mean, I do know the area around the tunnel and around the area there fairly well, a little bit at least. Ryan sat more upright in his chair and took another sip of water. 'See, me and Cheryl used to talk all the time on the phone or online and that. We also used to go on walks in each other's towns.'

Patterson looked at him quizzically. 'How's that? "You used to go on walks."'

'With online maps and street views of the local area where we both lived,' Ryan explained. 'Her in Glasgow and me in Sheffield. See, now and then, we would say to each other, 'Would you like to go on a walk? And then one of us would say, your place or mine? And then, we would go on a kind of virtual walk around each other's areas. Google maps. Virtual like. We would walk down to the shops. So you could say I've been to Gibson Street a few times, and I 'ave. Online, I mean. She'd point a few places out to me. Where the university was, and so on. There was also this shop where she got her magazines on Gibson Street. She pointed that out. So yeah, I knew Gibson Street a little, and I remember seeing this flower shop next to the newsagent. Cos once I asked her if she would like some flowers.' Ryan started crying again. 'I remember seeing it. I never thought I'd go there for real to be laying flowers down for Cheryl.' Ryan shook his head. 'I knew Gibson Street, the bridge, and the river, so I knew where to go immediately. But not because I had been there before. Cos I had seen it online. Honest, I had never been to Glasgow before in real life.'

Ryan seemed to have an explanation for everything.

'So, how is your grandfather?'

'Eh?'

'You said your grandfather was ill, taken to hospital. How is he?'

'Oh aye, he did have a stroke. A mild one, but it was still a stroke. He's doing OK, thanks.'

'You said your mum texted you. I don't suppose you would still have that text?'

Ryan started to shake his head but then stopped.'Hang on, I might just do as it 'appens.' He pulled an expensive-looking phone from his jacket pocket and started to scroll through messages. The solicitor and Patterson glanced at each other, both with differing thoughts. Sure enough, Ryan turned the phone around and, with a beaming smile, showed a message from his mum at 7:26 am on Sunday, the 30th of November. *Ryan, call us. It's an emergency. Your grandad has had a turn.*

Patterson took the phone and studied the message. Either Ryan had gone to elaborate measures, or the message was genuine. Partly through frustration, Patterson decided to end the interview there and then. He needed a break. He also wanted his team to check CCTV and Ryan's story immediately. It wouldn't take long to prove or disprove Ryan's version of events.

Ryan was taken to a holding cell while these enquiries were carried out. Patterson still had a bad feeling about Ryan, but now it wasn't because he suspected Ryan might be guilty; this time, it was because he suspected Ryan might be innocent.

Chapter 25

Disappointing Dunard

Afterwards, Patterson went upstairs to update his boss on the interview with Ryan. As he walked into his superior's office, Dunard looked back at him with what appeared to be undisguised contempt.

On his desk, and not for the first time, was an array of newspapers.

'Morning, sir,' said Patterson, wondering what the problem was this time.

'I take it you've seen these?'

'Seen what?' replied Patterson, only now remembering the curious remark by Maxwell on the train saying something about the papers.

'These!' replied Dunard pointing at the tabloids. 'Oh, you haven't, eh? Well, have a look at what the press is informing the world today.'

Patterson reached across and took one of the papers. On the front page, it said 'EXCLUSIVE! *Murder victim's boyfriend gives interview about devastating loss.*'

There was a photo of Maxwell kneeling down looking at the flowers outside the tunnel.

Patterson looked up at Dunard.

'Read on; it gets better.'

Patterson read on, and it did indeed get better. The inside two-page spread was mainly about Ryan dealing with the death of Cheryl. However, a sidebar had the headline 'My boss is an idiot.'It claimed that Patterson thought his fellow officers were imbeciles and that his superior, Dunard, was indeed an idiot. There followed a series of other things Patterson was alleged to have said, which confirmed the police were incompetent.

'But I didn't say any of those things; it's all made up!' protested Patterson. Then the realisation struck Patterson. 'Of course, that was why he stayed at the Marriott, and the photographer was at the tunnel. Ryan must have done a deal with the newspaper.'

'Oh, well done, Sherlock. Just figured that out, have you? Obviously, he's done a deal,' replied Dunard. 'The later editions of the other papers have picked up on the original *scoop.* Needless to say either that I'm not happy with this. Not happy at all. At the same time, I guess I should congratulate you.'

'Congratulate me?'

'At least you caught the bugger; that's the main thing. How did the interview go?'

'Well, he's confessed to being in Glasgow

on the day of Cheryl's disappearance. Actually, I thought you would have watched the interview yourself.'

'No, I'd have liked to, but something came up, unfortunately.'

Patterson knew his superior was making excuses again. On the one hand, Dunard said this case was vital for him and the station, yet he couldn't even be bothered to watch any of the interview with a prime suspect.

'So, Ryan was in Glasgow at the time of the murder, was he?'

'Ryan was in Glasgow when Cheryl went missing. It turns out he drove up to Glasgow shortly after Cheryl got on the train from Sheffield.'

'Did he indeed? He hasn't confessed to the murder yet?'

'No.'

'Well, I guess that may take a bit more time. As I say, despite the papers, I have to congratulate you on a job well done. Even I didn't expect you to get a result this soon.'

'Sir, Ryan's confessed to driving up to Glasgow, that's all.'

'That's all? It's quite a big confession, is it not? Ryan must have had a reason to do that and also keep it quiet. By the way, how did you know he drove up to Glasgow?'

'It was actually this morning. I was stuck in a traffic jam and saw McKinnon speeding by on his bike. Because of the traffic, though I was in the car and Brian was on his bike, he reached the station before I did. It occurred to me that the same thing could have happened with Cheryl and Ryan. With Cheryl stuck on the train, Ryan could easily have driven up to Glasgow and been in the city when Cheryl went missing. Plus, there were a few things Ryan said and did that made me wonder about him. One was that he said he didn't have a driving licence. I sensed, for some reason, Ryan was lying about being able to drive, and there must have been a reason for that.'

'Well, hopefully, this newspaper business will be forgotten soon enough once we announce we have caught Cheryl's murderer.'

'The thing is, I'm not entirely sure Ryan's guilty.'

'Not sure? What? He's driven up to Glasgow, told no one, and you don't think he's guilty?'

'No, I don't, to be honest. I don't believe he murdered Cheryl. It's more complicated than that.'

'Complicated how?'

'Well, if Ryan did drive up to Glasgow and murder Cheryl, when did he murder her? Cheryl was held over three days. Yes, Ryan drove up here on the Saturday, but I don't believe he was here for the three days Cheryl was held. As he said, he may have driven down to Sheffield the next morning.'

'Why on Earth would you believe that?'

'For one thing, Pettigrew has just called his employer, a building firm. Apparently, Ryan turned up for work on Monday morning.'

Dunard let out a sigh and looked to the ceiling.

'Of course,' continued Patterson, 'that's still to be verified, but so far, well, a lot of Ryan's story holds up. I've also just spoken to McKinnon. We already have confirmation from the hotel he was staying in that Ryan was there when he said he was. He arrived very drunk just before one am and then left the next morning at around eight-thirty. Ryan also says he drove back down to Sheffield on Sunday morning because his grandad had a mild stroke and was taken into hospital. Apart from showing me the text from his mum, the hospital has confirmed his grandad was admitted with a suspected stroke in the early hours of Sunday morning. As I say, a lot of his story checks out.'

Dunard looked suitably crestfallen. 'Bollocks.'

'The thing is, sir, Ryan is a very immature thirty-three-year-old. He says he drove up to Glasgow on the spur of the moment, got drunk, didn't see Cheryl, didn't even tell her he was in the city, and then drove back south without seeing her. It is just the kind of thing he would do. Now, I'm still not saying for certain that Ryan is innocent. However, in my opinion, the likelihood is that although Ryan is an idiot, he's not a murderer.'

Dunard didn't like what he was hearing but knew his DCI may have a point. 'I've just announced a press conference for midday. I need something to give to the media.'

'Why don't we still give them Ryan, for now at least? He may be innocent, but he has still lied to us, not to mention making false accusations about what I said. So let's use him. We say, or more precisely, you say, we have a suspect in custody. We keep Ryan in custody for 24 hours. In the meantime, we can thoroughly check his story just to be absolutely sure he is either guilty or innocent.'

'I don't suppose you've any other leads besides Ryan?'

'Actually, we may have one lead. Four council employees worked at the railway tunnel the week before Cheryl's murder. One of the workers, Tommy Beaton, has a conviction for sexual assault. I interviewed him yesterday. At the moment, it doesn't seem he had access to the tunnel gate keys. However, in my view, it seems too much of a coincidence work was being carried out at the tunnel in the days before Cheryl was murdered.'

'What about the other three?'

'We've interviewed them, but I believe it's Beaton we should be concentrating on.'

'And you think Tommy Beaton may have had access to the keys?'

'The foreman says he handed the keys in every night to the council offices. McKinnon's on his way to the offices now to verify his story. It could even be someone else at the council offices who had access to the keys, but if Ryan is innocent, then Tommy Beaton is our next prime suspect.

'Anything else?'

'We've not really much to go on, forensics-wise. Cheryl was literally washed clean when she was swept downriver. We've checked out DIY shops that sold the type of metal rods we believe helped tie Cheryl down, but nothing has come up so far. Same as for the other items used, such as the masking tape. I've also called the flatmates in this afternoon for an interview. I suspect they're hiding something, but I don't know what.'

Dunard shook his head. 'I still can't believe Ryan Maxwell may be innocent. I thought we had our man. Make sure his story stacks up 100%.'

'Of course.' Patterson rose and went towards the door.

'By the way,' said Dunard, 'Are you sure you didn't tell Ryan I was an idiot?'

'Of course not, sir. It's a complete fabrication.' And with that, Patterson left the office.

Chapter 26

You Can Call Me Becky

As Patterson was leaving Dunard's office, McKinnon was arriving at the council offices on the outskirts of Easterhouse. Like many newbuilds in the area, the council building was designed first and foremost with practicality and economy in mind rather than aesthetics. It was flat-roofed and flimsy, giving the impression one good gust of wind and the whole building would collapse.

McKinnon parked in a huge, busy car park and then walked to the council office entrance. He pressed an entry button and was met with a robotic-sounding female voice coming out of an intercom.

'Yes? Can I help you?'

'I'm DC McKinnon. Strathclyde police. I'm here to see Rebecca Price.'

A buzzer sounded along with a click, and McKinnon pushed open one of two highly polished glass doors. On entering, an immediate warmth contrasted with the cold outside. There was a smell of new carpet, polish and plastic. The only sounds heard were the odd distant conversation, a phone ringing and the polite tapping of keyboards.

In front of McKinnon stood a large and imposing circular reception desk pleading for someone to walk up to it. McKinnon duly obliged. As McKinnon walked forward, a woman sitting behind the desk slowly appeared as if she was rising out of the floor; her eye level came into view above the top of the counter, and she watched McKinnon with wary eyes.

Only when McKinnon was within smiling range did her manner change, and she put on a welcome demeanour. Yet, her smile was functional, devoid of any sincerity.

'Can I help you?'

McKinnon repeated the line he had just said thirty seconds ago.

'I'm DC McKinnon. Strathclyde police. I'm here to see Rebecca Price.'

'Rebecca? One moment.' The receptionist lifted a phone to her ear and punched a two-digit number on a keypad.

'Becky? There's a DC McKinnon Strathclyde Police here to see you.'

The receptionist put the phone down and smiled again at McKinnon. This time it seemed to have more warmth as if someone had decided to switch the heating on.

'If you'd like to take a seat over there, DC

McKinnon.'

She pointed to one of two extra-large teal fabric armchairs behind him. McKinnon smiled in return, turned and sat down, immediately looking and feeling like a small boy in the over large chair.

Rebecca Price was a tall, smiley, red-headed lady who gave off a vibrant, upbeat energy and a genuine, friendly manner. She appeared delighted McKinnon had deemed to give her a visit. She walked in front of McKinnon, escorting him back to her office, frequently turning her head to engage in small talk. She asked if McKinnon wanted a coffee or tea, and McKinnon gladly accepted a tea. They stopped off at a small room which had a kettle and cups on a sideboard.

Once in her large office, McKinnon sat down and, after asking permission, placed his tea on her desk.

'Now,' Rebecca said with a loud sigh, 'I believe you're here regarding one of our maintenance teams?'

'That's right, it's in connection with the Cheryl Kerr investigation. I don't know if you've seen about her murder on the news; it happened —'

'Oh yes, yes,' Rebecca interrupted. 'I did see that. Absolutely awful. No one is safe nowadays, and you're the one who is trying to catch her murderer?' Rebecca stroked her long red hair as if was a ginger cat sitting on her shoulders.

'Not me exactly. There's a team of us involved in trying to catch whoever did this. The thing is, Mrs –'

'Miss, divorced, thank god, you can call me Becky.' Perhaps McKinnon imagined it, but Becky seemed to be more than friendly.

McKinnon smiled. 'The thing is, Becky, you had four employees working at the tunnel during the week before Cheryl Kerr was found. I was just, that is, my colleagues and I were wondering who had access to the tunnel keys?'

'How do you mean?'

'The tunnel was blocked by large steel gates. They could only be opened with two keys, I believe. I believe you have the keys to those gates stored here?'

'Yes, we have all the keys we use across the city securely locked away in a safe.'

'So when the work was being carried out at the tunnel, presumably someone, one of the workmen, handed the keys in here? Every night?'

'That's right, whenever there's a job on, there's always a job on as a matter of fact; the keys were handed in by whoever is the foreman each night, usually between four and five.'

'And who is the foreman of this team?'

'Gerry McBride. He's a diamond. Been with us years, so he has. '

'So, Gerry would come to pick up the keys in the morning. Then come back at night and hand them in?'

'Yes, exactly.'

'Who else has access to these keys?'

'No one, really. Except for Debbie. She deals with the different teams and administrative affairs. Actually, you're perhaps better off talking to her. I don't deal with the hands-on business if you like. Hang on, I'll bring Debbie in. As I said, she's the one that deals with handing in keys and stuff like that. If you'll wait there...'

Becky left the office and, a while later, came back with a woman who looked to be in her early twenties.

'This is Debbie. Debbie, this is DC McKinnon; he's investigating -' Rebecca stopped herself, 'a crime. He needs information about who hands in the keys whenever a maintenance job happens. Like when Gerry McBride is on a job, does he always hand back the keys every night?'

'Absolutely. Gerry always hands the keys in every night. Why, has someone said something?'

'Why would someone say something?' asked McKinnon

'No, I mean –'

'I'm just trying to establish whether the keys were handed in every night. Especially when the team worked at the Kelvinbridge tunnel site two weeks ago.'

Debbie nodded enthusiastically. 'At Kelvinbridge? Absolutely, they were handed in every night.'

'By Gerry McBride? Every night?'

Debbie suddenly seemed unsure how to answer, as if she was wondering whether to ask the audience or go for the fifty-fifty.

'I just said he did.' Whether she was telling the truth or not, Debbie gave the impression she was telling a lie. At the same time, McKinnon could tell that this wasn't a regular occurrence. He thought he would try another approach. 'OK, tell me about the protocol Debbie, the procedure of giving out and handing back keys. Let's take Gerry as an example. Just talk me through it. What would happen?'

'Well, in the morning, Gerry usually arrives around half eight. I'd ask where he was working and then hand him the keys. If it was a new location, I would have been given the keys beforehand to give to him. If keys were needed, that is. It was the same for all the teams.'

'And at night, Gerry would come back and hand the keys over to you, and you'd lock them away?'

Debbie hesitated again, and she was clearly holding something back.

'Please, Debbie, you need to tell me the truth. It's important.'

'Well, to be completely honest with you. It isn't strictly true that Gerry brought the keys back every night.'

'No?'

'He would sometimes get someone else to hand them in. As a matter of fact, when they were at Kelvinbridge, he would usually do that.'

'Who would Gerry give the keys to?'

'Tommy Beaton.' Debbie turned to Becky. 'You know Tommy? Tommy Beaton would bring them back. I know it was supposed to be Gerry, but sometimes, he gave the keys to Tommy to bring back.'

'Tommy Beaton?' said McKinnon. 'Why was that, do you think?'

'I don't know. I never asked, and I didn't see the harm in it as long as the keys were handed in.'

'So, in effect, Tommy was often the keyholder?'

'You could say that, aye.'

Do you have a signing-in book for the keys? A logbook of some kind?'

'Yes.'

'Can I see it?'

'Of course, I'll get it.'

Once Debbie came back with the logbook, McKinnon checked over the dates. All he could see were signatures for Gerry McBride and not Tommy Beaton.

Debbie spoke without any prompting. 'Tommy signed it for Gerry. That's why it always says Gerry and not Tommy.'

'There's a day here, the 26th of November, where there is no signature at all.'

'OK,' said Debbie, a little tearful as she looked at Becky. 'Don't get on at me, but it's possible, sometimes, I assume, because Tommy couldn't get here on time, the keys weren't handed in at all.'

'Debbie!' Becky wasn't happy.

'Please, Becky,' said McKinnon, 'for now, let's concentrate on getting the truth. No more lies, Debbie. This is serious. So, sometimes, Tommy Beaton kept the keys overnight?'

' Sometimes, at least one time, I guess so.' Debbie was still on the point of tears in making the confession.

McKinnon stood up. 'OK, well, thanks for your help. Both of you. We may need to speak to you again, Debbie.'

Debbie nodded as Becky still glared at her.

McKinnon made his way out of the building, escorted by Becky. As he stepped back out into the fresh cold air, he was warmed by the notion that his visit could well have thrown up a new vital piece of information.

Chapter 27

Confirmation

It was quickly shown that Ryan Maxwell, despite being in Glasgow for a time, could not have murdered Cheryl Kerr. As far as could be made out, his story was more or less true.

After Cheryl had left for Glasgow on the train, CCTV from outside Sheffield station saw Ryan sitting in his car for around ten minutes. Presumably, this was him contemplating whether to drive to Glasgow or not. Having decided to do so, he then drove towards the motorway heading north, just as he had stated. In fact, through licence plate recognition, almost every moment of Maxwell's drive from England to Scotland was recorded. He arrived in Glasgow just after 3:05pm. At that time, Cheryl's train was just approaching Motherwell. CCTV from Central Station and the pub opposite the station confirmed that Maxwell went for a beer. Although, when Maxwell said he got 'talking to a bloke', he was talking to two women who were undoubtedly another reason he returned to the same pub.

Almost everything gained from CCTV, from the train station, the pubs, the hotel, and the multi-storey car park, tallied with Ryan's account of that day. He spent most of the night on a pub crawl, clearly getting more drunk as the night went on. He was refused entry to two pubs before hailing a taxi, clearly worse for wear, just after midnight. He was driven to a hotel on the Clyde waterfront, booked in, and left early the next morning. He was seen entering the multi-storey car park and, although probably still over the limit from the night before, drove back down south.

It was the CCTV of him back in Sheffield that absolutely proved Ryan's innocence more than anything. Whilst Cheryl was known to still have been held in the tunnel the whole of Monday and Tuesday morning, Ryan was back in Sheffield working. There was no doubt about it. Ryan Maxwell was innocent.

The disappointment that Ryan wasn't the person who murdered Cheryl was tempered by the news McKinnon brought back from the council offices. Patterson decided to relay this new development to the team and stood in front of the incident board.

'Just to let everyone know, it appears that Ryan Maxwell may have a cast iron alibi for the murder of Cheryl Kerr. We'll hold him a little longer but almost certainly let him go later today. The good news is that due to the good work of Brian here, it appears that Tommy Beaton may have had access to the tunnel keys. Given this is someone who has a conviction for sexual assault and who was at the tunnel in the week leading up to Cheryl's murder, I want him brought in for further questioning ASAP. Claire, find out where he is working today, and then you and Jack bring him in. In the meantime, I'm going to be interviewing Cheryl's two flatmates again, so if they can tell us something new. OK, just wanted everyone to know where we're at. Carry on with what you were doing.'

Chapter 28

Jenna Taylor

As Pettigrew and Simpson set off to bring Tommy Beaton back to the station for a formal interview, Patterson prepared to interview Cheryl's two flatmates, Jenna Taylor and Jonathan Dunbar. Patterson's goal was to find out whether either were hiding anything. Patterson had a strong suspicion that was the case. This feeling was intuition borne of experience, and many experienced detectives had the same skill. That feeling could still be nothing or result in finding another small piece of the jigsaw that would help explain the murder of Cheryl Kerr.

Patterson also wanted to interview the two flatmates individually. His impression at Bank Street was that Dunbar always wanted to say what Taylor wanted him to say. So Patterson decided to interview Taylor first at ten o'clock in the morning and Dunbar a couple of hours later at midday. He thought he would extract more from the later interview with Dunbar than with

Taylor. He could also compare what Dunbar told him with what Taylor told him earlier. No doubt, the flatmates had already collaborated on the telling of events. Although this, giving the exact same account, could be another sign that one or both was lying. It was something Patterson was prepared for.

Patterson came down to meet Jenna Taylor in the station's reception area. As he had hoped, Taylor had arrived alone.

'Hello, Inspector. How are you?' Taylor's manner was bright and breezy. She smiled as she spoke, always keeping eye contact and seemed as confident as she had appeared at Bank Street.

'Thanks for coming, Jenna; I've an interview room set aside just along here.' Patterson led Taylor through a couple of doors and along a corridor. 'As I said on the phone, this shouldn't take long; it's just some formalities we have to go through. Get it down on record.'

'Is it wrong that I'm looking forward to it?' Jenna asked.

'Not at all, but If I knew that, I would have charged an entrance fee,' replied Patterson matching Taylor's apparent jovial mood, 'It's just through here. Oh, would you like a coffee or tea?' Jenna accepted the offer of a tea.

Patterson walked Jenna through to the small interview room. She sat down as Patterson went to get her tea, and Patterson got himself a tea for a change. Sitting opposite each other, they first talked about Jenna's studies and how the investigation was going. Jenna still seemed very relaxed, just as Patterson wanted her to be.

Patterson went through the formalities of taping the interview and reassured Jenna, as he did with everyone, it was as much for her benefit as his own.

'Right, Jenna, the reason for this interview is I want to go over some of the facts you have already told us and learn a little more about Cheryl, if possible.'

'Of course, what is it you want to know?'

'Let's start with how Cheryl was when she left for Sheffield. I mean, did she appear concerned about anything? Worried?'

'No, she seemed fine as far as I could tell. Excited. She had been talking about Ryan for God knows how long. Now, they were finally going to meet; it was a relief for all of us.'

'They only knew each other online, Ryan and Cheryl? He never came to visit?'

'No, Cheryl talked about it, but she decided to go down to Sheffield first.'

'And you weren't concerned about that? Cheryl visiting a relative stranger down in England?'

'A little, but Ryan seemed fine. I told her to keep in touch, of course, and I told her to meet him in a public place the first time. She knew to do that anyway. They met in a bar in town, apparently. He was a good-looking guy. I know that doesn't count for anything, but he was well fit, at least from the photos he sent.'

'Coming back to Bank St, how did Cheryl, yourself and Jonathan end up in the same flat?'

'We knew each other at university and were all looking for someplace to stay, so we decided to look for a place together. Then we saw the flat in Bank Street, which was perfect.'

'Were you and Jonathan an item then?'

'God, no, we're not really an item now. Well, sort of, but we were just good friends.'

'You seemed close when I was at the flat.'

'Perhaps, we're more like friends with benefits, if you know what I mean.'

'But you like him?'

'Yes, Jonathan can be a bit weird sometimes, but he's all right.'

'What was your relationship like with Cheryl?'

'Good. We're very similar. We both had the same interests. Both studying chemical engineering. We both love music, occasionally going to clubs. That kind of thing. We even look alike.' Taylor gave a small laugh. 'She is, was, a right laugh. I loved her.' Taylor's demeanour saddened, and she brought a hankie from her handbag.

'So there was never any animosity between you?'

'No, never. Well, we sometimes had small disagreements about whose turn it was to do the cleaning and so forth as you do but nothing major.'

'What about Jonathan's relationship with Cheryl? What was that like?'

Taylor shrugged. 'Fine, they got on; I wouldn't say they were that close, but they got on.'

'Cheryl and Jonathan never became, how do you say, friends with benefits?'

'No! God, no.'

'Why are you so adamant about that?'

'They just wouldn't. Cheryl wasn't Jonathan's type.'

'What was his type? You?'

'Well, yes.'

'Yet, you just said Cheryl and yourself were very similar.'

'Yes, in some ways, but not in every way. Cheryl was different.'

'Do you think Jonathan was Cheryl's type?'

'No. I don't.'

'Why?'

'I just don't. Jonathan is too bookish for Cheryl. Ryan is more her type, she was always into older men.'

'When did you and Jonathan become close?'

'How do you mean?'

'Well, when you became more than friends.'

'Inspector, I came here because you asked, and I'm willing to answer your questions, but I really don't see what that has to do with anything.'

'Oh, of course,' said Patterson. 'I apologise if I'm prying, but that's what I'm paid for. I'm asking these questions because I wondered if the situation with Jonathan and yourself made things awkward in the flat. Awkward for Cheryl?'

'Awkward for Cheryl? No. I don't think it made things awkward for Cheryl. Or for anyone for that matter.'

'If Jonathan and Cheryl had got together, how would you feel about that?'

'It wouldn't happen.'

'Why wouldn't it happen?'

'It just wouldn't. I told you Cheryl's not his type.'

'The thing is Jenna, Jonathan told us –'

'Jonathan? You've been talking to Jonathan already? I thought you were interviewing him after me. You mean you've been talking to him? I knew it. I –'

'Jenna, calm down; it was just a slip of the tongue. We haven't -'

'So what's he been saying then? You shouldn't listen to a word he says. He's a fantasist. I knew the little swine would have got in touch with you.'

'Jenna, please, listen, let's just say…OK. We know more than you think.'

Jenna started to become tearful though Patterson wondered if the tears were genuine. Jenna composed herself just a bit too quickly, and it was noticeable her eyes weren't wet. She then began speaking again in a controlled voice.

'Listen, it doesn't mean anything but OK; Jonathan and Cheryl may have slept together just before she left for Sheffield.'

'May have?'

'They slept together. Jonathan confessed to me. The thing is… I know she's dead, but Cheryl could be a right bitch sometimes. I'm sorry, but it's true. She was a cheating cow. I'm not glad she's dead, but well, you know…'

'No, I don't know, actually.'

'What goes around comes around.'

'What does that mean?'

'Just saying, that's all.'

'Jenna, did you have anything to do with the murder of Cheryl?'

'No! For God's sake, how can you even ask that? Yes, we fell out before she left, but I wouldn't kill her. I wouldn't kill anyone!'

'I thought Jonathan was just a friend with benefits, as you say. Why would it matter if Cheryl slept with Jonathan? Do you have feelings for him?'

Taylor hesitated in answering as if she was asking herself the same question.

'Maybe I do. I like Jonathan. I like him a lot, as it happens. A lot, lot if you must know. I know he comes across as a geek, but…besides, Cheryl practically seduced him.'

'It takes two to tango, does it not?'

'Oh, Cheryl knew what she was doing, believe me. I knew she was after him for God knows how long. And all the time, she's going on about this Ryan. You know, she once said to me Ryan was talking about marriage. Marriage! Cheryl had no intention of marrying Ryan. The poor sod. She was just stringing him along. She was a conniving bitch. I swear she only started sleeping with Jonathan to get at me.'

'Yet, now, you and Jonathan are still *close*.

'Now that Cheryl is out of the way, yes.' Taylor composed herself again before continuing. 'Sorry, I didn't mean it to sound like that. What I meant was that when Cheryl went down to Sheffield, it gave Jonathan and me a bit of space, some time to ourselves, to sort things out, and that's what we did. Jonathan was going to tell Cheryl to keep her distance when she returned.'

'So the day Cheryl disappeared, Saturday the 29th of November, where were you, during the day and night, I mean?'

'I told you, at the flat. Me and Jonathan both stayed in the whole day. That's the truth. So Jonathan was with you the whole day at the flat? '

'With me, the whole day. He went out for a while but just to the shops.'

'You just said you both stayed in all day.'

'You know what I mean. I stayed in, but Jonathan went to the shops to get some snacks and milk and things.'

'What time was that?'

'Can't remember exactly. I'd say around three, maybe just after. He was out for about twenty minutes. I told you we were waiting for Cheryl to come back later the whole time.'

'See, Jenna, the problem I have is I believe that whoever murdered Cheryl knew she would get off at Kelvinbridge around that time. Not many people did know that. In fact, possibly the only people who did know were Jonathan and yourself.'

'So what are you saying? That Jonathan and me murdered Cheryl? That's ridiculous. Actually, if you're going to make accusations like that, I think we should end this interview now. I want a lawyer present.'

Patterson agreed to stop the interview. He hadn't time to arrange for a lawyer that day and thought it better to interview Taylor again at some point with a pre-arranged lawyer. For now, it was clear that, at the very least, Taylor and Dunbar, one or both, had a motive for murdering Cheryl. There was certainly tension in that flat. Jealousy. Whether they had actually committed the murder and how they had done it remained a mystery. It was all circumstantial for the moment. However, given what Taylor had told him, he was now even more curious as to what Jonathan Dunbar had to say.

Chapter 29

Jonathan Dunbar

Patterson hinting to Jenna Taylor that he had secretly spoken to Jonathan Dunbar and therefore knew more than she realised was a fairly obvious trick. So much so that Patterson was surprised that Jenna had fallen for it hook, line and sinker. His original intention was to use that trick on Jonathan since he would know Jenna had been interviewed before him.

As it was, it was Jenna who had told Patterson more than he had expected to hear. Now, anything Jonathan had to say to him was almost a bonus. However, he feared Jenna would now tell Jonathan to cancel his interview. As such, he was slightly surprised to see Jonathan Dunbar arrive in good time. Jonathan also had no desire to have a lawyer present. Patterson got the impression that Jonathan hadn't even spoken to Jenna. It was Patterson's lucky day.

Patterson gave Jonathan the same warm welcome he had given Taylor. Jonathan was noticeably more nervous than Jenna though that seemed the default mode. As with Jenna, Patterson also made small talk, to which Jonathan replied with short, quick answers. Once in the interview room, Patterson explained the formalities and began.

'Right, let's get down to business,' Patterson started. 'As I said to Jenna, this interview is simply a formality. I'd like to know more about Cheryl and when she went missing.'

Jonathan looked at him blankly.

'Jenna said you all met at university; is that right?'

'Yes. We were all taking similar subjects. We started hanging out together.'

'And since you were all looking for a place to stay, you thought you could live together as well?'

'Yeah, it seemed a good idea.'

'*Seemed* a good idea?'

'It was a good idea. We saw the place in Bank Street, and it was just what we were looking for.'

'Jenna seems a bright girl.'

'She is very bright. More intelligent than me, at least.'

'And Cheryl?'

'She's bright too; she knows, knew, what she wanted in life. Jenna and Cheryl are quite similar, in fact.'

'Two peas in a pod?'

'Sorry?' Patterson wondered if that phrase

had become outdated to younger people.

'I mean, they were similar in a lot of ways. You became closer to Jenna once you shared the flat, not before?'

'No.'

'Why was that, do you think?'

'What do you mean?'

'I mean, what attracted you to Jenna?'

'Well, she's a good-looking girl, for one thing. Bright, as you say. Good fun to be with. I like her; we get on.'

'Did you not get on with Cheryl?'

'Yeah, I got on with Cheryl as well. I got on with both of them, in fact. We all got on with each other. Like I said, that's why we got a flat together.'

'How did you feel about Cheryl?'

'As in?'

'I mean, did you like her?'

'Yeah, she was all right. She would spend most nights studying. She was closer to Jenn than me.'

'And when you and Jenna became an item, that wasn't a problem?'

'No, why should it be?'

'You were never attracted to Cheryl?'

'Attracted? No.'

'Never?'

'I don't know what you are getting at.'

'I'm not getting at anything. I just want to know more about your relationship with Cheryl.

Except that when I interviewed Jenna earlier... Anyway, I won't go into that yet. Let's get back to –'

'Why? What's Jenna been saying?'

This was too easy, thought Patterson, and for a moment, he wondered if he was the one who was being played.

'Listen, Jonathan. I want to get one thing straight. Regardless of what Jenna may or may not have said, I'm not here to judge, and I'm certainly not accusing you of anything; I –'

'Why would you accuse me of anything?'

'Exactly. I know you liked Cheryl. You liked her a lot. Yet, you two never got close?'

'Well, yeah, close, but not that close.'

'You just said a minute ago you weren't that close, that she was closer to Jenna.'

'And? Stop trying to mix my words. She was closer to Jenna; that's all I'm saying.'

'You had words with Jenna about Cheryl, didn't you? An argument. Jenna said she was jealous of Cheryl. She didn't like the fact you were attracted to her.'

'Was she? She didn't say anything to me.'

'I think she did. She got upset with Cheryl about something. What was it? Did you suggest a menage a trois?'

Jonathan laughed. 'Menage a trois. Where did you pick that one up?'

'I'm just saying, you were sharing a flat with two, let's face it, attractive young women.

Both very similar. Jenna was telling me about it.'

'About what?'

'There was tension, arguments. Between the three of you.'

'Sometimes, we argued. We were sharing a flat together. What about it?'

'What about it? Cheryl Kerr ended up murdered! You don't think it's relevant you were fighting with her beforehand and –'

'I wasn't fighting with her.' Jonathan sighed and put his hand through his hair. 'Listen, I don't know what Jenn told you, but it wasn't like that. You want to know the truth? You're right about the threesome, but Jenn suggested the menage a trois, as you put it. Jenn was the one who was attracted to Cheryl, not me. Listen, I know she's dead, and Cheryl was OK, but, truthfully, she could be a right pain sometimes. I argued with her a few times, so what? She got on my nerves. Jenn though, Jenn was the one who fancied her.'

'And you didn't?'

'No, I didn't, as it happens, not in that way?'

'So you weren't open to the three of you... becoming closer?'

'No, I wasn't. It was complicated; that's why we argued.'

'Complicated? How? Come on, Jonathan, you need to tell me the truth.'

'OK. You want to know the truth? I hated Cheryl, couldn't stand her! She was a stuck-up cow. I liked Jenna, though, still do, I think. It was like this. I liked Jenna. Jenna liked Cheryl. I hated Cheryl. Cheryl liked me.'

'Jenna said you and Cheryl slept together.'

'Did she?'

'She did. Did you sleep with her?'

'Yeah, I did.'

'Yet, you just said you hated her.'

'Have you never been tempted to have sex with someone you didn't like?'

The image of Emma Booth floated through Patterson's mind. 'It seems to me like there was a bit of tension in that flat.'

'Yeah, and the rest. To be honest, I was praying Cheryl would end up going down to Sheffield to live with that Ryan bloke.'

'Jonathan, did you have anything to do with the murder of Cheryl Kerr?'

'No, of course, I didn't!'

'OK, let me ask you another question. Do you think that Jenna could have had anything to do with the death of Cheryl?'

'No! Listen, I came here to help you, but if you're accusing Jenna or me of killing Cheryl, I want a lawyer present.' Dunbar stood up.

'Jonathan, sit down. I'm not accusing you of anything. I promise you. I have to ask these questions. I just want to know what the situation was like in the flat with the three of you. If you don't answer the questions now, you'll only have to come back later. Please.'

Dunbar sat down again.

'Now, as I said, I just want the facts down on record. See, I'll be honest, I get the impression Jenna and yourself are hiding something.'

'OK, yes, you're right.'

'Am I?'

'We are hiding something, but it's not what you think.'

'Then tell me.'

'I'll tell you. There's something else you should know –'

There was a knock on the door, and McKinnon entered the room.

'Brian, not now!'

'But sir, something's happened.'

'I don't care; get out. I'll be with you in a couple of minutes.'

'But –'

'No, but's, out!'

Dunbar smiled at Patterson. 'Just can't get the staff nowadays, eh?'

Patterson smiled back at him. 'What were you going to tell me?'

'Nothing to tell.' Dunbar stood up. 'Listen, if you want to interview me again, you'll need to give me time to notify a lawyer. Otherwise, I would advise you to keep your distance, or I'll have you done for harassment.'

'OK, Jonathan, if that's the way you want it, thanks for your time today. I'll get one of my colleagues to escort you out of the station.'

Once outside the interview room,

Patterson instructed a colleague to do just that before turning his attention to McKinnon. ‘Well done, Brian, your timing is impeccable. So what’s so important that you deem it necessary to interrupt my interview?’

‘It’s Tommy Beaton, sir. He’s been murdered.’

Chapter 30

Two Keys

The first question Patterson asked himself when he heard about the murder of Tommy Beaton was if it could be connected to that of Cheryl Kerr. It was possible his murder may be the result of an unrelated argument, a burglary, or god knows what. Yet, even as Patterson arrived where Tommy Beaton lived and walked up the tenement stairs in Cowcaddens, he couldn't help but gravitate toward the idea there was indeed a connection between the two murders.

Suited and booted in crinkly white paper, Patterson entered the flat and was greeted by a nod from Pettigrew and Simpson.

'He's in there,' said Pettigrew indicating a door on the left.

Patterson walked into the indicated room and saw Tommy Beaton lying face down between a green fabric settee and a small teak dining table. Beaton's head lay towards the window, his feet towards the door, his left arm stretched out above his head while his right arm was slightly twisted behind his back. He was wearing light denim jeans but no shoes, only black socks. A dark patch of congealed blood on Beaton's grey shirt had seeped through from the wound in his lower back. There was also a small pool of dark-stained blood on the light-coloured carpet. A broken cup lay near the body, with some liquid like spilt tea or coffee also staining the carpet.

Beside the body, Tasmina Rana was kneeling, lifting up the shirt and taking samples. She asked if the table could be moved and then, with better access, moved around the body to make some more calculations. As he waited for Tasmina to give her preliminary thoughts, Patterson walked out of the sitting room and into the hallway. It was small, tidy accommodation. A kitchenette faced onto the living room while there were only two other rooms, a bathroom and a bedroom leading off the short hallway.

Having a quick look around, there was no apparent sign of disturbance anywhere else. In the bedroom, the bed was made up with no clothes lying around. Beaton appeared to be a neat and orderly occupant for a man living alone. The bathroom had a sink and bath that could have starred in a cleaning advert. The kitchenette was the same, with surfaces clear of mess and wiped down. Opening the fridge, there was an assortment of healthy food, yoghurt drinks, orange juice, signs of a healthy life that would be cut violently short. Patterson walked back through to the living room and went up to Pettigrew.

'How long have you been here?'

'About an hour,' Pettigrew replied. 'I phoned the council to see where Beaton was working today and was informed he hadn't turned up for work again. So while you were interviewing the flatmates, Jack and myself came here and found him like this.'

'How did you get in?'

'The door was open.'

Patterson nodded as the pathologist stood up.

'Well, it looks like a well-placed knife in the back did the trick,' said Tasmina Rana. 'I'd say a three-inch, three-and-a-half-inch blade. One single entry wound. Pierced his heart. He died almost instantly. Almost instantly as he's tried to reach back to get the knife in his back. So he was facing away from his attacker, stabbed, and fell down into this position. I can see no other marks of violence on the body for now. For an approximate time of death, it was sometime last night, between six and midnight.'

'OK, thanks, Tasmina,' Patterson said as a thousand thoughts raced through his mind.

'I'll let you know more findings as I get them,' Rana said as she cleared away her instruments.

Simpson came into the room.

'No murder weapon?' asked Patterson.

'None found so far,' said Simpson. 'No sign of forced entry either and no real sign of a struggle. Apart from the broken cup, which probably happened when Beaton fell and knocked it over. So what do you think?'

'I think,' said Patterson, 'that Beaton probably knew his killer or, to be more exact, the murderer and Beaton knew each other. A possible scenario is that Beaton and his killer are chatting on the settee; Beaton gets up, turns to walk around the sofa, and his killer stabs him in the back.'

Simpson joined his two fellow officers and asked aloud the question all three officers had been asking since they arrived. 'The question is does this have anything to do with the death of Cheryl Kerr?'

'I'd say it's unlikely to be a coincidence,' Patterson said, 'After all, you just talked to Beaton a couple of days ago.'

'Yes, perhaps someone saw us talking to Beaton and wanted to stop him talking any more.' said Pettigrew.

'Talking about what, though?' asked Simpson

'And who could have wanted to stop him talking?' asked Patterson

'One of the other workers?' said Simpson.

'If so, which one?' asked Pettigrew.

'Right, I want the other three other workers who were at the tunnel brought in immediately and questioned. First of all, let's see who has an alibi for last night.'

'Sir?' The three officers turned to see McKinnon walk into the room. He proudly held up a clear plastic bag as if he had just won a goldfish. However, instead of a goldfish in the bag, were two keys, one big, one small. 'I found these in the bedside cabinet. They have the same dimensions as the keys used to open the tunnel gates at Kelvinbridge.'

Patterson took the bag and looked at the keys. He then looked back down at the body of Tommy Beaton. After his interview with Jenna Taylor and Jonathan Dunbar, and if they were indeed the keys to open the tunnel gate, then Patterson not only had one new suspect for the murder of Cheryl Kerr but three.

Chapter 31

Avenues of Investigation

Later that Monday, Tommy Beaton's three co-workers at the Kelvinbridge tunnel, Gerry McBride, Calvin Robertson and Andy McGregor, were brought in for questioning. However, all three had cast-iron alibis for the night before. These alibis were checked and double-checked. However, the more they were investigated, the more it confirmed none of the men could have carried out the murder of Tommy Beaton.

There was one important development. The keys found in Beaton's bedside cabinet were indeed those which unlocked the tunnel gates at Kelvinbridge. The only prints on them were Beaton's. Further enquiries soon revealed the shop where Beaton had these new keys cut from the originals. It appeared that he had copies made during the third day he and his co-workers had been at the tunnel. This corresponded to the date, the 26th of November, when he didn't hand the keys into the council offices.

All this provisionally linked Tommy Beaton to Cheryl Kerr and the murder of Tommy Beaton to the murder of Cheryl Kerr. Could Tommy Beaton be the murderer of Cheryl Kerr? It was certainly a possibility, but then why was Tommy Beaton murdered? Before and after Cheryl's murder, Tommy Beaton's whereabouts in the days leading up to and during Cheryl's murder were thoroughly scrutinised again. CCTV from the area around the tunnel was gone over once more, outside his working hours. However, Beaton was never seen on CCTV. His shopping habits were also investigated, but there was no evidence Beaton had recently visited a DIY store or bought anything found at the murder scene.

More importantly, in the following days, forensic evidence didn't bring up anything of interest from the flat or belongings of Beaton. If Beaton was the murderer of Cheryl, then it was likely some of her DNA, fibres, or hair would have found its way back to his accommodation or clothes.

Despite this, the fact remained Beaton had a set of keys cut that gave access to the tunnel. The shop owner distinctly remembered Beaton himself having these two keys cut. Given they knew the murderer must have had access to the tunnel, this made Beaton suspect number one, albeit a dead suspect number one. However, Patterson was also thinking about Jenna Taylor and Jonathan Dunbar. He now knew that one or both had a motive and in Patterson's experience, motive, more than anything else, led to the murderer. As such, while Beaton's previous whereabouts were being thoroughly investigated, so were Jenna Taylor and Jonathan Dunbar's.

Back at Partick Police Station, as Patterson stood in front of his fellow officers, Patterson asked the rhetorical question that was now foremost in his mind.

'Why did Beaton have those keys cut?'

'Because he wanted access to the tunnel,' said Pettigrew.

'And why did Beaton want access to the tunnel?' Patterson asked.

'Because he planned to abduct Cheryl Kerr or whoever happened to come along that Saturday afternoon. We know he already has a conviction for rape. He thought, rightly as it turned out, the tunnel would be a good place to take a victim,' said Simpson.

'There is one other possible reason he had those keys cut,' said Patterson. 'What if Beaton gave the keys to whoever murdered Cheryl Kerr.'

'Which brings up another question,' said McKinnon. 'If Beaton had the keys cut to give to someone else, what were they still doing in his bedside cabinet?'

'Because whoever murdered Beaton gave him the keys back,' said Simpson.

'No,' said Patterson, 'it's more likely that whoever Beaton gave the keys to murdered Beaton and then put the keys there to try and frame him,' said Patterson.

This seemed as logical an explanation as any, and the more Patterson thought about it, the more it made sense.

'OK, let's assume the murderer isn't Tommy Beaton but someone else. That someone else wanted access to the tunnel because he planned to abduct and sexually assault someone there. An abandoned railway tunnel would be a perfect location for that.' Patterson thought about this more, taking his theory along its logical path. 'So, whoever murdered Cheryl sees the council workers working at the tunnel and sees an opportunity to get the keys.'

'So, he persuades Beaton to get a set of keys cut? Why would Beaton agree to that?' asked Pettigrew.

'Money,' said McKinnon.

'That's certainly one possibility,' said Patterson. 'The keys were cut on the 26th of November. Cheryl was abducted on the 29th. Brian, check Beaton's bank account and see if any money was put in his account during that time. If it was a significant amount, he wouldn't want to have it on his person or even in his flat. So, let's take this idea further, Cheryl is murdered, and the tunnel is revealed where she was held.'

'So Beaton hears about this and realises he's given the keys to the person who murdered Cheryl. Surely, he would go to the police immediately,' said McKinnon.

'Not necessarily,' said Pettigrew, 'that would mean Beaton owning up to his misdemeanour.'

'Yes, but keeping quiet about something like that? Surely, he would still go to the police.' said McKinnon, perhaps letting his own morals trespass on those of Beaton.

'Eventually, yes,' said Patterson. 'Which is all the more reason to murder Beaton before his conscience gets the better of him, and the murderer of Cheryl Kerr does so,' Patterson said. 'OK, I think we're getting somewhere with this. However, it still leaves us with one major problem. We now have a double murderer to catch. We can only hope he-'

Patterson was interrupted when DC McLean came into the office. 'Sir, we've just had a call from Central Division. They've found a body in the grounds of Glasgow Cathedral.'

'So, what's that to do with us?'

'The detective in charge says there are some similarities to the murder of Cheryl Kerr and thinks you should have a look.'

'Spoke too soon,' Patterson muttered as he added to Pettigrew and Simpson, 'Come on, looks like we're going to Glasgow Cathedral.'

Chapter 32

Glasgow Cathedral

Dating back to the 12th Century, Glasgow Cathedral was like Glasgow's keystone placed at the top of what was now High Street, itself a historic thoroughfare. With its brickwork blackened by time, the cathedral had a constantly gloomy air, as if not impressed by the ever-expanding younger buildings springing up all around and across the city.

Patterson's car drove up the winding High Street with Pettigrew beside him and Simpson in the back seat. As the cathedral came into view, so did the large police presence, which had sealed off a significant area around the medieval building.

Patterson was led around the cathedral by a uniformed officer and to a cemetery near the rear of the building, passing through temporary metal barriers erected by workmen carrying out renovations. The three officers were then led to the back of the cemetery and an overgrown grassy area.

The relatively small rectangular area of the cemetery was bordered by the cathedral on one side, a wall with memorial stones, and two other walls north and south. These barriers, natural and unnatural, all made the cemetery pretty inaccessible. A smiling man in his thirties with regulation shirt and tie walked towards them, holding out his hand to Patterson.

'DCI Patterson?'

Patterson nodded and shook the man's hand.

'DI Flynn. I'm the one who gave you a call. The body is just down here. Watch your feet; there's broken glass and some needles lying around.' The DI had a slight Geordie accent.

Patterson was led towards the far corner of the ancient cemetery. Behind some heavily overgrown grass and thick bushes covered in frost lay the severely battered body of a naked young man. The body was tinged blue, a mix of bruises and cold. The young man's eyes were closed, but his mouth was slightly open as if he had died trying to say something. One of the first things Patterson noticed was the circular ligature marks around the wrists and ankles.

'Was he found like this?' asked Patterson

'Yes, the pathologist has already been and gone. In his estimation, he's been here since the weekend, probably Saturday. So what's today, the 8th of December? So, possibly, he's been here since the 6th. The pathologist believes he died from asphyxiation. He says the victim also had severe hypothermia. Small wonder if he had been stripped naked in this weather for around two days.'

'Do we know who he is yet?'

'Yes, he still had his wallet on him. It had about thirty quid in it, so we can rule out robbery as a motive. His name's Lucas Ryba. 24. Polish national. He had a travel pass and some other bits and bobs. His address is given as Garturk Street in Govanhill.'

'What is this area, anyway?' asked Simpson.

'Just as it looks, an old cemetery. Someone from the cathedral told me most of it dates back to Victorian times; some of it is even older. It's pretty secluded, as you can see. More so at the moment, what with the workmen doing some building on the other side of that fence; this area has been completely shut off for the last couple of weeks.'

'Are the workmen here every day?'

'Couldn't tell you at present. They might not have been working the weekend. Even if they were, it's unlikely they would have seen the body since it was pretty hidden.'

'Who did find the body?'

'A vagrant. We know him; he's harmless. He came here to have a drink and a bit of peace and quiet early this morning and wandered over to this corner.'

Patterson looked around. The area was overlooked by the imposing Glasgow Royal Infirmary. Although decidedly Victorian in its construction, it was almost as gothic as the cathedral. Many small windows looked down onto the cemetery, yet, no doubt, it would be fairly dark and difficult to see anything at night.

'Who would know about this place?' asked Patterson.

'Well, junkies sometimes come here, as you can tell by the needles, drinkers, prostitutes use it, and kids are known to roam around here, drinking etc. As I say, though, it's been fairly closed off due to the building work. So what do you think? Could this murder could be linked to Cheryl Kerr?'

'How much do you know about the Cheryl Kerr case?'

'Just what I've heard and read. I'm a friend of Rafe Weaver. Actually, he's the one who I called first. He said I should give you a call.'

Patterson looked over the body again, and something caught his eye next to the deceased young man. A small, neat, round hole in the ground just above the right shoulder. Patterson looked towards the left shoulder; sure enough, another small hole was just above it. Looking down further, he found the other two holes he expected to see around the feet.

Patterson turned to DI Flynn. 'Yes, on first

impressions, I believe this murder could very well be linked to that of Cheryl Kerr.'

'So, I guess this will be handed over to you then. What happens now?'

'Well, right now,' said Patterson, 'If you give me his address, I'm going to give Garturk Street a visit.'

Chapter 33

The Hidden Dirt of Glasgow

Glasgow had successfully reinvented itself as a city of culture in recent years. Yet, go past the shops, museums and restaurants of the areas the tourists are directed to, and you would soon find the hidden dirt, new and old.

Those were the thoughts of Patterson as he turned left off the relatively wide expanse of Victoria Road, into the more cramped thoroughfare of Alison Street, and left again into Garturk Street.

Govanhill had always been a bustling and diverse area with much activity, shops and businesses. Pockets of vibrant life were dotted all over the city's south side, like villages that had ended up connected to one other.

Garturk Street was relatively narrow, with tall tenements on either side. So tall that light seemed to have difficulty finding its way down to street level. There was rubbish strewn across the pavements and road. Many windows were boarded up with dark brown metal casings, which, on a positive decorative note, matched the dark brown painted doors.

Patterson got out of his car, walked across to the close entrance and took the small bunch of keys he had been given by DI Flynn out of his pocket. He quickly found the right one and successfully opened the main door.

Walking up the close always gave him a feeling of déjà vu simply because he did it so often. Hearing the echo of his footsteps on the stairs and the slightly claustrophobic feeling (maybe that was why it was called a close) often gave a sense of foreboding. You never knew what or who you would find waiting for you on the next landing. Patterson reached the second floor and the door with 2A on it. Once again, he correctly picked the right key the first time and walked into the flat's hallway.

He found himself standing inside a grubby flat, making the shabby close look well-kept. A pale green threadbare carpet almost reached the hallway's edges. A sour, rank smell entered Patterson's nostrils without asking for an invitation. It was like milk well past its sell-by date or a vomity kind of smell, which Patterson wasn't to know was actual vomit, well past its sell-by date.

The standard flat was split into bedsits with five doors in total. One half-open door led to a small bathroom, and another open door led to a kitchen. The three closed doors were presumably the accommodation, the actual bed-sitting rooms. Patterson tried one of the keys in the first door on the left and was pleased to hear it click open. His lucky day, he thought.

The room was the height of luxury, if that was a decidedly low height consisting of a room with a ceiling and floor. A small window looked out onto the tenements across the street and to the shaded street below.

There were three beds crammed into the small space. It reeked of an odour even more foul than in the hallway.

Patterson wondered if the other three rooms would be like this. If so, that would mean nine people were staying in the flat. Another landlord taking advantage of immigrant workers to get the maximum return on his investment.

The curtains were half-closed, and Patterson pulled them open to let in more light and opened the window to let in fresh air. Most of the prison cells he visited were better than this cramped room.

Clothes and empty food containers and cans were strewn across the floor. Power cords crisscrossed the carpet, and newspapers in a foreign language, presumably Polish, lay abandoned.

It was hard to tell which bed belonged to Lucas Ryba. However, picking up a bible on a small bedside table by one of the beds, he looked at the inside cover, and it conveniently said Lucas Ryba in neat handwriting. A picture of the Virgin Mary was also pinned to the wall by the bed. It appeared Lucas was religious.

In the bedside table drawer, Patterson found postcards from Poland and old copies of work contracts for a Harrington's work agency. There were also leaflets for a St Mary's Church in Shawlands. Patterson took one of the leaflets and a light blue copy of a work contract. He then looked under the bed and saw more loose clothes and food debris strewn along the floor alongside a couple of folded-up holdalls.

Patterson walked out of the room and knocked on one closed door and then another. There was no answer. Presumably, work was a blessed escape from the accommodation. The rank smell seemed to get stronger again, and Patterson was led by his nose to the bathroom. He pushed open the door further and saw a pile of yellow gooey sick lying next to the toilet bowl. Starting to feel ill, Patterson made to leave the flat. He had seen and smelled more than enough.

Chapter 34

History, Religion and the Glasgow Subway

The post-mortem of Lucas Ryba took place on Thursday morning. There were tiny haemorrhages in the lungs, heart and brain, indicating Lucas had indeed died of asphyxiation. Piecing together Lucas's last movements, it was believed that he left work in Govan on Saturday late afternoon and ended up in the graveyard behind Glasgow Cathedral a short time later. Over two days, he was stripped, beaten and repeatedly sexually assaulted in the same way that Cheryl Kerr had been.

It was now Friday morning, and Patterson stood in front of the incident board.

'OK, here's where we are,' began Patterson as he addressed his fellow officers. 'For now, I'd like to put aside the murder of Tommy Beaton and concentrate on the murders of Lucas Ryba and Cheryl Kerr. Specifically, I want to explore any connection between these two crimes. So, first things first,' Patterson pointed to the new photo pinned on the board, a passport photo of Lucas Ryba. 'Lucas Ryba was a 24-year-old Polish national who had been in this country for around 8 months. He stayed in shared accommodation in Govanhill, Garturk Street; overcrowded accommodation, I may add, now being investigated by the city council. On Saturday afternoon, the 6th of December, Lucas left his work at a bottling plant in Govan around 5pm and walked to the subway station at Govan Cross. There he got on a train to Bridge Street. This was his usual routine where Lucas would normally catch a bus from Bridge Street to Victoria Road in Govanhill. There he would walk along to the shared flat on Garturk Street. However, on this particular day, after leaving Bridge Street subway station, he somehow ended up in the grounds of Glasgow Cathedral. Now —'

'Are we sure he got off at Bridge Street?' asked DC McLean.

'Yes, we have CCTV of him entering Govan Cross station at 5:16 PM and exiting Bridge Street at 5:34PM. He then goes out of camera range. This means he doesn't go to the bus stop on the main road. He is not picked up by any CCTV in the immediate vicinity. So the first mystery we have to solve is why and how he ended up at Glasgow Cathedral. Any suggestions?'

Pettigrew spoke first. 'Well, getting to the cathedral from Bridge Street is quite a trek by foot. You have to walk north, cross the river, head through town, presumably go past Glasgow Cross and up the High Street. I would say it takes about forty minutes on foot at a rough estimate.'

'He still could have done that. Or else he could have got a bus or taxi,' said Simpson.

'But then either way, walking, bus or taxi, we would have picked him up on CCTV,' said McKinnon

'That's right,' said Patterson. 'If he had started walking north towards the cathedral, he would have been picked up crossing Glasgow Bridge and several other places. It's unlikely he got a taxi since, for one thing, it would have cost more than his weekly travel pass. However, we'll check out the taxi firms, just in case. So connection number one, like Cheryl Kerr, Lucas just disappears from view after leaving the subway station. Of course, we know Cheryl Kerr was held in the nearby tunnel, and Lucas was held in the cathedral grounds. So again, I want t know how Lucas ended up at Glasgow cathedral?'

'Maybe someone gave him a lift.' said Pettigrew.

'Yes,' said Patterson. 'Since we have no CCTV of Lucas after he leaves Bridge Street, I think he may have got into a car that took him to the cathedral.'

'If he did get a lift, presumably, that means he knew whoever took him to the cathedral.'

'Possibly,' said Patterson, 'but that brings us to the next question. Putting aside how he got there, why would he go there?'

'To meet someone? To be with someone? Presumably, he arranged to go there with the person he got in the car with,' said McKinnon.

'As I understand it, the grounds are often used by prostitutes,' said Pettigrew 'or maybe it was a girlfriend? If his flat was overcrowded and they wanted privacy, perhaps that's why.'

'In this weather?' said Simpson. 'Maybe in the Summer, but now? It would be bloody freezing.'

'OK, if we're looking for connections between the two murders,' said Pettigrew, 'and if we believe Cheryl was abducted and led to the tunnel against her will, then shouldn't we think Lucas was taken from outside the subway station against his will?' asked Pettigrew.

'But how?' said Simpson, 'it was a busy time in the centre of town, or just about. Surely someone would have seen something.'

'I agree,' said Patterson, 'I believe Lucas must have known his attacker in this case. I think if he got in a car, he got into the car willingly.'

'McKinnon and McLean, I want you to go over CCTV and try to match any vehicles seen outside Bridge Street station when Lucas left the station to any cars parked near Glasgow Cathedral later that night.'

'Now,' said Patterson, 'Is there anything else we can say connects these two murders?'

'The subway,' said Pettigrew. 'Both Cheryl and Lucas used the subway just before they were murdered.'

'Yes, but almost half the city uses the subway at that time,' said Simpson.

'Nevertheless,' said Patterson, 'That's certainly a connection we must keep in mind. It may be significant. What else?'

'The locations,' said McKinnon.

'How's that?' asked Simpson

'There's a historical aspect to both locations, the tunnel and the graveyard. Plus, whoever knew about the graveyard at the back of Glasgow Cathedral must know the city fairly well. Perhaps he has knowledge of historical places.'

'Yes,' agreed Patterson. 'I would say that whoever carried out these two murders has a good knowledge of the city and possibly a knowledge of history, specifically Glasgow history.'

'You know, there is another possible connection,' said McKinnon.

'What's that?' asked Simpson.

'Religion.'

'Religion?' asked Simpson, ' I don't see how the railway tunnel is religious.'

'Not the tunnel so much,' said Pettigrew. 'But weren't Cheryl and Lucas both held spread-eagled on the ground?'

'So?'

'Well, it's almost like they were crucified.'

'Brian, that's nonsense,' said Simpson.'

'No,' said Patterson, 'We have to look for any possible connections. Lucas was found in a cemetery next to a cathedral. There could indeed be a religious aspect to this we can't dismiss out of hand just yet.'

'In that case,' said Pettigrew, 'something else could give a religious connection to the murders.'

What's that?' asked Patterson

'Cheryl had a wound, a gash in her side.'

'You've lost me,' said Simpson.

'Jesus on the cross? He was pierced in the side by a spear?' Don't you know your bible?'

Simpson shook his head. 'I think we're going off on a tangent here.'

'I think I may have to agree with you there, Jack,' said Patterson. 'Nevertheless, I'll ask the pathologist to double-check the findings on that wound. Anything else?'

There was silence from his fellow officers. 'OK, that'll do for now,' said Patterson.' I've printed out the assignments for the rest of the team. Davies, if you'd like to do the honours and hand them out. As always, if you've any questions about anything, just ask.'

As Davies handed out the assignments to the wider team for that day, Patterson thought there were more potential connections between the two murders than he had anticipated.

There was a possible historical angle, the Glasgow Subway connection and possibly even a religious motive. The religious angle did remind him of one thing. He had arranged to meet Lucas Ryba's priest, Father Eugene Gillespie, at the weekend. As he still thought of the connections between the two murders, he wondered which, if any, could turn out to be significant.

Chapter 35

Cessnock

Two months had passed since Sarah McKay found out her fiancé was having an affair. Now, as Sarah walked towards meeting him for the first time since then, she didn't mind admitting how nervous she was. The fact was, Sarah couldn't help missing Billy. The truth was, she still loved him. In the back of her mind was the thought that if Billy truly, truly regretted what he did, then perhaps, perhaps mind, she could give him another chance.

They arranged to meet in a small cafe near Partick Cross they had frequented many times before in happier days. Billy was already there when Sarah arrived, and she sat down with a stern face, trying as best she could to disguise the pleasure she felt in seeing Billy again. After ordering a latte, she looked across at her ex and waited to see how genuine his attempt at forgiveness would be.

'Sarah,' he began, 'Thanks for agreeing to meet me. I know you must be hurting, but I am too...and I hope one day you'll forgive me, but I just had to see you before I leave.'

At first, she didn't understand the 'before I leave' bit but decided to stay quiet rather than ask and possibly, make it more real.

Billy continued. 'I'm moving to Northern Ireland next week with Peggy.'

Sarah sat numb. Surely he was joking. Wasn't he begging to get back with her just a few weeks ago?

'Billy, you don't need to play games with me; if you want us to get back together, just say so but don't tell me silly stories.'

'That's just it, Sarah; I realise now I'm not sorry for what I did. I love Peggy with all my heart, and hopefully,' he smiled coyly, 'She loves me just as much.'

Sarah couldn't believe what she was hearing. Did Billy want her to beg him to come back? Was that it? If so, she would swallow her pride and do as he wanted. He was really beginning to scare her now. 'OK. I still love you, Billy. Is that what you want to hear? I don't know why, but I still love you. I mean, I miss you. I can understand if you made a mistake. I can even forgive you. It might take a little time, but I'm prepared to try.' She made a move to hold Billy's hand, but he pulled it away and shook his head. 'It's you who doesn't understand, Sarah. I'm sorry, but like I said, I'm in love with Peggy and as soon as we arrive in Portadown – '

'Portadown?'

'Peggy has family there. As soon as we arrive in Portadown, we're going to the first registry office we can find.'

Billy had obviously lost the plot. What had the cow done to him? Knocked him over the head and drugged him? She could feel tears start to roll down each of her cheeks. Sarah tried to think of a way to make Billy stay, yet in her heart of hearts, the way he spoke, she already knew there was little she could do. One more time, though, as the other customers in the cafe looked on at this soap episode being played out in real life, Sarah begged Billy to stay. Alas, it was all to no avail. Billy was adamant. He had fallen head over heels in love with Peggy, and that was all that mattered. The clock couldn't be turned back.

'Nevertheless,' Billy said, suddenly perking up and smiling, 'You can keep the engagement ring. See it as a going-away present if you like. No hard feelings, eh?'

Sarah sat in silence and with an open mouth. She then carefully looked in her handbag and took out the engagement ring she treasured so much. She then threw it as hard as she could at Billy's face. It glanced off his left cheek, cutting it, before landing somewhere at the back of the café. An 'Oh!' went up from the watching audience, and a trickle of blood started to run down Billy's face.

'Fuck your ring and fuck you,' Sarah said

before walking out of the cafe into the bitter cold wind outside.

Sarah didn't know what she was doing or where she was going. Her head was spinning. She just walked in a direction that could have been any direction, not caring that she was bawling her eyes out and attracting stares from passers-by. On the spur of the moment, she crossed the road and turned left into Kelvinhall subway station. She still had no idea where she was going.

The first train to arrive was on the inner circle, which meant it would take her to the south side first before the city centre. She got on, surprised to see the carriage was almost empty on an early Friday evening. She sat, half numb with cold and the bitter reality of what Billy had said to her. In a slight daze, she looked up at the subway map. Where would she get off? Govan? Kinning Park? Bridge Street? Or would she stay on the train until it took her round to the city centre? Then she noticed Cessnock. Where the hell was Cessnock? What the hell was Cessnock? Had she ever been there in her life? Yes, she would get off at Cessnock, and that's what she did. Sarah wouldn't just lose Billy that night. Sarah would lose her life.

Chapter 36

Father Gillespie

On Saturday morning, Patterson arrived at St Mary's Church to meet Father Gillespie. St Mary's Church was a modest, modern building tucked away up a side street near Shawlands Cross. It had a low, flat roof and no windows. Only a small, simple cross above the door gave any idea it was a place of worship. Walking inside, it was a different matter. Patterson immediately felt the cool interior that seemed to be the trademark of most churches. There was a muffled silence, too, that was agreeably churchlike. Inside were rows of simple wooden chairs instead of pews. A stained glass window stood behind the altar, yet this wasn't a window but attached to the wall like a glass painting. The altar was a raised platform with a statue of Jesus on one side and the Virgin Mary with a raised hand on the other, like a mother calling her son in for tea.

As Patterson stood surveying the church, he was unsure if this was where Father Gillespie was to be found or if he should have looked for a rectory-type building nearby. To his relief, a priest emerged from a small door to the left of the altar.

Father Gillespie walked up to Patterson quickly, holding out his hand and wearing a beaming smile. To Patterson's eyes, Father Gillespie was a healthy, looking, fresh-faced man in his late fifties. His smile could be called a minister's smile, and he had the healthy glow and quick movement of someone who kept active in advancing years.

'DCI Patterson?' Patterson acknowledged it was him. 'How do you do? You're here about Lucas? I still can't believe it. So young too. You know I was only just talking to – Anyway, come this way, we can talk better through here. Did you manage to find the church alright?'

Father Gillespie talked fast, slightly overwhelming Patterson with words. He has a well-spoken Glasgow accent. Patterson was glad to have an opportunity to say something in reply.

'Yes, I found it quite easily, thanks.' Patterson followed the priest through the small door on the left and, to his surprise, into a large bright conservatory that had presumably been added on to the church. Tables and chairs were scattered around, with the largest round table in the centre of the room. Father Gillespie walked to a table against a wall and switched on a kettle next to a dozen or so cups.

'Tea? Coffee?'

'Coffee, thanks, milk, one sugar,' Patterson replied.

Patterson sat at one of the smaller round, grey, Formica-topped tables next to the centre table. The smell of sawdust and paint reminded Patterson of school, then again, everywhere of late seemed to remind him of school. Soon, the kettle started to make a rumbling noise as if preparing for take-off, then clicked off. Father Gillespie made the coffees and brought them over to Patterson's table. Patterson's mug was adorned by a logo for Howell's Builder's Merchants, while Father Gillespie's had a photo of a tropical sandy beach with a blue sky. Gillespie was smiling again and sat down in a chair opposite Patterson.

'Now, how can I help you?' said the priest.

'The reason I'm here, Father. Should I call you Father?'

'You can call me whatever you like; my name is Eugene, but Father is fine with me if it's fine with you.'

'Right. As you know, we're investigating the murder of Lucas Ryba. For the moment, I'm trying to find out more about his background. How well would you say you knew him?'

'Lucas came here every Sunday and often came to the midweek mass too. He was an enthusiastic member, I can tell you that.' Gillespie shook his head. 'Still can't believe we're discussing him in the past tense.'

'So would you say you knew him quite well?'

'Quite well, yes; he would often come here for a talk afterwards with other church members.'

'Talk about what?'

'Oh, you know, religion, obviously. His Catholic faith. The Church. God. The meaning of life. Anything and everything, really. Lucas was always wondering how he could be a better person. A better disciple if you like.'

'Did he ever mention his personal life? Had he any problems, or did he mention people bothering him in any way?'

'No, when you called saying you wanted to meet about Lucas, I've been racking my brains about why anyone would want to harm him. I can't say for elsewhere, but Lucas was well-liked by everyone at the church here.'

'So, he never talked about his personal life?'

'Oh, he did mention a couple of things. He didn't like his job, and he was also homesick. He often talked about that. He was always thinking about going back to Poland. One other thing was he didn't like where he was staying either. I remember he said everyone drank too much. Lucas wasn't one for socialising.'

'Yet, he often came here for talks?'

'Yes, I got the impression here was one of the few places he could feel at ease and be himself.'

'Have you never been to his accommodation?'

'No, I can't say I have.'

'Well, it was pretty squalid. Overcrowded. Frankly, I'm not surprised he wanted to return to Poland.'

'Really?' Father Gillespie seemed surprised. 'That's terrible. If I'd known it was that bad, I would have tried to find him a better place to stay. Then again…'

'What?'

'Well, as I say, Lucas hadn't been that happy these past few months. Homesick. I advised him it was perhaps better if he went home to Poland. He didn't seem settled here. He worked in a factory somewhere in Govan, I believe. He wasn't happy in that regard either.'

'You see, Father, we believe it's possible that whoever killed Lucas may have known him. Was Lucas not close to anyone here? Apart from yourself, I mean.'

'You know, I don't think so. Lucas was well-liked, but I honestly couldn't say if Lucas was particularly close to anyone here.'

'Have you ever heard of someone called Cheryl Kerr?'

'Cheryl Kerr,' Gillespie looked puzzled. 'Was that not the name of the young woman murdered in Kelvinbridge?'

'That's right. You see, we believe the murders of Lucas and Cheryl are linked.'

Patterson brought out the photo of Cheryl he now carried around with him. 'This is Cheryl. Have you ever seen her before?'

The priest studied the photo and shook his head. 'I'm sorry, no.'

'If the person who murdered Lucas knew him, then that person could also have known Cheryl. Are you sure you have never seen her before?'

Gillespie studied the photo intensely again before shaking his head. 'No. I'm afraid I haven't. Poor soul. So you really think whoever killed this woman murdered Lucas as well?'

'We believe so.' Patterson took a drink of coffee before asking the next question. 'I have to ask everyone this, but where were you on Saturday around 5 pm.'

Father Gillespie thought for a moment. 'I believe I was here if I remember correctly. In the church. Yes, I'm sure I was.'

'Can anyone verify that?'

'I'm afraid not. I was here alone. Preparing my sermon for Sunday mass.'

'OK, well, that's all for now.' Patterson took a final gulp of his coffee. 'If you do think of anything that could be of interest, please give me a call.' Patterson handed him his card. 'I best get going.' Patterson rose from his chair, realising his visit had been fruitless.

Father Gillespie rose to escort him out of the church.

On the way out, Patterson stopped at the main entrance to thank the priest again. There was a notice board just to the left of the main door, and Patterson looked at it. There was the usual array of events and notices you would expect to see on any church noticeboard. A bring-and-buy sale, a cleaner wanted, the times of a bible study class....yet, one item, in particular, caught his eye.

Interested in history? Then come along to our historical society. The Friends of Old Glasgow. 51 Crown Circus every second Tuesday of the month at 7:30pm. Free to Join.

'I haven't heard of them before.'

'What's that?'

'The Friends of Old Glasgow.'

'Oh, I wouldn't expect you to. We're just a small group.'

'We?'

'Oh, yes, I'm a member. I love my history. It's great fun. You should come along one night.'

Patterson nodded. 'I might just do that. I don't suppose Lucas Ryba was a member of this society, was he?'

'Lucas? No, why?'

'Nothing, just a thought. Anyway, I appreciate your time, Father. Thanks for your help.'

'Not at all. The sooner this person is caught, the better, and if I think of anything else, I'll get in touch.'

'I appreciate that. Thanks again, Father.'

Patterson left the church and made his way to his car. The Friends of Old Glasgow? A historical society? Maybe his visit to Father Gillespie wasn't as fruitless as he first thought.

Chapter 37

Walmer Crescent

After being able to spend most of Sunday at home with Stephanie, Patterson was back in his office on Monday morning. McKinnon entered the office after a short knock. McKinnon's urgency gave Patterson a sense of foreboding. So much so that Patterson guessed what he was about to say.

'What, another one?' asked Patterson.

McKinnon nodded. 'Fraid so. In Walmer Crescent.'

'Walmer Crescent? Where's that?' asked Pettigrew.

'Cessnock,' replied McKinnon.

Patterson sighed and picked up his jacket from the back of the chair. 'Well, Brian, notify Jack and Claire; it looks like we're going to Cessnock.'

Walmer Crescent curved behind a row of shops on Paisley Road West that could be described as the centre of Cessnock. Walmer

Crescent was a Grade A building built by Alexander 'Greek' Thompson, so named because of the Greek influence in his architecture. As you would expect for a listed building, Walmer Crescent was in reasonably good condition. Both ends of the elegant crescent were closed off, with police activity centred around a house in the middle of the crescent.

Once dressed in his obligatory white paper suit, Patterson walked up the short flight of stairs to the front door with Simpson and Pettigrew close behind. Inside, there was a strong smell of paint and turpentine. All around were building materials, and the house was clearly undergoing major renovations.

Patterson looked into a large front room to the left and saw two workmen in cream overalls, possibly decorators, standing with dazed expressions. Patterson showed his ID to a uniformed officer inside the hallway.

'Where's the body?'

'It's just up here, sir.' The officer led Patterson up a wide staircase covered in a dirty grey, paint-splattered canvas. There were three floors, and it must have been luxurious accommodation in its day. Even in its present state, it was still an impressive house.

On the third floor, Patterson was led into a large bright room with windows looking down onto the crescent and the back of the shops. The floor consisted of floorboards which looked newly varnished.

In the corner of the room lay the naked body of a female who appeared to be in her early thirties. She had long blonde hair, and her glazed-over eyes looked up at the ceiling. Her body was covered in bruises and lacerations, and her arms and legs were spread wide apart.

Patterson immediately looked for small holes in the floor, but none could be seen. However, ligature marks were still apparent around the woman's ankles and wrists, showing she had been tied up at some point. Patterson looked at a radiator underneath the window and a heating pipe on the other side of the body. He noticed both had chipped paint with small shavings on the floor. Perhaps the murderer had attached cords to each of these to keep the young woman's arms and legs apart.

'Any idea who she is?'

'Yes,' said a young police officer in uniform who was first on the scene. 'Her handbag was found over there.' He pointed to another corner of the room. 'The officer handed Patterson a driving licence. Her name is Sarah McKay. 33 years old. Lived in Partick.'

'Not reported missing?'

'We believe so, but only from last night.'

'Who found the body?'

'A couple of workmen who are renovating the building. They had been away for the weekend, came in this morning and found her. The doctor has been, and death has been declared. We're still waiting for the pathologist.'

'What made you call Partick?'

'I don't know, sir. You'd have to ask DCI Foley. I believe he's in the back garden at – Oh, here he is now.'

A middle-aged detective who Patterson vaguely knew walked into the room.

'Mike, isn't it? DCI Foley, don't know if you remember me. How you doing? As soon as I saw the body, I suspected this one was yours.'

'Yes, it's Dave, isn't it? I think we crossed paths regarding the Clydeside antique warehouse murder.'

'Of course; how you doing? Yes, this looks like the same murderer I've been dealing with, I'm afraid.'

'Looks like you've got a job on your hands, then. The murders must be stacking up.'

'Yes, if this is the same guy, this is the fourth victim.'

'I got called here about forty minutes ago. We're just waiting on the pathologist—' he turned to the uniformed officer waiting by the two senior officers.'

'John, go outside and keep guard. Don't let anyone in unless they have reason to be here.' The young officer departed.

'So this looks like the same perpetrator, does it?' asked Foley.

'Definitely looks like the same guy. The

lacerations and bruises on the body. The ligature marks on the wrists and ankles. First indications are it's the same person.'

Foley nodded. 'I've had a quick look around. It seems the back door has been broken into. As you can see, the place is being renovated. The builders work Monday to Friday, so no one was here over the weekend.'

Simpson and Pettigrew came up the stairs, and Patterson made the introductions.

DCI Foley said his hellos and then just as quickly said his goodbye. He obviously didn't want to get roped into something when he could be getting on with his own work.

'I was saying to DCI Foley, this is almost certainly our man. Too many similarities for it not to be.'

Pettigrew nodded. 'And this is a listed building,'

'Is it?' asked Simpson.

'Yes, it was built by a well-known Glasgow architect, if I remember correctly,' said Patterson.

'There's something else that could be significant,' said Pettigrew, 'Cessnock subway station is right at the end of this crescent. In fact, it's practically part of the crescent.'

Patterson took off his glasses and pinched his eyes. 'Right. Claire, double check the pathologist is on the way. Jack, find out who the next of kin is. Her name is Sarah McKay lives in Fortrose Street in Partick according to her driving licence.' Both officers departed, and Patterson looked down at the victim's body. Her face and lips were blue, and her mouth was slightly open. Patterson knew it was more than likely she had been asphyxiated the same way Lucas Ryba was.

The pathologist confirmed the time of death as late on Sunday night or the early hours of Monday morning. There were also signs of sexual assault, broken ribs and torture. Simpson informed Patterson the victim's parents lived in Springburn.

'You two stay here for now,' Patterson told Simpson and Pettigrew. 'You both know the routine. Find out what you can. If Dunard gets in touch, tell him I'm going to the parents, and I'll see you both later.'

Patterson headed out of the building and to his car. He suddenly felt slightly dizzy and stopped for a moment on the pavement. He held on to the railings trying to steady himself. His anxiety was making itself known again as if dropping in for a quick cuppa. This was now the fourth victim. Patterson had to find the murderer soon, or it was only a matter of time before someone else lost their life.

Chapter 38

Poverty, Gap Sites and Memories

Patterson got in his car, flicked open his mobile phone and phoned Booth. On her answering, he asked where she was, and Booth replied that she was in Byres Road. Patterson informed her there had been another murder and told her to meet him outside where the parents of Sarah Mckay lived, at Carleson Street in Springburn.

Springburn had a proud industrial heritage and particularly in the building of steam trains. What Govan was to shipbuilding, Springburn was to train building. In its heyday, locomotives were despatched to the four corners of the British Empire. With the dual demise of steam trains and empire, Springburn was now typical of many areas in Glasgow. Its rich industrial past was replaced by poverty, gap sites and memories. Carleson Street was just off the main road that cut through the area. It had relatively modern houses on a pleasant sloping road uphill. Seeing Booth's car had arrived before his, Patterson got out of his vehicle and walked over to Booths.

On seeing him approach, Booth made to get out of the car, but Patterson motioned for her to stay inside. Patterson then walked around to the passenger side, a move which Booth met with a smile. He entered the car and closed the door.

'Morning, sir.'

'Morning Emma.'

'What's happened?'

'A body was found in Cessnock. Walmer Crescent. Looks like the same murderer as that of Lucas and Cheryl. This is where the parents live. Number 15. The victim was Sarah Mckay. 35. Apart from that, we don't know much except she lived in Partick. There's no need to tell you; this will be very difficult. The parents are going to be devastated. At the same time, we must ensure it is Sarah McKay. So the parents and someone else will have to identify the body later.'

Booth nodded solemnly. In a few moments, Patterson and herself would be changing the lives of two people forever.

'Is there anything else I should know?' asked Booth.

'Sarah was found badly beaten, probably sexually assaulted like the other victims. Of course, don't mention any of that to the parents. As far as they're concerned, all you know is Sarah was found in a house in Cessnock, and the death is suspicious. As usual, once I'm gone, I need you to learn everything you can about Sarah. If you feel you need to bring in anyone else, just say. There are a lot of victims piling up in a short space of time. For now, our number one priority is to give the parents all the support they need. Only ten days till Christmas as well. Get family members round, friends, well, you know the score.'

'Of course,' Booth said, but then her mood suddenly brightened. 'It's good to see you again.'

Patterson noticed her sudden change of mood with surprise and disappointment. He decided to have a word with Booth without further delay.

'OK. Emma, that was something else I've been meaning to say to you.'

Emma seemed to take this as a positive rather than a negative. Yet, Patterson didn't know how to put what he wanted to say into words. 'Emma, I know we got close to one another before, but I need to know that you realise our relationship is, and always will be, strictly professional.'

'Of course, why would you think differently?'

Patterson looked at her again; he just couldn't figure her out. Booth seemed genuinely surprised.

'I'm serious, Emma.'

'So am I. Listen, I know as well as you do know we got a little closer than we should have before, but I know it's in the past. Besides, nothing happened.'

'I know nothing happened. Just as long as you know that. I don't want there to be a problem.'

'With all due respect, sir, it seems to be you who has a problem.'

'Then what was that comment the other day about "I know you still want me"?'

'It was a joke!'

'Was it?'

'Oh, for crying out loud. Of course, it was!'

'OK, I just wanted to make my position clear.'

'Trust me, you've made it loud and clear.'

'Good. I just got the impression you thought there is a chance something could happen between us.'

'Sir, apart from anything else, why would you think anything could happen between us? Frankly, do you really believe I could be interested in you? You're almost old enough to be my dad, for crying out loud.'

Patterson thought for a moment and realised she may have a point. 'OK, right, I just wanted to say…I mean, OK, anyway, we have to get on with this. I don't need to tell you what to do.'

'No, you don't,' Booth said.

'Right,' Patterson said and got out of the car. For a moment, he wondered if Emma would join him. It seemed to take an age before she got out of the vehicle. Once she did, Patterson started walking toward the parents' house. He felt quite agitated and knew he needed to calm himself down. Thankfully, remembering what he was about to do soon put his situation with Booth into perspective.

Number 15 Carleson Street was within a small block of flats. Patterson walked up a flight of stairs to the communal front door and waited for Booth to join him.

Booth eventually caught up.

'You OK?' Patterson asked.

'Fine,' Booth said without making eye contact with her boss.

Patterson rang the doorbell. As with every police officer, this was the part of the job he hated the most.

As the two officers waited for a reply from the intercom, Booth looked across at Patterson. 'You know, this was how we first met.'

'How d'you mean?'

'In Drumchapel. At the mother of Susan McLaughlin's place. Don't you remember? You came to the flat, and I was already there. That was the first time we met.'

'Is this another joke?'

Booth smiled as a tinny female voice came through the small, round tannoy. 'Hello?'

'Mrs McKay? I'm DCI Patterson, Strathclyde Police.'

There was a moment's silence as Mrs McKay

was obviously wondering why the police would be at her door. Then there was a continuous buzz and a click, and Patterson pushed the door open. As Patterson and Booth walked up the first flight of stairs, Mrs McKay and her husband had come out onto the landing to look down at them over the thin, black metal bannister. Their worst fears were already becoming a reality as they saw the grave looks on the police officer's faces.

The parents looked like a respectable couple in their mid-fifties. The mother was a small woman with blonde hair, while the father looked a bit like Patterson, tall with short grey hair and glasses. Both parents continued to look with curiosity and fear as Patterson and Booth walked up the stairs.

'What's the matter?' the mother said before Patterson and Booth had reached the first-floor landing. 'Is anything wrong?' The words echoed around the small close.

'May we come in?' said Patterson.

This only served to heighten the fear more than the curiosity. A thousand scenarios already going through the couple's minds as they ushered Patterson and Booth through a narrow hallway and into a comfortable living room. The loud, upbeat noise of daytime television filled the space.

Patterson and Booth sat down on a large settee as the parents entered the room after them. The father switched off the TV, and now the only noise was the ticking of a clock on the mantlepiece.

'Has something happened?' Mrs McKay again asked, wanting Patterson to say there was no need to worry, that everything was fine. Instead, Patterson's continued silence and grave manner were already conveying the first act of the news that was their worst nightmare.

'Would you both like to sit down?' said Booth, and the parents did as they were told, sitting on the two separate armchairs in the room.

'I'm afraid I have some very bad news to tell you.' Patterson began.

At this, the mother started crying, 'Please don't tell me it's Sarah. Please don't.'

Patterson looked to the father, who had a look of shock on his face.

Patterson then noticed the framed photograph of a smiling young woman on the mantlepiece who was identical to the woman he had been looking at only an hour earlier.

'I'm very sorry. We found a body this morning, and we have reason to believe it is your daughter Sarah.' The mother wailed and started sobbing her eyes out, and Booth immediately went and knelt beside her holding her hand.

Patterson looked at the father again, who was now blankly looking into the middle distance. He appeared to have aged 20 years in a matter of seconds.

'I'm very sorry.' Patterson continued.

The father spoke for the first time.

'What makes you think it's Sarah? I mean, she was only here the other day. Are you sure it's her?'

Booth continued to try and console the mother, putting her arm around her and saying words to try and alleviate the emotional pain and distress.

Patterson brought out the driving licence.

'This was found near her body in a handbag. Do you know if this belongs to your daughter? She had other documents belonging to Sarah McKay, which makes us believe it's Sarah.'

The father continued to question as the mother continued to cry. 'But how? What happened? You found her this morning? How?'

'I need you both to prepare for even more distressing news. We're treating Sarah's death as suspicious for now. We believe she could have been murdered.'

The father looked at Patterson as if he was mad, but tears started to form in his eyes. He removed his glasses and wiped away the first tears of many that would appear for the rest of his days.

'Murdered?'

'At the moment, we're still trying to fully establish exactly what happened. I promise you'll be the first to know as soon as we know more. I need to ask you both a few questions straight away.'

'Where was she found?' It was the mother that asked the question.

'In a house in Walmer Crescent. It's on the south side.'

'How?' the mother asked again.

'As I said, we're still trying to establish all the details. Can I ask if Sarah ever mentioned Walmer Crescent?'

'No, I don't think so,' replied the father, looking over at Mrs McKay, who shook her head.

'Never. I don't even know where Walmer Crescent is,' added Mr Mckay.

'As I said, it's on the city's south side. Cessnock,' said Patterson.

'Cessnock? Where the hell is Cessnock?' the father asked in a daze.

'It's part of Govan. Paisley Road West. Would Sarah have any reason to go there? Did she have any friends there?'

'No, not as far as we know,' said the father.

'When was the last time you saw your daughter?'

Mr McKay looked across at his wife, who answered. 'It was Thursday, late Thursday afternoon. She came for her tea.' Mrs McKay talked while catching her breath through sobs and tears.

'Did Sarah say anything about what she was doing on Friday or at the weekend?'

'No.' Both parents shook their heads again, and then Mr McKay looked up as if suddenly remembering something. 'Oh, wait a minute, she said she was going to meet her ex-boyfriend. Billy.'

At this, the mother looked at her husband in surprise. 'She was meeting Billy? You didn't tell me that!'

'I'm sorry, but Sarah thought it best you didn't know. You see, Inspector, my wife doesn't like the boyfriend Sarah was going out with.'

Mrs McKay was suddenly angry. 'Is it any wonder? He cheated on Sarah and with a woman old enough to be his gran!'

'And Sarah definitely said she was going to meet her ex-boyfriend on Friday, Mr McKay? You're quite sure about that?' Patterson cut in.

'Well, that's what she said. I'm sorry, Ruth, I would have told you, but Sarah made me swear not to.'

Patterson brought out a notepad. 'What's the name of the ex-boyfriend?'

'Billy. Billy Richardson.'

'Did Sarah say where she was going to meet him?'

'I think she said a café in Partick. Near Partick Cross. Near where she lives, in fact. I can't remember the name.'

'Do you happen to have Billy's address?'

'Aye, I think I've got it in the kitchen somewhere, he lives in Spittal, hang on,' Mr

McKay went into the hallway. Patterson listened to Mrs McKay, still crying.

'Emma, could I have a word with you for a moment?' Patterson said quietly.

Booth rose and followed Patterson out of the room. As Patterson stood in the hallway, he could hear Mr McKay rummaging around in a drawer in the kitchen.

Patterson spoke quietly. 'I'll need to chase up this boyfriend. You'll need to stay here. As usual, see what you can find out.'

Booth nodded as Mr McKay came from the kitchen. He handed a piece of paper to Patterson.

'This is his address here. It's Lochlea Road.'

Thanking Mr McKay, Patterson took the piece of paper and followed the father through to the living room along with Booth. Patterson renewed his questions.

'Did Sarah mention any issues recently, mention anyone following her, her boyfriend perhaps or someone else, anything at all suspicious you can think of?'

Again both parents answered in the negative, and Patterson felt he better start tracing the boyfriend. 'OK, I know this is a difficult time, but if you can think of any reason someone would want to harm Sarah or anything else, just let Emma know.'

Patterson rose from the settee. 'I'll leave you in the hands of Emma here for now. I'll see myself out. I'm afraid we'll probably need a couple of people, one of you or another family member or friend, to identify Sarah formally sometime soon.' The parents didn't respond. Anyway, if you need anything, just tell Emma, again, I'm very sorry for your loss.'

Patterson turned and left the flat, then walked back to his car. He called the station to get Simpson and Pettigrew to accompany him to Spittal.

Chapter 39

Join the Club

The ex-boyfriend of Sarah McKay, Billy Richardson, was at home and immediately brought in for questioning. CCTV confirmed his version of events that after meeting Sarah at the cafe, he returned to the flat of his fiancé Peggy 'O'Brien in Tollcross. Her testimony also confirmed he had spent the entire weekend there. Billy Richardson could not have murdered his ex-girlfriend Sarah McKay.

CCTV also showed that after Sarah had left the café, she walked to Kelvinhall Subway station. From there, she got on a train and got off at Cessnock. CCTV outside Cessnock station showed her hesitating before walking down Cessnock Street and going out of camera range.

Further enquiries showed she apparently knew no one in that area. So, could she have gotten off the train on a spur-of-the-moment decision? Did she walk down Cessnock Street in a distressed state with no definite place to go? For Patterson, it was certainly a possibility. After all,

Billy Richardson said he had just told Sarah he was moving to Northern Ireland with Peggy.

The autopsy of Sarah McKay showed that, like the other victims, she had been beaten and sexually assaulted over time. Her arms and legs had been kept apart by a cord wrapped around her wrists and ankles and then tied to a radiator and a pipe, just as Patterson had surmised at the crime scene. As had been determined with Cheryl Kerr and Lucas Ryba, the sexual assault was carried out using a large dildo-type object thrust into her repeatedly. Her abduction and murder were almost identical to the previous crimes.

As his fellow officer sat around the incident room, Patterson initially wanted to convey his thoughts on how Sarah ended up in that particular house in Walmer Crescent.

'We know that after Sarah exited the subway station, she walked down Cessnock Street,' Patterson said. 'The back entrance to the house in Walmer Crescent had been broken into and left open. So the murderer must have done this shortly after the workers had left the building on Friday afternoon around 4:30 pm and before Sarah wandered down Cessnock St on Friday evening at 6:17 pm. The murderer also knew the house would be empty over the weekend.'

'I still don't see how he got Sarah from Cessnock Street to the back of the house in

Walmer Crescent?' asked McKinnon.

'Presumably the same way he led Cheryl Kerr to the tunnel. All he had to do was place a knife to her back and lead her to the house via the broken back door,' said Patterson. 'Putting aside how he came to trap Sarah, her murder has thrown up one or two interesting connections to previous murders we've already touched upon. I now believe the murder of Sarah allows us to be a little more definitive about those connections. First off, the location. Sarah McKay was murdered in an A-listed building. Coincidence? I doubt it. So we can now cautiously say there is usually a historical connection to the murder location.

'Second. The subway. All three victims used the subway just before their deaths. Again, we can almost certainly state this is not coincidence. Putting these two facts together, it appears this murderer looks for a historical location he can take his victims shortly after they leave the subway.'

'How many subway stations there are?' asked Simpson.

'I believe there are fifteen stations if memory serves me correctly; any particular reason for that question?'

'Well, if he is targeting people exiting subway stations, couldn't we just have more patrols and security around those stations?'

'Enhanced security across all subway

stations is already in place. I've been able to call on extra personnel from other forces to do this. However, it still doesn't mean they're 100% secure. So those are the two lines of enquiry I want us to concentrate on. The subway and the historical connection. That's to say, as we've said before, we're looking for someone with a good knowledge of history and Glasgow. This brings me to one last point. I visited Father Gillespie yesterday, Lucas Ryba's local priest. As I was leaving, I noticed a small flyer on a noticeboard. It was for a historical society called The Friends of Old Glasgow. It turns out Father Gillespie is one such person interested in history. Of course, it may be nothing, but it means Father Gillespie is someone we should certainly be keeping a closer eye on.'

'How are you going to do that?' asked Simpson.

'One of us is going to become a member of this Friends of Old Glasgow, and when I say one of us, I mean you, Jack.'

'Me? Why me?'

'Because you're a foreigner,' said McKinnon.

'Not exactly,' said Patterson,' but you have the advantage of being an out-of-towner. It means you can have an oven-ready back story about being transferred up here from down south. You're keen to learn more about your new home so you want to join the club.'

'So, what exactly do you want me to do?'

'Just try and find out anything of interest about Father Gillespie. Keep your eyes and ears open at this historical society and see what turns up. You never know; you might even enjoy it.'

'Yeah, course I will,' said Simpson.

'Well, they're having a meeting tonight, so that's your entertainment for the night sorted. Anything else, cancel it. They meet at Crown Circus, which is not far from here, at 7:30. Go along, be your charming self and then report to me in the morning with what you find.'

Patterson picked up the typewritten sheets with everyone's tasks for that day. He gave them to McKinnon to hand around. 'OK, everyone, you all know what you need to do. Let's get on with it.'

Chapter 40

The Friends of Old Glasgow

Simpson turned his car left, distancing himself from the fuzzy lights of Byres Road takeaways, pubs and cafes and entered the relative darkness of Dowanside Road. An angry, howling wind blew small darts of snow across the windscreen of his car, making it hard to see. Nevertheless, Simpson soon managed to find the narrow road that led up to the elegant Georgian terrace that made up Crown Circus.

Some premises on the hilltop crescent were still privately owned. However, most had been converted into offices and let out to small businesses and organisations such as The Friends of Old Glasgow.

Simpson gratefully found a parking space on the crescent and sat in the car for a moment, summoning up the courage to confront the blizzard outside. As he eventually got out of the vehicle, Simpson was immediately covered in flakes of snow, which flung themselves onto him as if hugging a long-lost friend.

He looked up at the first building in front of him. On a white stone pillar, the number 27 was marked in large simple numbers. Knowing the Friends of Old Glasgow met in number 51, Simpson quickly strode to his right, scanning the different pillars for the correct number. Wiping the snow from his eyes, he finally saw the number he was looking for and ran up the wide granite steps to the main door.

Simpson rang the doorbell, hoping it would be answered quickly. It wasn't. He waited for what seemed an eternity until, eventually, the door opened with a long, theatrical creak. Feeling the cold more with every passing second, Simpson looked inside. A small man in a tartan bow tie and grey checked waistcoat stood before him.

'Mr Simpson, I presume?' Simpson hadn't felt the need to change his name.

'Friends of Old Glasgow?' Simpson replied.

'The very same.' The man, whose smallness Simpson observed may have been due to him being noticeably hunched over, proceeded to motion Simpson to enter. 'Come in, come in,' he said, making a movement with his hands as if trying to waft his visitor's presence inside.

Simpson gratefully stepped over the threshold with some snowflakes chancing their arms and gate-crushing the building entrance. Simpson shook some of the snow off, wiping down his arms, legs and front and additional wetness from his eyes.

'Some night, eh?' the small man said as he shut the door.

With the door closed, Simpson looked around and found he was standing in a cramped hallway as if it too, was hunched over. The faint light initially made Simpson think the place was lit by candles. However, there was no flickering, only an overall yellow dimness. The lack of space in what was once a private hallway of a well-to-do Georgian family was further hindered by a large table presumably used as a reception desk in the daytime. To his immediate right, Simpson looked at a carpeted staircase that led to darkened upper rooms and, to the left of the stairs, a small corridor that led elsewhere.

There was a smell of dampness and general oldness of air. It reminded Simpson of places that always stayed in the past, never quite adjusting to the present day.

As Simpson continued to look around, his host looked up at him.

'I see you have a keen eye, Jack, a historian's eye, no doubt. That's always good to see. Here, let me take your coat.'

'Thanks,' Simpson replied. As he handed his coat over, he listened to the snow and wind lashing the building, whistling through cracks, and rattling windows. This sound formed a constant backdrop to all conversation.

'My name is Malcolm, by the way, Malcolm

Brodie. I'm the president of The Friends of Old Glasgow. It was me you talked to on the phone when you enquired about our little association.' Brodie's voice was very polite; it was what Simpson had come to learn as upper-class Scots.

Simpson held out his wet hand, then quickly wiped it on his jacket before holding it out again.

'Pleased to meet you, Malcolm.'

Malcolm Brodie shook his hand, not appearing to be bothered by its wetness. Brodie then hung up Simpson's jacket, sparkling with melting snowflakes, on a coat peg next to an array of other wet jackets.

'I hear by your accent you're from down south?'

'Yes,' answered Simpson, 'Manchester.'

'Ah, Manchester. One of my favourite cities. I adore Quarry Bank Mill, you know it? Marvellous building.'

Simpson had never heard of it. 'Yes, it is,' he replied.

'Come through and meet the other members. We're a friendly bunch here; there's no need to be nervous.'

Simpson followed the elderly man through the narrow corridor next to the staircase. It had a thick, ancient-looking carpet and wooden walls hung with black and white photos of an earlier Glasgow in modern silver frames. As he walked along, Simpson rubbed his wet hands on his trousers again to dry them some more. Malcolm Brodie walked slowly in front of him with a slight limp.

'You'll have to excuse my lack of speed, Jack. Old bones, you see.'

'No need to apologise,' said Simpson. He estimated Brodie must be in his seventies.

The elderly man turned left and led Simpson into a large, bright room with the air of a gothic library. Two walls were covered in large bookcases filled with books with spines of cloth and leather. The room was dominated by a large, dark brown rectangular table around which eight people stared at Simpson. Brodie motioned for Simpson to sit in one of two empty chairs while Brodie sat on the other, positioned at the head of the table.

'Ladies and gentlemen of Old Glasgow,' Brodie announced, 'I'd like you all to warmly welcome our latest member Mr Jack Simpson.'

Looking around the table, Simpson noticed the eight people were a mixed bunch, young and old, male and female. Some of the looks Simpson received were amiable; others were not. Simpson felt the whole atmosphere intimidating, slightly creepy, and he wondered just what Patterson had got him into.

'Now, first things first, perhaps we should all give a short introduction of ourselves to Jack, and when I mean short introduction, I mean short!'

Simpson quickly gathered that Brodie liked being the president, the head of the table who kept his pupils in check.

'Now, I'll begin,' said Brodie, 'then Jack, if you'd like to introduce yourself, and then we'll go clockwise around the table.'

'Clockwise, how dae ye mean clockwise?'

It was a young man on the left who asked the question. This was one of the members who had looked at Simpson with clear animosity.

'What do you think I mean by clockwise, Louis? Clockwise as in clockwise. That way.' He made a circular stirring movement with his hands.

'Just asking. Ah, didnae know if ye meant that way.' He made a circular motion with his own hands but in the opposite direction.

Brodie sighed. 'Anyway, Jack, my name is Malcolm Brodie. I'm the president –' At this, the young man loudly coughed, and Simpson noticed a few other faces smirking. '– And I'm the president of the Friends of Old Glasgow.' Brodie went on to say he was now retired after he had been a professor of medieval history at Glasgow University. He now dedicated his time to his love of history and teaching others about the subject. 'Now Jack, if you'd like to begin by introducing yourself and then, as I said, we'll go – he shot a look at the young man – clockwise round the table.'

Simpson really did feel like the new boy in

class as the eyes of the other members bore down on him. He cleared his throat and began.

'OK, well, hello, everyone. My name is Jack Simpson. I work for an insurance firm in Salford, but I've just been transferred to Glasgow for six months. So I'd like to learn more about the city while I'm here and thought this would be a good place to start.'

'Excellent,' said Brodie, and he motioned to a small, friendly-looking woman on Simpson's left to introduce herself.

'Hello, Jack. My name is Iona McDonald. I'm from the north of England too, from Grimsby. I've been in Glasgow just over a year now, and also, like you, I just want to learn more about where I'm staying. Oh, and I've always been interested in history.' Iona McDonald smiled shyly and turned to the young man on her left as a way of saying your turn.

'Hi Jack, I'm Louis Gallacher. I'm a history guy. In fact, I've got my own YouTube channel *Gallacher's Glasgow*. You should check it out; if I say so myself, it's pretty good.' He looked at the older woman on his left.

'Hello. My name is Tess McLintock.' She stared at Simpson in a very friendly manner, making the Mancunian a little uncomfortable. 'I can't say I'm that into history, but my beloved husband is, so you know... Anyway, if you need anything, just ask; I'm always available.' She didn't look to her left but still stared at

Jack, smiling as the man beside her gave her a withering glance and started talking.

'Hello Jack, welcome to the club. My name is John McLintock. I'm the poor sod who is married to Tess here.' This drew a withering look in return from Tess. 'Only joking, my sweetest. My main interest in history is the early reformation period, specifically under Charles the second's reign and –'

'Yes, that's fine, John,' interrupted Brodie, 'short introductions only, thank you. Ofi, go ahead.'

The smartly dressed black man sitting very erect then spoke. 'My name is Ofi Obiaka. I'm from Nigeria. I have been in Glasgow six months, and I am very pleased to meet you!' Obiaka spoke with a loud, cheery voice.

Next to speak was Father Gillespie. 'Hello, Jack. My name is Eugene, or Father Gillespie, as I'm known to my flock. As you can probably tell by my attire, I'm a catholic priest, and as with the others, I'd like to welcome you to our club.' He then looked at the tall, dark-haired man on his left.

'Hello, Jack. My name's John McKenzie. I'm 29 and want to travel the world, promote peace and marry Shania Twain.' Brodie glared at another disruptive influence in his class.

'Good,' said Brodie, 'That's the introductions done. I think you'll like our little club, Jack. Glasgow's a fascinating city. It was once considered the second city of the Empire, you know –'

'Oh, here we go. Second city of the Empire! Unbelievable.'

'Well, it was Louis,' protested professor Brodie. 'It's a fact.'

'I don't know why you'd like Glasgow to be associated with an Empire that murdered its way around the world and was built on slavery, not to mention –'

'Oh, give it a rest Louis. Why don't you take your student politics and shove it up your arse.' It was Tess McLintock's turn to interrupt.

The language used surprised Jack as then someone else spoke. It was Iona. 'I think we should all try to put aside our bickering for one night; it's not fair on Jack.'

'Well said, Iona, the voice of reason as always,' said Brodie. 'I also suggest we get straight on with tonight's subject, shipbuilding!'

Tess McLintock rolled her eyes as Brodie, reading from a sheet of paper, began an introduction about the history of shipbuilding in Glasgow. After ten minutes, he stood up and pulled through a table on which sat a large television. They watched a forty-five-minute documentary detailing shipbuilding's importance in Glasgow. By now, Simpson was cursing Patterson to the high heavens, but he tried to pay attention to the programme as best he could in case questions were asked later.

Once the programme came to a close, Brodie clapped his hands together. 'Right, I hope you all found that interesting; We'll have a discussion later, but first, let's have some tea.'

'About bleedin' time,' John McKenzie muttered as everyone got up to stretch their legs.

Simpson stood up too, and Ofi Obiaka quickly came over to Simpson. 'Pleased to meet you again, Jack. I'm Ofi.'

'Pleased to meet you, Ofi,' said Simpson, 'Have you been coming here long?'

'Five months. I like it. It get me out the house.'

'Right,' said Simpson as Ofi suddenly walked away, and Tess McLintock came towards him.

'Hello, Jack. I love your accent, by the way. Reminds me of Sean Bean.'

Simpson smiled. 'I believe he's from Yorkshire. I'm from Manchester.'

'Whatever, welcome to the dead zone,' she said, casting a withering eye over the other occupants in the room.

Simpson felt he had some magnetic force pulling others towards him, and next, Iona McDonald wandered over. 'Hello, Jack, pleased to meet you; if you're unsure about anything, just ask. I know everyone seems to be shouting at everyone else, but they're all right, really. I'm just going to help the prof with the teas and coffees. What is it you want, tea or coffee?'

'Tea, please, two sugars, ta.'

'Right, see you in a bit,' said Iona walking away towards the Profesor and the kettle.

John McKenzie then came up to him.

'Welcome, Jack. I bet you're already regretting coming here tonight. Don't know why I come myself, to be honest. Hey, we should go for a drink sometime. I know a few good bars around here.'

'I might take you up on that,' replied Simpson.

Next, it was Louis Gallagher's turn to come up to Simpson. 'Sorry aboot that earlier ma man. It's jist that every night the prof keeps banging on about the second city of the Empire bollocks. Does ma heid in. But anyway, we're all right here. How ur ye finding it so far?'

'Well, everyone seems friendly enough.'

'Aye, there's a couple of bawbags, but maist are awright. What about yerself? Ur ye intae yer footie? Just don't tell me yer a hun.'

'Hun?' Simpson knew fine well that hun meant protestant but feigned ignorance.

'Louis, enough of that nonsense,' It was John McLintock that spoke, coming over. Louis quickly walked away as if he couldn't stand to be near John McLintock. 'I'm sorry about that, Jack, but it's the West of Scotland disease. Bigotry. If anyone asks what Glasgow team you support, just say Partick Thistle; trust me, it's easier. Anyway, I suppose you support a Manchester team. John McLintock, by the way, how do you do?'

'Hello, John. Fine. It was an interesting documentary. I didn't realise shipbuilding went that far back in Glasgow.'

'Oh, yes, way back. 17th century I believe, at least, of course, it really took off with the dredging of the Clyde. Is there any specific period of history you're interested in?'

Simpson shrugged; he had no interest in history. 'No, not one specific period; I like all of it, really.'

'Right, as I was saying earlier, I particularly love the reformation period and –'

As John McLintock told Simpson about the particular areas of history he was interested in, Simpson looked over at Father Gillespie. He was the only one who hadn't come across and introduced himself. He was chatting away with Tess McLintock, who was standing very close to the priest. By the body language, Simpson got the impression that he was flirting with her or, more exactly, they were flirting with one another.

As John McLintock continued to talk, Iona McDonald came across and interrupted. 'Teas up, everyone. Come with me, Jack. Here's your tea. There are biscuits if you want. We sometimes have a whip-round to pay for the biscuits and sugar, by the way, it's not much. How are you finding it so far?'

'Good,' said Simpson, and he really was pleased everyone was so friendly. He walked with Iona and took a couple of biscuits.

Iona McDonald kept by his side. 'Yes, I know, it can seem a bit dry, all this history and stuff, but we also go out for day trips as well. No doubt we'll soon be heading to a shipyard somewhere or down the riverfront. It's actually quite interesting. The other week we went to Glasgow Cathedral. I found it fascinating. Have you been there yet?'

'Glasgow Cathedral? No, can't say I have.'

'The interior is stunning. Beautiful stained glass windows. I love my stained glass windows I do. Oh, and we saw this old cemetery around the back. Some of the gravestones were right ancient.'

'Really,' said Simpson, 'I'm sorry I missed that. Have you been anywhere else recently?'

'Let's see, we went to the city chambers not long ago. That was good. And then we went to the Burrell Collection. That is a must, by the way. If you haven't been, you really should go. Where else have we been?' Iona thought for a few moments before saying. 'I know, we can look in the souvenir book. We have a souvenir book for wherever we go. It's over here.' Iona took Simpson to an A4 folder full of postcards, flyers, notes and photographs. Simpson looked through them and recognised one place immediately.

'Where's that? Looks like a nice street.'

'It is. It was built by a famous architect in the city.' She looked at the back of a photograph. 'That's right, Walmer Crescent; we were there last month. Simpson's interest was piqued by this. The Friends of Old Glasgow had recently visited two places where murders had occurred. Then Simpson noticed another photograph. He picked it up. Iona saw Simpson looking intently at it. 'Oh yes, that was a few weeks back. We visited this old railway tunnel at Kelvinbridge. That's not that far from here. It's disused now, but that was fascinating too. We do visit some fascinating places. I'm positive you will enjoy it here, Jack if you stick it out, that is. It's all really quite interesting.'

'Yes,' said Simpson slowly,' it sounds very interesting indeed.'

Chapter 41

The Review

It was now the 17th of December, and Simpson stood before the incident board to give his findings on the Friends of Old Glasgow. Since there was limited space on the incident board, Simpson placed a whiteboard in front of it balanced on a chair. On this whiteboard were the names of the eight members of the Friends of Old Glasgow and a short line about each.

Father Eugene Gillespie – 54, a catholic priest from Glasgow

Iona McDonald – 29, admin assistant from Grimsby

Ofi Obiaka – 24, an asylum seeker from Ibadan, Nigeria.

Louis Gallacher – 27, Youtuber from Glasgow

Tess McLintock – 50, a housewife from Glasgow married to John McLintock

John McLintock – 53, insurance worker

from Glasgow, married to Tess McLintock

Malcolm Brodie – Club president, ex-professor at Glasgow University

James McKenzie – 42 – a self-employed businessman from Perth

His colleagues, including Patterson, sat around the main incident room waiting for Simpson's presentation.

'Now,' Simpson began, 'some of you may be wondering why I have listed the names of all eight members when we're chiefly concerned with Father Gillespie. There is a simple reason for that. It turns out that The Friends of Old Glasgow have visited all three of the murder locations we're investigating. Namely, the Kelvinbridge tunnel, Walmer Crescent and Glasgow Cathedral.'

'Your point is?' asked McKinnon

'My point is that, in my opinion, we're not just looking at one suspect here; we're looking at eight.'

DC McLean was the first to interject. 'Er, hang on, how do you work that out? As far as we know, Father Gillespie is the only one to have known a victim, Lucas Ryba. Surely, if the society has visited three murder locations, it's even more reason to believe Father Gillespie is the prime suspect rather than anyone else.'

'Not necessarily,' explained Simpson. 'I mean, of course, we're especially interested in Father Gillespie because he knew Lucas. However, since all eight members visited all three murder locations, we can't rule any of these members out. All eight had the opportunity to survey these sites for future crimes. Therefore, I believe all eight should be put under investigation.'

'Put under investigation, how?' asked Pettigrew.

'We should look into each of their backgrounds more.'

Pettigrew shook her head dismissively. 'We're all impressed by your detective work Jack, but this is a historical society. Historical societies visit places of historical interest. That means there is a good chance they would have visited at least one or two of our locations in any case.'

'But all three? And they're not exactly top tourist attractions in the city. I can understand them visiting Glasgow Cathedral, but a disused railway tunnel and Walmer Crescent?'

It was Patterson's turn to speak.

'I agree with Jack to some degree. I feel the visits to the murder sites by this society could well be significant. At the same time, let's not forget we're probably looking for a man and a physically fit man. So, in your opinion, Jack, out of these eight, who would you say realistically could have possibly carried out any of these killings?'

'Realistically? If we're looking for a man,

that would mean Ofi Obiaka, Louis Gallacher, James McKenzie, or Father Gillespie.

'What about Professor Brodie?'

'He seems quite frail. I doubt he could have carried out these murders.'

You're also forgetting John McLintock,' said Pettigrew.

'And Tess McLintock,' said McKinnon.

'Tess? I thought we were looking for a man?' asked Simpson.

'We could still be looking for a couple. Tess and John McLintock together is a possibility,' said Pettigrew.

'OK,' said Patterson rising from his seat, 'Tell you what, Jack and Claire, I want you to look into the backgrounds of all eight members for now and see what turns up. We'll especially keep an eye on Father Gillespie. In the meantime, I think I'll pay Professor Brodie a visit. As the so-called president of this society, he may be able to give us more information about the other members. Brian, keep looking out for any previous crimes that could be linked to this investigation. I think that could still be key. OK? Let's get on with it.'

With that, everyone drifted away, and Patterson returned to his office to find out the address of Professor Brodie.

Chapter 42

Professor Brodie

Professor Malcolm Brodie lived in a modest tenement flat near Firhill stadium, the home of Partick Thistle Football Club. On ringing the bell to the flat, the neighbour from across the landing came out.

'He's no in,' the elderly lady said.

'You wouldn't happen to know when he'll be back, do you?'

'What's it about?'

Patterson brought out his warrant card.

'Ah don't,' the neighbour said, but ye might catch him up Ruchill Park. He goes up there maist mornings for a walk.'

'OK, thanks,' said Patterson, who then made his way out of the tenement close.

It was only a five-minute walk to Ruchill Park. The park was spread over a hillside where a play park and well-kept gardens sat on the summit. On entering the park gates, Patterson saw an elderly man sitting on a bench near the top of the hill. There seemed no one else about on what was another bitterly cold day. Patterson made his way up a winding path which led towards the park bench, conscious of being studied by the elderly man looking down towards him. Finally, quite out of breath, Patterson reached his destination.

'Professor Brodie?'

'Aye?'

'I'm DCI Patterson, Partick Police. I wonder if—'

'Is something wrong?'

'No, nothing's wrong. Do you mind?' Patterson indicated the space on the bench next to Brodie. After getting a nod from Brodie, Patterson sat down.

'Phew, that's some climb,' Patterson said, opening his jacket now hot and bothered even though a cold wind blew.

Again Brodie nodded without saying anything and continued to look at Patterson with curiosity.

'Is there something I can help you with?' Brodie asked.

'That's what I'm hoping. As I said, there's nothing to worry about; I – '

'How did you know I was here?'

'Your neighbour told me.'

'Oh, Ivy, I can't do anything without her knowing about it.'

'I think she was just trying to be helpful,'

said Patterson, 'Anyway —' Patterson stopped as he suddenly noticed the view. It looked over the jagged early morning skyline of northwest Glasgow. As far as the eye could see were spires, tower blocks and tenements. There were gable ends painted in childish colours, smoke billowing from long, thin chimneys, and everywhere there were windows, each immersed with a story of one life or a thousand lives past and present. In the distance, a clear blue sky lay above the white-topped Campsie Hills.

'That's some view,' said Patterson

'Exceedingly so,' replied Brodie, 'Listen, I don't want to be rude, but could you tell me what it is you want?'

'It's about your historical society, The Friends of Old Glasgow? I'm interested in one of your members.'

'Who would that be ?'

'Father Gillespie.

'Eugene?'

'Eugene, yes. I'm trying to build up a picture of a young polish lad, Lucas Ryba, who was murdered recently. Father Gillespie was his priest. Do you know Eugene well?'

'Quite well, he's been coming to the society for a couple of years. He has an excellent knowledge of history. Yes, I like Eugene. We get on. I heard about that young laddie on the news.'

'Yes, it's not so much Eugene; I'm just trying to build a picture of Lucas Ryba's life. You see, I believe Lucas was quite religious.'

'Right,' said the well-spoken elderly man, still looking at Patterson as if the policeman was selling something and he wasn't buying. Patterson started to button up his jacket again. The warmth generated by the hike up the hill was quickly disappearing.

'Can I ask about the other members of your society?'

'What about them?'

'Would you say you know them well, too?'

'Not particularly well, I know them, but I wouldn't say as well as I know Eugene.'

'Are the meetings the only time you see the members?'

'Well, we sometimes go on trips around Glasgow. Historical trips.'

Patterson nodded. High up, the elevated park was exposed to freezing winds. Patterson noted that, unlike himself, Brodie was wrapped up warm with a thick coat and bright red and white tartan scarf. The edges of a green and yellow bow tie also poked out the middle of his jacket.

Patterson listened to the sound of the wind and then those universal city sounds; the revving of an accelerating car, the cries of schoolchildren, police sirens faint, loud and faint again. There were the cries of seagulls, dogs barking, and an occasional jet flew overhead as it circled to land at Glasgow Airport. Each sound was accompanied by the ever-present background hum of restless traffic.

'Do you ever see Eugene outside of the society? I mean, outside the day trips?'

'No, not really. Actually, I tell a lie; Eugene invited me to a service one Sunday. Not my kind of thing; I'm agnostic, but I accepted, and it was pleasant enough.'

'These history trips; who chooses the destinations?'

'Well, I do. I always choose somewhere linked to the subject at the meetings. For instance, we've just talked about shipbuilding, so I thought of taking the group down to the Finneston Crane and the transport museum. Maybe we'll go along to Govan. I haven't decided yet.'

'The thing is, professor, I believe your group has visited three locations recently linked to three murders.'

'Really? What locations would they be?'

'I believe you went to Glasgow Cathedral, Walmer Crescent and the old railway tunnels at Kelvinbridge.'

'How do you know that?

Patterson didn't answer and asked another question instead.

'You didn't go inside the tunnels when you visited, did you?

'No, they're closed off. Besides, it would probably be too dangerous to enter them. We just stood outside, and I gave a short talk. Then we walked along to the old Kelvinbridge station and along the River Kelvin to the old Botanic Gardens station. It was rather a pleasant day if I remember.'

'Did all eight current members go on that day trip?'

'I can't recall exactly, but I think so, yes. We've had the same members for a while, apart from one new member who arrived this week.'

How much do you know about the other members?'

'A little. Listen, I'm not comfortable with these questions. If you think I'm going to betray the confidences of my members, you're wrong.'

Patterson kept his hands deep in his coat pockets. He was beginning to think there wasn't much he could learn from the professor. Yet, unexpectedly, Brodie started talking again.

'I will say this to you, and this is in the strictest confidence mind, but if there is one member you should keep an eye on, it's Louis Gallacher.'

'Louis Gallacher?'

'He's quite young, but he can sometimes be a bit of a scallywag.'

'In what way?

'Well, his language, for a start. I've told him so many times, but he never listens. And he always seems to be going on about the British Empire. Saying it's this and that. He's so biased. He never appreciates the good our Empire did. A good historian is always objective. Louis drives me to despair sometimes.'

'Why do you think we should particularly keep an eye on him?

'Well, I don't mean keep an eye on him, as it were, but it wouldn't surprise me if he was in some kind of group. You know, protest group, activists, causing mischief.'

'Has he said anything that makes you think he's done anything wrong recently?'

'No, absolutely not, but I'm just saying if you're asking whether there is one person worth watching, it's him.'

'OK,' Patterson thought for a moment. 'Anyway, I just thought I'd have a chat. Thanks for your time. Can I walk with you down the hill?'

'No, I think I'll stay here for a while longer if you don't mind. It takes me an age to walk down this hill. My legs, you see.'

'Of course,' Patterson rose from the park bench. 'There is one thing you could do for me, professor. Would it be possible to arrange a meeting with the members of your society in the next couple of days? Get them all together; I'd like to speak with them.'

'What about?'

'Just some members may remember seeing something when visiting the locations. Someone hanging around, that sort of thing.'

'I'm not sure I —'

'It wouldn't take long. If you could tell them to come along to Crown Circus, say this Thursday night, it would be good and if you could keep the real reason quiet. I know it's short notice, but if you could.' Patterson handed him his card. 'I'd really appreciate it.'

'Why the secrecy?'

'It's just that I'd prefer it that way. If you give the real reason, someone may decide to not turn up.'

‘OK, I can try. Actually, I did want to bring the members together some night to arrange our New Year get-together. See, we always have an extra get-together sometime around New Year. I suppose that could be a reason.’

‘Well, let me know ASAP,’ Patterson said.

Brodie looked at the card he was handed and nodded.

‘See you soon, professor,’

Again, Brodie nodded without saying anything as Patterson turned and made his way down the hill.

Chapter 43

St George's Cross

As soon as Patterson arrived back at the station, McKinnon approached him.

'Sir, I may have found something regarding previous crimes.'

'OK, give me a minute to get a coffee and then come to my office.'

No sooner had Patterson sat down at his desk than McKinnon knocked on the office door and entered. 'As I was saying, I may have found something.'

'Go on,' replied Patterson looking through the paperwork that had landed on his desk while he was away.

'Well, back in October, near the end of October, I don't know if you remember, but there was a murder at St George's Cross? Near the subway station, in the underpass.'

'It kind of rings a bell; what about it?'

McKinnon handed Patterson a couple of sheets of paper. 'This is the police report. They still haven't got anyone for it. The conclusion was that it was a mugging gone wrong.'

'And?'

'Well, when the victim was found, he still had his wallet on him, with about £70 inside it.'

'So, what made them think it was a mugging gone wrong?'

'There seemed no other plausible explanation, and they had nothing else to go on. No witnesses, nothing. It was assumed the mugger must have panicked after the victim fought back, and the attacker stabbed him before running away, leaving the wallet and a couple of other bits of valuables.'

'What makes you think different?'

'It was just a curious incident all round. It's unusual for a mugger to end up killing someone.'

'You think? What about CCTV?'

'Not working.' This piqued Patterson's interest more than anything as it was the kind of detail, the sort of luck or info, the killer may have known.'

'Anything else?'

'If you look at the autopsy report, the victim was stabbed in the back, precisely where Tommy Beaton was stabbed on the lower right-hand side. I know this could be a coincidence, yet the knife wound was the same size as Beaton's, made by a three-and-a-half-inch blade. Same size of knife, same area of penetration.'

'I thought you said the victim fought with

his attacker? Wouldn't he have been stabbed in the front?'

'You'd think so, but it was surmised that as the victim tried to run away, he was stabbed in the back.'

'Who was the victim?'

'Alec Donaldson. Lived in a flat on West Princess Street. Divorced. Fifty-four –'

'Fifty-four? Doesn't fit our victim profile, does it?'

'I didn't realise we had a victim profile. So far, our murder victims have been a young woman in her early twenties, a polish man in his mid-twenties and a woman in her mid-thirties.'

McKinnon had a point. 'So what's your thinking, Brian? You really think this murder could be linked to our investigation?'

'Well, this murder happened a month before the killing of Cheryl Kerr. We know it's possible the murder of Cheryl wasn't our killer's first crime or first attempt. If he did learn from a previous attack, then the murder of Alec Donaldson could fit the bill. It is exactly the kind of incident that is not thought through. Our killer places a knife at the back of McKenzie. Tells him to walk somewhere –'

'Walk where exactly?'

'Well, if we assume the murderer takes his victims to a place with some historical link, it would be a similar place around St George's Cross.'

'Is there such a place around St George's Cross? The only place that comes to mind is, say, St George's Mansions, along at Charing Cross. That's a fair distance to walk holding a knife to someone's back.'

'There are some other possibilities. There are some historic buildings on Maryhill Road. Plus, the underpass just about leads directly onto Queen's Crescent, a place with some architectural significance. It has a couple of B-listed buildings.'

'It's townhouses, isn't it? Georgian. Yes, that's a possibility. So you want to check them out?'

'With your permission. I'd like to take Pettigrew if you can spare her and look around the area. See if we see or find anything of interest.'

'OK. Fine by me,' answered Patterson. 'Who was the lead investigator, by the way. Into the murder of Alec Donaldson, I mean?'

'Dave Shaw. Maryhill.'

'Shaw? Have you spoken to him?'

'Not yet.'

'Well, do so. He could be a big help to you, and good work, Brian.'

'Thank you, sir.' With that, McKinnon turned to leave the office.

'Oh, and how is the fitness regime going, by the way? I noticed you didn't have your riding gear on when you arrived this morning.'

'Yeah, I've had to give up the bike riding for now, got a puncture.'

'Ah right, A puncture,' repeated Patterson quietly.

McKinnon could discern what Patterson was thinking and left the office before he could be asked any more questions. As McKinnon left, Patterson thought about the murder at St George's Cross. There could be a connection, and Patterson was reminded once more why he had McKinnon on his team.

Chapter 44

Asking for Assistance

Professor Brodie contacted Patterson to say he had managed to arrange an impromptu meeting for the Friends of Old Glasgow to meet on Thursday night at 7pm. He gave the excuse of it being about the New Year get-together. So it was that just before seven that night, Inspector Patterson stood in front of the eight members of the Friends of Old Glasgow, seated around the large oak table. Simpson stood by Patterson's side.

'First of all, I'd like to thank you all for coming tonight at such short notice. It's much appreciated. I do have a confession to make. You're not here to learn about the New Year get-together. Well, you are, but not just that. Please, don't blame the professor, but I made him arrange the meeting. I'd like to properly introduce myself: I'm Detective Chief Inspector Michael Patterson of Partick CID. This man on my right is someone I believe you have already met. Jack Simpson. His full title is Detective

Sergeant Jack Simpson.'

'Told ye he was dodgy as fuck,' Louis Gallacher said to the others.

'Please, Louis,' said Brodie, 'enough! Let the police inspector explain.'

'Yes,' said Tess McLintock. 'What exactly is all this about?'

'I'm just coming to that,' said Patterson. 'There have been four murders in recent weeks around the city. You may have read about or seen them reported on TV. Three of these murders happened in locations this historical society recently visited. I'm here to see if any of you saw or heard anything suspicious when you visited these sites. For instance, do you remember seeing anyone hanging around? Think back. Did anyone come up to you and start talking for any reason. Did you notice anything suspicious? Anything. I don't expect you to remember straight away but maybe in the coming days. I'd like you to think back to these visits and see if anything occurs to you, particularly if you saw anyone. If so, you can contact my colleague here or myself at Partick Police Station.'

'Ofi –' Patterson addressed the Nigerian before Gallacher interrupted him.

'Oh, here we go. That's right, pick on the black man. Unbelievable. I hope you've got your lawyer on speed dial, Ofi; your colonial masters are looking for a scapegoat, and you fit the bill exactly.'

Ofi looked frightened. 'I don't understand. Have I done something wrong?'

'There's nothing to worry about, Ofi,' said Patterson, 'I was just going to say if you have any trouble understanding what I'm saying, my colleague here will gladly explain later. Now —'

'Just where are these locations? I'm not sure where you mean?' asked Iona McDonald.

'As I said, you may have read in the papers about a murder in one of the old abandoned railway tunnels at Kelvinbridge. There was also a murder in the grounds of Glasgow Cathedral. A few days ago, a woman was murdered in Walmer Crescent. I believe, as a group, you visited all these places.'

'He does have a point. I, for one, have no problem cooperating with the police,' said Father Gillespie.

'Thank you, Father. I should say I kind of know Eugene already since he was the priest of one of the victims. Anyway. If you remember anything at all, just get in touch with Partick Police Station. I'd like to thank you all again for coming tonight, especially at such short notice. Unfortunately, I have to go away as I have a prior engagement. DS Simpson will stay and see if there is any information you can tell us immediately. If not, have a think and get in touch. Jack, if you'll do the honours.'

Jack took out his notepad as the eight members began chattering amongst themselves.

Patterson walked around to the head of the table and knelt down to talk to Professor Brodie.

'Thanks for this, professor. It's much appreciated.'

Brodie put his hand in the air. 'Oh no, it's all right. I quite understand. If you need any further assistance, just let me know.'

'Here,' said Patterson. 'I'll write down my home number so you can contact me at home or at the office if you hear any information.' Patterson brought out his pen but dropped it. Brodie picked it up for him. As Brodie handed him the pen, Patterson looked across and saw Louis Gallacher glaring at him with clear hate in his eyes. Patterson turned back to the professor.

'Are you sure that's necessary? I already have your card,' Professor Brodie said.

'I know, but my home number isn't on the card. Anyway, I have to get going, I'm afraid. Again, I really appreciate your help.'

Patterson watched as Simpson started to go round the table and left him to it.

Chapter 45

Queen's Crescent

The next morning, McKinnon drove with Pettigrew to Woodside and the site of Alec Donaldson's murder near St Georges Cross subway station. McKinnon parked on West Princess Street, where Alec Donaldson lived.

West Princess Street had seen better days. Nowadays, at best, it could claim to be shabby chic with an emphasis on shabby. Nevertheless, it had elegant, townhouse-style tenements near its junction with St George's Road.

Before getting out of the car, Pettigrew turned to McKinnon. 'Just to be clear, what exactly are we looking for again?'

'We're looking for anywhere the murderer could have planned to take Alec Donaldson when he presumably put a knife to his back. Maybe we should walk down to the subway station first and see the underpass.'

Both officers walked over to Queen's Crescent and around one side of its curved façades. This led to some steps, which, in turn, led to an underpass and, further on, the entrance to St George's Cross subway station.

They stopped at the covered entrance to the station. It was a relatively busy subway station, with people continually entering from all directions.

'Right, so Alec Donaldson gets off the subway here and starts walking towards his flat in West Princess Street,' said Pettigrew over the roar of traffic above.

'Aye,' said McKinnon, and they started walking back through the short, wide underpass. 'So Alec's walking, and presumably, his murderer is waiting for him here or around the corner at the end of the underpass.'

'Where was his body found?' asked Pettigrew

McKinnon walked out the underpass to the gently sloping path which led up to the beginning of Queen's Crescent. 'Here. However, if the murderer wanted him to walk to a specific location, he probably put the knife to his back in the underpass and told him to keep walking. My thinking is that by the time they get to this path, Donaldson decides to fight back, tries to run away but is stabbed in the back.'

'That's all rather hypothetical, is it not?' said Pettigrew.

'However the actual murder happened, it still occurred outside a subway station about a month before Cheryl Kerr's murder. There are definite possibilities that this is our murderer trying and failing to abduct someone.'

'Which is why we need to find a place he could be taken?'

'Exactly. Queen's Crescent has several listed buildings. I suggest we start looking there.'

'For what? An abandoned property?'

'Whatever. An abandoned property. Somewhere secluded.'

'I noticed a For Sale sign. We could try that first.'

'Yes,' McKinnon agreed. 'Let's go round the back lane.' They walked around and along a dirt lane parallel to the length of the Crescent's back gardens. The back garden gate of the house for sale was open, and they walked up to the back door. It was secure, as was every back door they tried.

They walked back from the lane to the front of Queen's Crescent. The crescent curved on two sides around an area of grass closed off with iron railings. In the centre were old bare trees topped with snow. There was an ornate, Victorian fountain that, although long since functional, could have been the centrepiece of any larger park.

They toured the wider area, even walking as far as the Mansions at Charing Cross and along Maryhill Road. There was still nothing to be seen. However, back at the station, McKinnon phoned the estate agent to find out how long the property for sale had been on the market. He was told it had been available for the last two months. Although, for a time, they had to carry out more repairs on the property. McKinnon asked what kind of repairs. He was told someone had broken in through the back door. McKinnon asked when the building was broken into, and he was told it was around the weekend of the 28th of October.

The day before Alec Donaldson was murdered.

Chapter 46

Backgrounds

It was the morning of Friday the 19th of December, and Patterson was contemplating the consequences of what McKinnon and Pettigrew had discovered at Queen's Crescent. A knock on the office door interrupted his thoughts, and Simpson appeared.

'Sir, I've been looking more into the backgrounds of the Friends of Old Glasgow, and a couple of interesting things came up regarding some members, although it's mostly rumours and conjecture.'

'Such as?'

Simpson took this as an invitation to sit down, and he started to go through what he had written down on a notepad. 'OK, well, let's start with Father Gillespie. I was talking to a woman who works at the church. She says Eugene Gillespie is quite a ladies' man.'

'Gossip,' said Patterson dismissively.

'I know; listen, I'm just going through what

I've found out in case it becomes relevant, gossip n' all. According to a cleaner, she's seen Father Gillespie confronted at the church by more than one irate husband.'

'Interesting, but as far as we're concerned, it's not a crime; anything else?'

'Ofi Obiaka. He's been working nights at a city centre restaurant. Not every night, but they call him in when the regular staff don't turn up.'

'What about it?'

'He's an asylum seeker; he's not allowed to work while his case is still being processed, which it is.'

'Not sure it's relevant, but OK, go on.'

'Iona McDonald. She's a busy lady. She's a member of about four different clubs and societies, learning everything from the tango to Gaelic.'

'Good for her, next.'

'James McKenzie. He is also another ladies' man. Only this time, there are some rumours he has been swindling women out of their savings. He's certainly not the successful businessman he makes himself out to be. He's currently unemployed.'

'OK, we'll certainly look into that.'

'Next, we have Tess and John McLintock. They're very active members of swinger's clubs.'

'How did you find out all this?'

'I haven't been up here this long without having made a contact or two?'

'I'm impressed. Anything else?'

'Professor Brodie, It appears he was forced out of his job at the university because of inappropriate behaviour.'

'What sort of inappropriate behaviour?'

'Nothing sexual. It appears he had a bit of a problem with gambling. In addition to borrowing from colleagues, he acquired a loan from the University, which he didn't pay back.'

'This is all very interesting, Jack, but I'm not sure it is of any use for our investigation.'

'I know, the thing is, a lot of these activities, such as Obiaka working in the restaurant, Iona McDonald with her clubs, John and Tess McLintock with their activities, means they all have alibis for at least one of the murders.'

What about Brodie? How does his gambling give him an alibi?'

'It doesn't. Except I contacted his doctor to verify his condition, and he does indeed have severe mobility problems.'

Patterson nodded. 'OK, so who does that leave us with?'

'Louis Gallacher.'

'So you think he is now more of a suspect than Father Gillespie? Why would you think that?'

'Because he's a ticket collector for the subway.'

*

Half an hour later, Patterson stood before the incident board with his colleagues gathered around.

'OK. As I said earlier, we can categorically say that the subway network is one of the main connections for these murders. In addition, Jack has just informed me that Louis Gallacher, a member of the Friends of Old Glasgow, also works for the Glasgow Subway.'

'So Louis Gallacher is now our number one suspect?' asked Pettigrew.

'Louis Gallacher is certainly of more interest, that's for sure.' Patterson pointed to a headshot of Gallacher. 'You need to familiarise yourself with what Gallacher looks like. If he turns up in any CCTV, particularly taken around the time of the murders, the locations and loitering around any subway station, all the better. We also need to find out if Gallacher has access to a car. If he does, I want all car registrations seen at every station around the time of the murders checked and cross-checked with any vehicle linked to Louis Gallacher. We also need to establish exactly where Gallacher was when these four murders, including that of Tommy Beaton, took place.'

Patterson looked around the room and noted, not for the first time, that Booth wasn't there. 'We've also set up a dedicated communications room for our investigation. Whenever one of the other forces in the city hears of an incident in or around a subway station, they're to contact us immediately. One other thing. We need to keep our information regarding the Glasgow Subway angle quiet. Even if it is just for a day or two. I don't want our murderer to know just how much we know. Plus, we don't want to start a panic among people travelling on the subway. If any journo does ask anything, direct them to the communications office.'

DC McLean spoke up. 'But sir, if someone is targeting passengers on the subway, surely the public has a right to know.'

'Of course, they have a right to know, and we will let the public know in time. However, this head start may make all the difference in catching this murderer. In the meantime, we continue to have extra security and patrols at every subway station. Again, I repeat, we keep all aspects of our investigation quiet. OK, I'll hand out your itineraries for today in a minute. Right, let's get on with it.'

Later, Louis Gallacher was brought in for questioning. Much to Patterson's dismay, Gallacher stonewalled every question. This could have been as much an indication of guilt as anything else. However, since there was no actual evidence linking Gallacher to any murder, Patterson had to let him go. Patterson knew all that did connect Gallacher to the murders was working for the subway and having an interest in history. In other words, nothing concrete. However, Gallacher didn't have an alibi for any of the murders. Mostly, according to Gallacher, because he was in his bedsit and didn't see anyone. He was never working during the relevant days. It was another coincidence Patterson didn't like, but for now, Gallacher was just another suspect along with Father Gilespie.

Patterson then thought about the two flatmates of Cheryl. Being distracted by the Friends of Old Glasgow, Patterson hadn't followed up on his interviews with them. However, importantly, their alibis had been checked for the murders of Lucas Ryba and Sarah McKay and were rock solid.

For the remainder of Friday, Patterson tried to bring the various lines of enquiry together. For once, he had a big enough team at his disposal, yet frustratingly, nothing concrete regarding leads or evidence.

He called it a day at around six and told the rest of his team to do the same. Forty-five minutes later, he drove up to his home, looking forward to having dinner and then going upstairs for a nap.

He was definitely getting old. He struggled

to get out of the car with aching limbs. Eventually, he managed to stand up, grab his papers, plus another couple of books he had gotten from the library, and lock the car door. As he opened the front door, the warmth of the house embraced him. Patterson shut the door and thought he could hear voices coming from the living room.

He hung up his coat and put his papers on the hall side table but held on to the books. He could still hear voices through the closed door to the living room and wondered who it was.

Patterson opened the living room door. He saw his two children, Callum and Aisling, with Stephanie, all looking back at him, smiling.

'Hey, this is a surprise,' said Patterson, 'I thought you two weren't coming till the 23rd?'

Both children rose to meet him and gave him a hug.

'We had the chance to come up a few days early, so we did,' said Aisling

'How are you, dad?' said Callum as he stood smiling at his father.

'Good,' said Patterson, heading towards the fake coal fire that blasted out real heat.

'I was just saying,' said Stephanie sitting stiffly on the settee, 'you're on another big case. This person who has been going around murdering people.'

'Yes, that's usually what I investigate, unfortunately,' said Patterson as he sat on the settee beside Stephanie.

The two children sat on two armchairs. Callum was tall like his father but, unlike his dad, was stocky in build. Aisling was slight and intense, with fair hair and a constant smile. Both children looked in good health.

As Patterson sat down, feeling exhausted, a moment of silence lingered to an almost uncomfortable length before Stephanie cut it off in its tracks.

'Dinner's nearly ready, Mike. I thought we could have it at the kitchen table, just like the old days.'

'Just like the old days?' Patterson smiled. 'Aye, that would be good.'

'Actually, I'll go and check on the dinner, won't be a sec,' Stephanie said as she left the room.

So, was your journey up all right?' asked Patterson

'Fine,' said Callum. 'We were able to change our tickets to today. Cost us a few quid more, but still. I got the train up from York, met up with Aisling's train from Plymouth in Edinburgh, and then we both travelled through to Glasgow.'

'Sounds a bit of a trek.'

'It was,' said Aisling, 'But we're here now. Mum was telling us that you went to the Maldives; sounds nice.'

'Aye,' said Patterson, 'It was good to get away.'

'What're the books you've got?' Aisling nodded towards the couple of books Patterson had laid on the settee next to him.

'These? Oh, it's just a couple of books I got from the library on the way home.'

'What are they about?'

'The Glasgow subway, it's to do with the case I'm working on. I thought reading up on the subway might be useful.'

'You know you can get all that information online now; there's no need to go to the library.'

'Well, it's still good to support your local library. I hope you two do the same. Besides, you can't beat a good old-fashioned book.'

Aisling went over, grabbed one of the books, then sat back down and started looking through it.

'So, how long are you two staying?'

'Just till the 28th.'

'You're not staying for the New Year?'

'I'm going down with Aisling to Southampton.' said Callum, will make a change spending it there, and I can see where she lives.'

'Here,' said Aisling looking up from the book, 'It says here, the Glasgow subway was opened in 1896 and is the third oldest underground in the world after London and Budapest.'

'How about that, eh?' said Patterson, 'Bet you can't get that information online.'

'Course you can, dad.' said Callum.

'It has around 12 million passengers a year. Didn't realise it was that busy,' said Aisling continuing to look through the book.

'Anything else of interest you can tell me about it?' asked Patterson

'Hang on,' said Aisling flicking through more pages. 'Oh, here. The subway only has two lines. An Inner and Outer circle, each around six and a half miles long. The Outer Circle runs clockwise, and the Inner Circle anti-clockwise.'

'Tell us something we don't know.'

There was silence as Aisling continued to skim through the book. Patterson and Callum looked at each other, smiling.

'Well, what about...' asked Aisling. 'It's locally known as 'The Clockwork Orange' because of its bright orange carriages; hang on, I'll try and find something interesting –'

'We're going to be here all night,' said Patterson smiling.

'Oh, here we are, on its first day of operation; a major accident meant it was closed for weeks.'

'There you go,' said Callum, 'and now it's one of the safest ways to travel.'

'I think the jury's out on that one for the moment,' said Patterson. 'Listen, I'm just going to have a word with your mum. Have you unpacked your things yet?'

'Not yet; we'll do it later,' said Callum.

'Right,' Patterson said as he went through

to the kitchen.

Stephanie was putting plates on the table, pots were simmering on the cooker, there was steam and heat in the air, and Patterson couldn't help smiling. 'How are you?'

'Fine,' said Stephanie, wiping her hands on a dishcloth. 'Everything is nearly ready. Just waiting for the Yorkshires to rise.'

He went over to her. 'Hey, relax; you're doing great. I told you everything would be all right.' He put his arms around her and kissed her lightly on the lips. Stephanie pulled herself away and went across to check something in the oven.

As she did so, Patterson had a curious sensation; it was as if he could taste mint, peppermint, peppermint with the slightest tinge of alcohol for a split second. He thought he must have imagined it, but the taste was definitely there.

'I'll just check if the kids want to eat now or later.' Stephanie said as she went back through to the living room. Patterson continued to wonder about the taste on his lips. Not so much the alcohol but the alcohol mixed with peppermint. He went over and opened a kitchen drawer where the napkins and tablecloths were kept. He fumbled around in the back of the drawer, and his fingers came across something hard. He pulled the object clear and found himself looking at a half-opened tube of extra-strong peppermints. The peppermints were the last thing he wanted to find. It really was just like the old days.

Chapter 47

Shields Road

The next morning Patterson arrived at Partick Station in a good mood. Spending the night before with Callum and Aisling had been very pleasant indeed. There were only three days till Christmas, and as with every year, Patterson wondered where the time had gone. Yet, for a change, he was really looking forward to Christmas. It would be nice spending it with Stephanie and the kids.

However, as Patterson worked through the day, he couldn't help thinking about the unexpected smell of alcohol from the night before. Was it his imagination? Then, there was also that taste of mint. In previous times, even though she would be clearly drunk, Stephanie would take peppermints in the vain hope it would mask the smell of booze. He couldn't understand it. Throughout the previous evening, Stephanie seemed completely fine. A little stressed, perhaps, but perfectly fine. In addition, the dinner was lovely, and it was great to have all the family around the kitchen table once again.

As the day wore on, and the more Patterson thought about it, the more he couldn't be 100% sure he had actually tasted alcohol when he kissed Stephanie. It did indeed seem to be his imagination. Then he realised something else. The peppermints had probably been in that drawer for months. Forgotten until Patterson found them again. The incident made him realise he had to keep his fears and doubts about Stephanie in check.

The day itself was, more or less, routine. Louis Gallacher's interview was scrutinised, his alibis were checked out, and they stood up to scrutiny. He had a driving licence, but there was no evidence of him renting or borrowing a car, let alone owning one.

Toward the end of the day, Patterson wondered if he should return his attention to the other Friends of Old Glasgow members. While pondering this, McKinnon came into his office looking down at a piece of paper, himself seemingly lost in thought. So much so that he didn't address Patterson at first but just stood still, looking down at the piece of paper.

'Something bothering you, Brian?'

McKinnon looked up as if suddenly jolted out of thought. 'Oh, I'm wondering what to make of this report that's just come in. It says a woman has gone missing.'

'What are you unsure about?'

'Well, it says she's only been missing three hours. Her husband called Govan. Says his wife comes home without fail every day at 3:30pm. Says she gets the subway to Shields Road subway station and then walks home. Govan obviously knew about our interest; hence they called it over.'

'When did you say she was reported missing?'

'Just a half-hour ago. What is it now, 6:30? As I said, she's been missing for only three hours. I'm not even sure you can call that missing. That's why I'm wondering whether to take it seriously.'

'Still best to check it out. OK. Give the husband a call and then transfer it through to me.'

'Right,' said McKinnon, and he left the office.

Soon after, the phone rang.

'Hello?'

'Sir, I've got the husband on the line. His name is George Fleming, wife's name is Sally.'

'OK,' said Patterson, 'Put him through.' After a click, Patterson started talking.

'Hello Mr Fleming, You called to say you think your wife is missing, is that correct?'

'Aye, she should have been home about three hours ago, and I haven't heard from her.'

'If you don't mind me saying, three hours isn't that long a time. Could she not have met a friend or something?'

'Naw, that's the thing, she's always back every day at the same time, without fail. I know it's a wee bit strange, but that's how she is. She's been working at that place for two year now, and not once has she been late.'

'What place?'

'Cooper's Bakery in town. Sauchiehall St.'

'Is that the big place on the corner? Near the bottom of Sauchiehall St?'

'Aye. That's it. On the corner with Hope St. Sally finishes at two-thirty, walks down to Buchanan St subway, gets a train to Sheilds Road and walks up tae oor hoose. Ah know three hours isnae a long time, but she's never been late in all the time she's been there. Ah, swear I know something's wrong, ah jist know.'

'Sally, that's your wife's name?'

'Aye. Sally, aye.'

'So Sally works at Cooper's every day?'

'Four days a week and every second Saturday.'

'And you're certain she comes home at the same time every day?'

'Course. Without fail, sometimes she's a wee bit early, but never late —'

'She always gets the subway? Never a bus or a taxi?'

'Always the subway. She's got a monthly pass, gets off at Shields Road, like ah says, she walks down to Buchanan St and gets the train from there.'

'Where do you live?

'McCulloch Street, Pollokshaws. It's a ten-minute walk from the subway station.'

'I know I'm repeating myself, Mr Fleming, but I need to be sure. You're adamant she always comes home at the same time? Without fail? Every day?'

'Aye, that's what I'm tellin' ye. For Christ's sake, ye have to believe me.'

The voice on the end of the line was clearly distressed. The good thing about keeping the subway angle of the murders away from the media was that there would be a spate of calls like this if they didn't. If this man knew a murderer was targeting the subway, he would be frantic. As it was, and with it only being three hours, Patterson surmised there was probably no need to be concerned, yet, another voice in his head said better safe than sorry.

'OK, Mr Fleming. It may not seem like it at the moment, but I assure you there is probably some rational explanation for Sally not coming home on time for once. In the meantime, we'll do our best to determine if anything is wrong. I just need to ask a couple more questions, and then I'll send an officer round to see you. So, Mrs Fleming would usually get off the subway at Shields Road and walk up to your home.'

'Aye, that's right.'

'Isn't there a pub on the corner at the top of

Shields Road? Is that still there?'

'Aye, she walks up Shields Road, goes past the pub, up a bit more and turns left intae McCulloch St. I'm looking out the windae now; still cannae see her.'

'Is there anyone else there with you? Family?'

'Naw, there's jist me and Sally, kids left home yonks back.'

'Could you give me a general description of your wife?'

'She's in her fifties, short black hair, eh, I dunno, stocky build....'

'Do you know what she was wearing?'

'Aye, she wears her uniform, well it's mair a top from the bakery under her coat, brown. She has a long dark green coat on, black trousers, black shoes, cannae mind what else, oh aye, she carries a large handbag, an' it's got an owl on it if that's any help.'

'OK, as I say, we'll do our best to find out if anything has happened to her. I'm sure she'll be fine. If you hear anything in the meantime, call us straight away.'

'Aye, course. Eh, and thanks. I wisnae sure you'd take us seriously with it only being a few hours, but like ah cannae help worrying.'

'No problem, Mr Fleming, I understand. As I say, a colleague will be round in the next hour. I'll contact you later, hopefully with good news; bye for now.'

'Bye.'

Patterson put the receiver down, entered the main office, and called for attention.

'OK, listen up everyone, we've had a report of a missing person, a Mrs Sally Fleming. She's only been gone a few hours, but apparently, this is very out of character. So, at the very least, we can use this as a practice run. Claire, I want you to find a contact number for Cooper's bakery on Sauchiehall St. It's probably closed now, but there might be a cleaner or night staff. Get in touch with someone and find out what time Sally Fleming left. I'm heading down to Shields Road subway station, Jack; you can come with me. In fact, Brian, you can come as well and walk up to Mr Flemings's house. Claire, I may also need you to get CCTV from Buchanan St and Shields Rd subway; contact Strathclyde Transport for that. First things first, make that call to the bakery.'

Claire went to her desk as Patterson called across to Simpson. 'Jack, you ready?'

'Coming,' he said as he grabbed his jacket, and with McKinnon following, all three men headed out of the building.

Chapter 48

A Rumble, a Whoosh and a Toot

After getting out of the car on Scotland Street, McKinnon was dispatched to walk up Shields Road and to the flat of Mr and Mrs Fleming while Patterson and Simpson walked towards the subway station.

It had some tough competition, but Shields Road was perhaps the most anonymous station on the Glasgow subway network. Situated on Scotland Street near its junction with Shields Road, you could easily walk past it countless times without realising it was there. Its architecture appeared to be working under the guise of less is more, whereas, for Shields Road subway station, less was simply less.

Meanwhile, Simpson was wondering why there was a subway station in what appeared to be the middle of nowhere. He wasn't to know that when Sheilds Road station was built in the late nineteenth century, the surrounding area of Tradeston was well-populated and bustling.

Since then, like other parts of the city, it had become isolated, decimated by the building of the M8 motorway. Especially for a period in the mid-sixties, when transport trumped people, and the wrecking ball always trumped buildings. Nevertheless, to some degree, Shields Road had recently gained new life as a popular park-and-ride facility. However, it was still one of the less-used stations in Glasgow.

Patterson and Simpson walked into the station that was bright but bare. A cold wind was funnelled through the small entrance to the single central platform below. Occasionally, a train could be heard entering or leaving with a rumble, a whoosh and a toot. Yet, few passengers came up or went down the softly whirring escalators. The slightly sour smell that was the trademark of the subway also made its presence known, wafting up from the damp tunnels below.

Patterson walked up to the ticket window where a young man was sitting, watching him with bored expectancy. In his early twenties, the ticket collector was thin with black hair and had his hand poised above the ticket-issuing button. His expression didn't change as Patterson showed his warrant card at the window.

'DCI Patterson, Partick CID. Do you work in the afternoon here?'

'Aye, mostly; how?'

'I'm trying to find a woman who, I believe,

comes past here regularly, around a quarter past three. She's in her forties....' Patterson then brought out a notepad on which he had jotted down some details earlier. Looking down, he continued, 'She's in her forties, has short black hair, is stocky, and has a brown work blouse under a long green coat. She carries a handbag with an owl on it. She –'

'Sally?' the young man uttered. 'You're looking for Sally. Why, what's she done?' he smiled but, on seeing Patterson's continued serious expression, added, 'I just saw her as usual, as ye say, about just after three.'

'You know her?'

'Aye, Sally, dunno her second name mind, but she works at a bakery in town. I see her most days. She comes by here regular, like ye said, sometimes says hello n' that. She's all right.'

'All right?'

'Aye, as a person ah mean. All right. Friendly.'

'And you say you saw her today at just after three?'

'Roundabouts, aye. She gave me a wee wave as per. You think something might have happened to her? She seemed fine when I saw her.'

'What's your name?'

'Darren. Darren Jamieson.'

'OK, Darren, so you definitely saw Mrs Fleming, Sally, pass here at around three-fifteen.

You're sure about that?'

'Absolutely. Like I said, she gave us a wee wave; I gave one back. I know her, no well, but I know who she is. It was definitely her. But, like I say'd, she seemed fine. Did she no' go home then?'

Patterson didn't answer but thanked the ticket collector and walked with Simpson out of the station.

Simpson started to say something, but Patterson cut him off with a finger in the air and brought out his mobile phone. He rang a number.

'Brian, you seen anything of interest?' He hadn't. 'OK, Listen, I need you to rustle up as many uniforms as possible to search this whole area. Tell Claire to come down as well. According to the ticket collector, Mrs Fleming was seen leaving the station at just after three. You can make the call from Mr Flemings. Don't mention about his wife seen leaving the station. No need to worry him anymore just yet. Also, keep your eyes peeled. Anything at all unusual, note it.' With that, Patterson put the phone back in his pocket.

Simpson turned to him. 'You think this could be our guy?'

'It's possible; hopefully, Sally's met someone she knows or something and is just acting out of character.'

'But if it is our friend,' said Simpson, 'Wouldn't he take Mrs Fleming to some historic place nearby? There doesn't seem to be anything around here that fits the bill.'

'You think?' replied Patterson. 'You see that big building over there?' Patterson pointed along and down the road.

'Yeah.'

'That's where we're going. 'Scotland Street School. It was designed by Charles Rennie Mackintosh. Please tell me you've heard of Charles Rennie Mackintosh.'

'I'm not a complete philistine. Wasn't he an artist or something?'

'Designer. Architect. Along with Alexander Greek Thomson, you could say he's one of Glasgow's most famous sons.'

'And that's a school he designed?'

'A school. Well, it's a museum now, dates back to Victorian times. I'll tell you on the way. Come on, let's just get there.'

With that, both men walked fast towards Scotland Street School.

Chapter 49

Scotland Street School

Outside the school museum, a sign hung on light green metal railings saying the building was closed due to renovation work. Patterson walked up to the central gate under a low, thick stone archway, hoping the main entrance wasn't locked. It wasn't. Patterson pulled the gate open and walked into the front schoolyard, followed by Simpson. Their feet made a soft crunching sound as they walked on the frosted ground, and surfaces glistened under the orange sodium streetlights from the main road.

Even in the darkness of a winter's early evening, it was still possible to make out the design of the building. There were no bright lights inside, only a dim yellow glow. Now and then, the building would be lit up in flashes by the headlights of passing cars on the main road.

The building had the look of a baronial castle, complete with two round jutting towers on either side that enclosed stairways.

Everywhere were elegant, slightly elongated windows typical of Mackintosh. Patterson stopped and looked around before turning to Simpson.

'Well, what do you think?'

Simpson shrugged. 'There's a lot of windows.'

Patterson stared at him. 'And you say you aren't a philistine? This is one of the finest buildings in Glasgow, if not Scotland. I'll need to bring you back here one day so you can appreciate it in its full daylight glory.' Patterson looked around once more. The building had three entrances, corresponding to the old school days. In bold stone lettering above each door, it showed girls entered on the left, infants in the centre and boys on the right. Patterson first went up to the infant's central entrance and pulled at the dark green door. It was locked.

'Go and try the girl's entrance, Jack.'

Simpson walked over to the large door on the left and pulled. He looked across at Patterson and shook his head. Patterson turned and went to the boys' entrance on the right. He pulled the door towards him, and it opened. He motioned for Simpson to come over.

Simpson walked over, and Patterson whispered. 'This is a museum. There should be security here. Anyway, keep your wits about you.'

Patterson opened the door further, and

both men walked inside. They found themselves in the museum's large reception area. As they stood, the door behind them closed with a loud, echoing thud. Patterson and Simpson looked at each other, silently blaming each other for the noise. Once the door had shut, there wasn't a sound to be heard. Everywhere seemed to be in semi-darkness. Patterson again wondered where the security was. There were some important historical artefacts in the building. If he and Simpson could just walk in, then who else could?

'Now what?' said Simpson quietly.

'We explore.' Patterson had visited the museum a couple of times with his family, but the last time had been many years back. 'There are a lot of rooms in this school if I remember correctly. Old classrooms, exhibits. We start with the ground floor. You go to the left, and I'll go to the right, and hopefully, we'll meet in the middle somewhere around the back. Remember, the first sign of trouble, shout.'

'Thanks, I wasn't planning on keeping quiet.'

Simpson then set off left, past the main reception desk and down a corridor as Patterson went to the right. It was still relatively easy to see in the half-darkness of the dimmed lights. Patterson passed a blackboard resting on an easel with a food menu written on it. Meanwhile, Simpson walked over a hopscotch game printed onto the floor.

Patterson knew there was probably no one in the building, but it still had to be checked out. He turned a corner and was suddenly confronted with a man staring back at him. Startled, Patterson stepped back before realising he was looking at an exhibit. The model of a janitor sweeping the floor. Looking further along the corridor, he saw Simpson walking towards him.

'Anything?'

'Nothing,' Simpson replied. 'I think this could be a false trail.'

'Probably, but there's no harm in looking. Let's head upstairs. The main staircase is around here, I think. Yes, there it is.'

They walked up a wide staircase with highly polished bannisters that reflected light even in the semi-darkness. On the walls were photographs of Victorian schoolchildren looking ragged and curious. Reaching the next floor, there was another long corridor with doors lining each side. Simpson entered the first door on the left and found himself in a preserved school classroom. The wooden school desks rose on different levels, going higher the further back they went.

Both men entered the other classrooms. Nothing was found. After checking all the rooms, Patterson walked into a cloakroom near the end of the corridor. On pegs hung girls' Victorian school uniforms, white pinafores and dresses. Still, there was nothing of interest.

Except when Patterson was walking out of the cloakroom, something caught his eye. It looked like the edge of a flat ladies' shoe sticking out from the far corner bench. Patterson walked forward and looked at the other side of the hung uniforms.

On the floor lay a woman resembling the description of Sally Fleming. She looked back at him with an open mouth and petrified eyes. Her blouse was soaked in blood.

'Simpson!' Patterson called as he quickly went over to the woman with her head half raised, propped up against a tiled wall.

Patterson heard Simpson's footsteps enter the room as he bent down to Mrs Fleming. She was still alive, but her breathing was laboured, and she looked at Patterson with an unfocused gaze.

'Call an ambulance!' Simpson brought out his mobile phone and did so.

Patterson knew Mrs Fleming was in a bad way and losing a lot of blood. He took a couple of the pinafores off the pegs and, ripping open her blouse, pressed them against the stomach wound.

'Stay with me, Sally; you're going to be fine. An ambulance is on its way; just stay with me.'

Mrs Fleming tried to say something. 'Don't try to talk; just stay calm; as I say, an ambulance is on its way.'

Patterson kept talking to Sally, trying to

keep her conscious, repeating that an ambulance was arriving soon, but he knew he was losing her. 'Look at me, Sally. Look at me! Don't try to move; we'll get you to the hospital in a minute.'

Mrs Fleming was still trying to say something.

'Sally, please don't try to speak; you just need to keep calm,' Patterson's knees felt wet and, looking down, saw an ever-growing pool of blood around him. Mrs Fleming again tried to say something. She was whispering, and Patterson bent down to try and hear what she was saying.

Her eyes started to close. Patterson pulled her down straighter on the floor and still tried to stem the flow of blood until the ambulance crew arrived and took over. Patterson watched as they continued to try and save her, but it was all to no avail. Sally Fleming died.

Shaking through a mixture of effort and despair, Patterson continued to stare down at the dead body of Mrs Fleming as the ambulance crews noted down the time and confirmed other details with one another.

Simpson looked across at his distraught DCI and put a hand on his back.

'You OK? Did she say something to you?' asked Simpson.

'Louis,' Patterson said quietly. 'She just said "Louis".

Chapter 50

The Search

There was a sombre mood at Partick Police Station the next morning. Reflecting on the previous night, it had been especially traumatic for Patterson. On the one hand, he had been praised for his efforts in almost saving Mrs Fleming. Yet 'almost saving' was absolutely no comfort.

If any 'positive' did come out of the night, it was that with Mrs Fleming's last word, she had named her killer.

Louis.

It wasn't absolutely certain that Louis was Louis Gallacher, but it seemed too much of a coincidence to think otherwise.

A few more details had also emerged about the night before. The security for the building consisted of a sole security guard hired by an agency. It emerged that said security guard had developed a habit of sneaking off to the local pub. When asked why he had left one of the main doors unlocked, he said it was 'in case he lost his keys'. The security guard and the employment agency were promptly dismissed, and the security arrangements for Scotland Street School were swiftly upgraded.

As for Mrs Fleming being stabbed, it was surmised that Gallacher had seen or heard the two officers enter the building; perhaps when the main entrance door closed with an unexpected slam. Whatever it was, Gallacher was aware the police were in the building and decided to murder Mrs Fleming before making his escape. Unfortunately for Gallacher, he didn't kill Sally Fleming outright, allowing her to say his name with her last whispered breath.

From Scotland Street School and the dying Sally Fleming, Patterson and Simpson raced around to Gallacher's Byres Road bedsit accompanied by armed officers. Gallacher wasn't there, and according to the other occupants of the flat, he hadn't been seen for a couple of days. Strathclyde Transport also said Gallacher hadn't been in to work the last two days.

The next morning Dunard gave a statement that the recent spate of murders were all connected to one person who appeared to be targeting the Glasgow Subway. The press immediately gave the killings the collective name of *The Glasgow Subway Murders*. This also led to more criticism of the police and questions about why they hadn't informed the public sooner. It was suggested, not without reason, that this could have saved the life of Sally Fleming.

An appeal was also put out across all media that Louis Gallacher was wanted in connection with an ongoing police enquiry, adding he was considered a dangerous individual and shouldn't be approached. The press quickly determined that the ongoing police enquiry was the Glasgow Subway Murders. Immediately, there were reported sightings, though none were confirmed. It appeared that Louis Gallacher had disappeared into thin air.

After what happened at Scotland Street School and its aftermath, it wasn't until the early hours of the morning that Patterson arrived home. Having had very little sleep, Patterson woke up still feeling exhausted. However, another day had begun, and a short time later, it was time for Patterson to start another briefing.

'OK,' Patterson began, 'I know it's been a trying time for all of us, but I believe we're on the final stretch of this investigation. Specifically, there is one person we need to find now, and that's Louis Gallacher.' Patterson pointed to Gallacher's photo.

'While we try to locate Gallacher, we also need to build a case against him, which means we need evidence. I know we have already checked – ' Patterson suddenly felt dizzy and steadied himself against a desk.

'You all right, sir?' asked McKinnon.

'Fine, Brian. As I was saying, we need to double-check his alibis again and, above all, find out where he is.'

Patterson took a sip of mineral water, removed his glasses and rubbed his eyes. He had a headache, his body ached, and he felt shattered. He put his silver-rimmed glasses back on and continued.

'There has to be some evidence linking Gallacher to these murders, no matter how small. His accommodation is being thoroughly searched and analysed as we speak. Hopefully, there will be something that will link Gallacher to at least one of the victims. As I said, what I want is that when we eventually find Gallacher, we already have a solid case against him so that charges can be brought immediately.'

DS Davies raised her hand as she was inclined to do before asking a question. 'Are we completely sure Louis Gallacher is who we want?'

'No, we're not, Leanne. That is precisely what we're trying to prove. It may still be possible that Louis Gallacher isn't our culprit. That's why we must analyse everything he has done for the past three months to prove or disprove his guilt. As for finding him, of course, all major and minor transport hubs have been notified. My own feeling is that Gallacher is lying low somewhere close to home. Sooner or later, he will have to show his face, and when he does, we'll have him. We also need to establish the motive for these murders. Initial thoughts, anyone?'

Simpson spoke first. 'Well, my impression of Gallacher was that he seemed to have a beef against everyone. On the one hand, he had a YouTube channel showcasing Glasgow, but I got the impression he also had a grudge against the city.'

'What do you mean by grudge?' Pettigrew asked.

'Well, on more than one occasion, he talked about slavery, the Empire, colonial masters… he thought Glasgow was an important part of all that.'

'OK,' said Patterson. 'We need to find out if he was a member of any organisation, anti-slavery, anti-poverty, anti-British Empire, anti-whatever. He may not have been acting alone.'

'What about his job?' said Pettigrew. 'All his victims were taken from the subway, and Gallacher worked for the subway. Maybe he had a grudge against his bosses or Strathclyde Transport.'

'Yes, Claire, that's a possibility which is why I'm meeting the head of personnel from Strathclyde Passenger Transport in about an hour from now. It could simply be that Gallacher used his knowledge of the subway to murder. For instance, the CCTV not working at St George's

Cross. That's just one of many questions we have to answer. Now regarding the search, I've split you all into teams, and I'll hand you the details in a few moments. Other officers will be arriving to help. Anyone not sure what they have to do, come and see me. Remember, we're nearly there. We find Gallacher, and this case should be as good as closed. OK, let's get on with it.'

Chapter 51

Meeting the Manager

Strathclyde Passenger Transport HQ was in St Vincent Street, located in an elegant building that, with its generous amount of windows and circular jutting tower, reminded Patterson of Scotland Street School. Inside, it was more functional than elegant. Patterson was led to a large, bright office to meet SPT's personnel manager, John Hendrie.

Hendrie rose from his desk and shook Patterson's hand. Hendrie was tall, broad-shouldered and in his late fifties with thick grey hair. His skin had a deep tan, and his teeth were shining white and over perfect. He wore a pale blue shirt and sober dark tie. He could have easily starred in an advert for a cruise holiday opposite an equally stereotypical female lead.

'Thanks for meeting me, Mr Hendrie.'

'Not at all; I was shocked to hear one of our employees may be involved in these murders. Although, I'm not sure there is much I can tell you myself. I took the liberty of inviting a colleague of Louis, who I am reliably informed he knew well. He's waiting in the office next door. I also have the work file on Louis Gallacher. I can give you a copy if you need it.'

'That would be helpful, thank you. Can I start by asking, how long has Louis worked for you?'

'He came to work for us in 2006. Initially, it was part-time through an agency, but he proved good at his job, so we kept him on. We've not long taken him on full-time. Around two months now.'

'Have you had any trouble with him, any problems?'

'No, none at all, as far as I am aware. As I say, we gave Louis a full-time contract not long ago. In fact, he was in this very building to sign the contract. According to my colleague, he seemed delighted by all accounts. In all honesty, reading his file, he's an excellent employee; good at his job, always available to do overtime when needed, he's liked by his colleagues, and he deals with the public well. Never had a problem. Otherwise, we wouldn't have taken him on.'

'You say you have a colleague of his in another office?'

'Yes, his name is Josh Sneddon. I'll go and get him.' Hendrie got up from his desk, left the office, and returned with Sneddon.

Josh Sneddon was in his twenties with short, neat brown hair. He wore a parka, jeans and a defiant look as if he was there under duress.

Hendrie brought a chair from the wall, placed it next to Patterson, and motioned for Josh to take a seat. Josh gave Patterson a wary glance as he did so.

Once Hendrie had sat back down at his side of the desk, he smiled at Josh in what he hoped was reassuring. However, Sneddon didn't find the bearing of over-white teeth reassuring.

'As I said, Josh, there's nothing to worry about. This is DCI Patterson from Partick CID. He's trying to locate Louis, and a little birdie told me you're quite close to him.'

'Was that wee birdie called Linda by any chance?'

Hendrie answered with a question. 'Are you not close to Louis, then?'

'Aye, Ah know him, but I don't know where he is if that's what yer' thinking.'

Patterson turned to face Josh directly. 'Josh, Louis may or may not be in trouble, but we still need to find him as soon as possible.'

'Aye, right,' replied Josh. 'You're wanting him for they murders that's been happening.'

'So, do you know Louis quite well?'

Sneddon shrugged. 'A wee bit, aye, you could say. I mean, Ah widnae say we're best buddies or anything, but we get on. We sometimes went for a drink together. Ah, mean, we went tae the pub even though Louis doesnae drink himself. Hates the stuff, so he does.'

'Hates the stuff?'

'Alcohol, he gets sick just smelling it, but he still came to the pub wi' me and had soft drinks.'

'So when you were together, at work or the pub, what did you talk about, as in what was he interested in.'

'Dunno. Just stuff. Football, news, dunno, the job, just stuff.'

'What did Louis say about the job? Does he like his job?'

Sneddon glanced at Hendrie.

'It's all right, Josh,' said Hendrie. 'I promise you can say anything. DCI Patterson just wants to know the truth.'

'Well, actually, he does like his job. We'd moan and stuff, just the usual, but he likes his job, really. We both do as it 'appens.'

'Did you work together at one station in particular?'

'Hillhead mostly, but we would get moved around a bit, the odd day here and there.' Sneddon looked at Hendrie again.

'The ticket collectors are mostly based at one station,' Hendrie explained further. 'Yet, they are sometimes sent to other stations to cover for someone else who hasn't turned up or if there is a busy day such as a protest march, football match, or what have you going on. Extra personnel help with crowd control, and trying to keep drunken hoards falling onto the tracks is always a challenge.' Hendrie smiled.

Patterson looked at Josh again. 'Do you know if Louis worked at Shields Road at all?'

'Oh aye, he's worked all over, same as me. I think I've done a stint at every station.'

'So Gallacher would probably have worked at Sheilds Road or St George's Cross, Cessnock....'

'Aye, all over. Like ah, say, it's part of the job.'

I can confirm that,' said Hendrie, 'it's more than likely Gallacher has worked at most if not all, the stations.'

'He has a YouTube channel, doesn't he?' asked Patterson.

'Aye, history stuff, that's right. Goes around Glasgow, filming places. No ma thing, but ah watched a couple of videos, and it's all professional. One thing you can say about Louis is he knows his history. Seriously, you can ask him anything, and he'll know the answer.'

'Would you say he was political?

'How's that?'

'Was he passionate about any cause, or was there something he was against?'

'He could get a little political now, and then, that's for sure. He would sometimes go off on one about something, but just like we aw dae.'

'What would he go off on one about?' prompted Patterson

'The usual,' Sneddon continued hesitantly, 'The rich getting richer, poor getting poorer, that kind of stuff. The environment and he had a thing about the British Empire for some reason. All that gumph. He could go on about it for ages. Personally, I couldn't give a rat's arse, but Louis, to be honest, he sometimes did ma heid in wi' it all. Ah, just let him get on with it, have his wee rant, and then it was like out his system, and we'd talk about other stuff.'

'OK. So have you no idea where Louis might be? Has he a girlfriend, or does he know someone you think he could be staying with?'

'Ah, really don't know. He doesnae have a girlfriend, as far as ah know. He isnae even that close tae his family, but you could try there. His mum and dad live in Johnstone, and he has a brother who lives in Wales. Ah, cannae think. Honest to God, if ah knew, ah'd tell ye.'

'OK, that's fine for now, Josh,' Patterson said. 'We appreciate your time. If you think of anything that could be of help, or anywhere Louis could be, give us a call on this number.' he handed Josh a card.

'Will do Batman,' Josh said before he and Hendrie rose from their chairs and left the office. As Patterson waited for Hendrie to come back, something was troubling him. He still couldn't work out the motive for these murders? Sneddon said Gallacher liked his job. If so, these murders weren't about having a grievance against his employer. Was Gallacher killing for the sake of killing? Hendrie came back into the room and sat down.

'So, what do you think? You think Louis could be staying with family?'

'We've already checked them out, and they seem concerned as anyone else in trying to find him.'

'You don't think Louis could be staying with Josh?'

'We'll certainly check that out, but I don't think so, to be honest. Even if Louis had been staying with Josh, he would be well gone by now. Anyway, I best get going.' Patterson rose from his chair. 'Thanks for your help again.'

'Not at all. I want this man caught as much as anyone. This publicity about the subway murders will not be good for passenger numbers, that's for sure. No one will be as pleased as me when he's finally caught.'

'There's one thing that puzzles me, Mr Hendrie. Josh said Louis was happy in his job. See, I thought one possibility was that Louis was attacking people who used the subway because he may have had a grudge against your company. Do you think that's possible? Could Louis have had any grudge against you, SPT?'

'Honestly? I don't think so. I talked to the staff member who gave Louis his long-term contract. As I said, Louis seemed genuinely delighted.'

This confused Patterson even more. 'And you gave Louis a permanent contract around six weeks ago?

'That's right. About six weeks ago.'

'Well, thanks for your time, Mr Hendrie. I'll be in touch again if I need anything.'

'By all means, and if there is anything I can do to help. Oh, here's the copy of Louis's work record.' Mr Hendrie handed Patterson the folder.

Hendrie then led Patterson back through the corridor towards the stairs. On the walls were photos and art prints of Glasgow buses, trams, the subway, and some transport maps.

Patterson stopped to admire them. One, in particular, caught his eye. It said Glasgow Subway, yet the map wasn't the present-day two oval loops but had subway lines running north, south and east.

'What's this?' asked Patterson.

'That?' answered Hendrie, 'Those were our plans to expand the subway network in the early seventies. As you know, the network mainly serves the south side, west end, and city centre. The east end, the whole of the northeast, in fact, is completely neglected. We've always been looking to change that.'

'Yes, but obviously, these plans never came to fruition?'

'No, I believe they got bogged down in beaurocracy and ended up being shelved. Ultimately, they decided just to modernise the network in the late seventies.'

'Pity, it would be good to see the network be expanded at some point.'

'Well, watch this space. Confidentially, there are currently plans for a couple of new lines going as far as Bridgeton to the east and north to Springburn. Whether they come to fruition or not remains to be seen.'

'So what's stopping you?'

'Money. As always, money. Or should I say funding? As it's a major project, it would not just take a lot of money but obtaining planning permission. We need everyone on board, including the Scottish Parliament at Holyrood, and they're never keen on any Glasgow project when the money could be given to Edinburgh. Still, as I say, keep your ears open; we're hopeful we can announce new plans very soon.'

Patterson nodded, then walked on with Hendrie to the stairs.

'There's no need to escort me further, Mr Hendrie; I can find my own way out from here.' With that, Patterson descended the stairs. Halfway down, he had to hold onto the bannister as he felt unsteady again. This reminded him of why that may be and the night before. Mrs Fleming. Watching Mrs Fleming die. Patterson took a deep breath before stepping outside. He knew he had to keep going a little longer and find Louis Gallacher as soon as possible. Otherwise, someone else could soon lose their life.

Chapter 52

The Bad Old Days

After visiting Glasgow Passenger Transport HQ, Patterson returned to Partick Station but didn't stay long. He still felt unwell and decided to had no choice but to head home early; he was no use to anyone in his state. 40 minutes after leaving Partick Station, Patterson pulled into the driveway of his home and, as usual, grabbed his papers, including the work record of Gallacher from SPT and went to his front door. With events catching up on him, he really was feeling completely shattered now and looking forward to having something to eat with his wife and two children before going upstairs for a well-earned sleep.

However, as he stood outside the front door, he thought he could hear shouting and wondered where it was coming from. The next-door neighbours? Somewhere down the road? Patterson opened the front door.

'You ungrateful cunts! Who do you think you are, talking to me like that!'

Patterson knew immediately that the slightly muffled and slurred voice came from Stephanie. A wave of despair rushed over Patterson. He shut the front door and put his papers and keys on the hallway table. He wondered who could be on the receiving end of her tirade. Suddenly, the living room door opened, and that question was answered by Callum and Aisling rushing out like two people fleeing a fire. Aisling was in tears. They looked in surprise at their dad standing in the hallway.

Aisling immediately hugged her father.

Callum shook his head, 'I'm sorry, dad, but she's an absolute psycho. I don't know how you can put up with her.'

'Sorry, dad, we have to go,' Aisling added. She wiped away some tears and let go of her father.

Patterson shut the living room door without looking inside.

'Just wait a minute and hang on,' Patterson said. 'I'll have a word with your mum. She'll calm down. She's just been worrying too much about everything lately.'

'Calm down?' Callum said, giving a short sarcastic laugh. 'There's no dealing with her when she's like this. She needs help.'

'She's getting help. She's trying. Honest. She's going to AA meetings. At least wait until tomorrow. She'll fall asleep soon. She always does.' Patterson then noticed his kid's bags in the corner of the hallway.

'We know she's got a problem,' said Aisling, 'But why's she so cruel?'

'She's not. Listen, trust me, both of you, go upstairs and wait for me. Like, I said, I'll calm her down. Just give me half an hour.' Patterson pleaded with them to stay, but Callum opened the front door, the cold air rushing inside. Patterson stood in the doorway, obstructing the children's escape.

'Please, it's Christmas,' Patterson said, and as soon as the words came out of his mouth, he knew it sounded pathetic.

Callum picked up some of the bags and brushed past his father, followed by his sister. Patterson realised Callum had already phoned for a taxi, for as soon as his two children were outside, one pulled up outside the house.

'If you're going to go, there's no need for a taxi. I'll drive you.'

The children ignored the offer.

'Mum needs to sort herself out,' said Aisling.

'I told you, she's doing that,' said Patterson, slightly annoyed at his daughter's condescending tone. 'Aisling, things don't happen overnight, no matter how much you want them to.' The taxi driver looked over, thinking he was simply watching a family saying their goodbyes to each other. Callum picked up his bags and strode over to the taxi.

'Where are you going to go?' asked Patterson.

'We have a friend in North Kelvinside; she said we can stay there.' replied Aisling, who picked up her own bags and followed Callum towards the taxi.

'Sorry, dad, we really have to go; we'll call you,' said Callum.

'Bye, dad,' echoed Aisling as they both entered the brightly lit rear of the car. The door closed with a familiar taxi clunk, and Patterson watched as the vehicle turned round and quickly pulled away. Only Aisling looked back but didn't wave.

Patterson continued to stand in the freezing night air before eventually walking back into the house and closing the door. There now seemed to be a silence in the building as loud as the shouts of before. Patterson leant over onto the small table in the hallway. He felt so tired and now mentally tried to prepare himself for drunk Stephanie. The drunk Stephanie he naively hoped he would never have to face again.

He opened the door and walked into the living room. Stephanie was sprawled across the settee as if she was trying to hide it. She had a glass of wine in her hand. She shot him a withering look.

'Have the little cunts gone?' Stephanie asked in a slurred, tired voice.

Patterson didn't reply. He just felt sad, so

incredibly sad at seeing Stephanie drunk again. As always, just when he had convinced himself Stephanie was off the drink for good, she was back on it again.

Stephanie looked up at him, smiling. 'What's the matter with you? You look like shit. Anyway, how was your day?' This was said in a friendly, upbeat voice as if nothing had happened and everything was perfectly normal. Again, Patterson didn't reply. The sadness made it impossible for him to speak. He walked out of the room and went into the kitchen.

Plates and food were scattered around the room. Patterson could see there had been some effort to make dinner, but it was obviously a half-hearted effort made by a half-drunk Stephanie earlier in the day. In any case, Patterson wasn't hungry anymore. He sat at the table and lowered his head onto the tabletop, slowly falling asleep, waiting for Stephanie to appear once again.

Chapter 53

A Message

Patterson woke up with a start, and it took him a moment to realise he was still in the kitchen with his head lying on the table. He looked at his watch and saw that it was 12:45 a.m. He also noticed it was the 24th of December, Christmas Eve. Patterson had been asleep for nearly six hours. He stretched and yawned, hearing bones stretch and yawn in turn, before walking through to the living room to see Stephanie lying on the couch, fast asleep. There was a strong smell of stale alcohol. A glass lay on the floor where it had fallen from Stephanie's hand. Patterson lifted the glass onto the table and then lifted Stephanie's legs onto the settee. She moaned and mumbled something unintelligible. He then went into the hall cupboard to get a blanket and a pillow. He gently slipped the pillow under her head and put the blanket over her. Unwelcome memories of what had happened earlier in the day came back to him as he turned and went upstairs to bed, where he quickly fell asleep once more.

Patterson woke up with a start, and again, he wondered where he was. His mobile was ringing on the sideboard. He flipped the phone open to hear Pettigrew's voice.

'Sir, sorry to ring you so early, but there has been a development with Gallacher.'

'What sort of development? What time is it?'

'It's just gone six. It's probably best if you get down here, and I can explain it better.'

Patterson mumbled an 'OK. I'll be there soon,' and slumped back down on the pillow. He was still so tired. His head was thumping, and, as always, one of his first thoughts was where Stephanie was. Holding tight onto the bannister, he walked downstairs to see Stephanie immobile on the couch. No doubt, she had woken up during the night but, after yesterday's events, decided it was best to stay on the sofa for as long as possible. Patterson walked back up the stairs to the bathroom and felt a little better and at least half-awake after a shave and a shower.

He dressed and, on leaving, went back to see Stephanie.

'Stephanie, Stephanie, come on, wake up; let's get you upstairs. I've been called into work.' Stephanie partially rose, and without saying anything more, Patterson escorted his wife up the stairs into the bedroom and into bed.

Stephanie kept her eyes closed as if trying to block out reality. Patterson kissed her on the cheek, returned downstairs, got his stuff, and left for the station.

With light traffic on the roads, it didn't take Patterson long to get to Partick Station.

As he walked into the main office, Simpson, McKinnon, and Pettigrew were already there.

'Morning,' said Patterson. 'So, has Gallacher been found then?'

'Not quite,' said Pettigrew, 'he's sent us a message.'

'A message? How's that?'

'He uploaded a video on YouTube,' explained Pettigrew.

'I thought we closed that channel down?' said Patterson.

'We did, but he's opened up a new one,' said McKinnon. 'I've uploaded it to the monitor; it's ready to play.'

'OK, just hang on a minute.' Patterson went across to the cafetiere and poured himself a coffee. Holding his mug of warm drink, Patterson pulled up a chair, his back leaning against a desk. Pettigrew noticed her boss looked exhausted as McKinnon pointed the remote at the screen.

An advert for an insurance company came on for a few seconds before McKinnon could skip past it. Next, Gallacher appeared on the screen. He looked surprisingly well. His light brown hair was short and neat, and he looked fresh-faced and healthy; his skin and eyes were clear. It certainly didn't look like he was sleeping rough. Behind him was a wall with distinctive yellow wallpaper with bright, multi-coloured leaves. Gallacher smiled before suddenly changing and speaking in an angry, loud voice.

'Fuck Glasgow. Fuck Glaswegians. Fuck your shitty little low-life town, your second city of the Empire bollocks. Fuck your fancy cafes and your poncy pubs and your bistros and conferences and your boutiques and whatever other bullshit you call it. Fuck the west end, south side, east end, north side. It's all bollocks. You know that? Absolute bollocks. I mean, some of us have to live here in this shithole. You can stick your cunty cunt of a city up your fucking arse. I've had enough. Fuck you. Fuck Glasgow. You cappuccino cunts.'

Then Gallacher suddenly changed from angry rant mode to smiling, genial host reminding Patterson of Stephanie.

'Hey, guys, how you all doing? There's a reason for that message which I'll explain in a second. I'm making this video today because I don't want any more people to get hurt. You don't want that. I don't want that, so I'm appealing to your better nature. Let's just stop this now.' Gallacher was pronouncing his words slowly and with less of his natural accent, as if reading aloud from a book in primary school.

'So, I'm guessing you're probably

wondering what this is all about? It's like this. This city is a disgrace. I have become aware of proposals to expand the Glasgow Subway. That's right. They are going to expand the subway. Why should you be concerned about this? Because if this extension goes ahead, a number of historic buildings in Glasgow will be demolished. We cannot allow this to happen. This is our history they're destroying. Your parent's history. Your children's history. Our history. Something we can never recover because once these buildings are gone, they're gone forever. That's why I'm taking direct action, but you can do your bit too. I'm appealing to all the good-hearted Glaswegians and anyone planning on visiting our city to boycott the subway. I repeat, do not use the subway. Don't give these scumbags your coffers so they can destroy our heritage. Get a bus, walk, taxi, cycle, whatever. Yes, if you did use the subway, you may save a few minutes on your journey. Is that worth destroying our history for? Now I know our city has its darker past. Its role in slavery will forever be a stain on all of us. Exceedingly so. But Glasgow is still our city, our home. People have already been hurt because of this very bad plan. So let's make sure no one else gets hurt. My message is that we will never stop our actions until these plans are stopped indefinitely. We cannot repeat the mistakes of the sixties and seventies when so much of our architectural heritage was demolished and destroyed forever. Play your part and stop using the subway. OK, guys; it's just a short video today, but I'm sure you'll agree it's a deadly important one. Remember, if you like this video, don't forget to hit those like and subscribe buttons if you haven't already done so. Hey, and remember, by destroying our past, they're destroying our future. Till next time guys, catch yous all later, from *Gallacher's Glasgow,* over and out.'

There was a moment's silence as Patterson and his colleagues pondered what they'd just watched.

'So, what do you think?' asked Simpson.

'I think I was kind of expecting it.' replied Patterson

'Expecting it?' asked McKinnon.

'Yesterday, I visited the Strathclyde Transport headquarters. The manager I talked to said there are indeed plans for a new subway extension. Obviously, Gallacher has become aware of these plans, possibly when he visited Strathclyde Transport HQ six weeks ago and decided to take direct action, as he calls it.'

'Well, he's obviously a nutter,' answered DC McLean.'

'He's basically saying that if these plans for an extension aren't stopped, he will keep on killing.'

'In some ways, this video changes nothing,' said Patterson. 'Yes, we may now know for definite the motive behind these murders, but our priority is still finding Gallacher.'

'Do you know anything more about these extension proposals then?' asked Pettigrew. She again noticed Patterson looked exhausted. His skin was pale, his eyes bloodshot, and she was even more concerned to see his hands trembling.

'Just that plans are in place. They had plans before, but they came to nothing. Probably couldn't get the money together or have the planning permission approved. This time, I got the impression they've done more groundwork to get these plans moving forward. In fact, Brian, get back in touch with SPT. Find out all you can about these new extension proposals and what buildings are under threat.'

'If there is such a long way before these plans become a reality, why is Gallacher murdering people now?' asked Pettigrew.

'So the plans are nipped in the bud,' said Simpson.

'Could we find out the location of Gallacher through that YouTube video?' Patterson directed his question at McKinnon.

'Doubt it,' replied McKinnon. 'It's not like tracing a mobile phone. There is also no real indication of where it was filmed apart from the wallpaper, which is quite distinctive.

'Yet, I think we can at least say it was filmed in someone's house or flat, ' said Patterson. 'So that is presumably where he is staying.

Whoever let him film that must also know of his plans which means Gallacher may well have an accomplice. It would explain a lot if he did.'

'So what do we do now?' asked Pettigrew.

'Like I said, this video changes nothing. For now, we carry on with what we've been doing. We must double-check all Gallacher's friends, family, and acquaintances. He has a friend, someone I met yesterday, Josh Sneddon. Go over to his address to check it out. McLean, find out who stocks that particular wallpaper and then see who has bought any in the recent past. OK, let's get on with it.'

Patterson returned to his office and sat down behind his desk. He still felt terrible. It was as if his whole body, his soul, was aching with pain and tiredness. Yet, somehow he knew he just had to get through the day. He wondered about Stephanie again, and the thought of her being drunk brought another layer of despair to the morning. There was a knock on his office door, and he looked up to see Pettigrew entering. She closed the door behind her.

'Claire, Everything all right?'

'Fine. I just wanted to check if everything is all right with you?'

'Me? I'm fine, a little tired. Why?'

'Well, you look worn out. I know it's not for me to say, sir, but why not take a day off? If the other night's events were traumatic, you're perfectly entitled to recuperate.'

‘ Take a day off? You’re kidding, aren’t you? I really don’t think this is the time, Claire. No, I’ve just had a couple of bad nights’ sleep, that’s all. I’ll be fine; thanks for your concern all the same.’

‘Are you sure?’

‘Yes, I’m sure. Now go start trying to find where that video was filmed.’

Pettigrew turned to leave the office. She stopped as someone else entered the office without knocking. Emma Booth. The two women looked at each other with curiosity as Pettigrew slid past her into the main office.

Patterson watched as Booth closed the door. Emma Booth was the last person Patterson wanted to see.

‘I’d like a word,’ Booth said.

Patterson looked up at her and sighed. ‘Please, Emma, unless it’s to do with the case, I really don’t have time right now.’

‘I’m leaving.’

Patterson took off his glasses and rubbed his eyes once again. He then indicated for Booth to take a seat.

‘You’re leaving?’ Patterson asked once Booth had sat down.

‘Yes, I’m going back to Stirling; a position opened up at the station where I used to work. I’ve spoken with my old boss, and he’s willing to take me back if you give permission to let me go immediately.’

‘Immediately? Well, yes, if that’s what you

want to do, of course, I give permission. Give me his details, and I'll contact him.' Patterson looked at Booth and suddenly felt a lot of compassion for her. 'Listen, Emma, are you quite sure this is what you want to do?'

'Yes, I need to get away from here. Not with what is going on between us.'

'Nothing is going on between us. That's the point.'

'But you seem to think there is.'

'Me? I don't. You do. I mean, maybe something's got mixed up in translation; I don't know anymore. There's no need to leave. However, I'm not going to stand in your way. Are you sure you want to head back to Stirling?'

'I'm sure. I've still got a few days' holidays due to me; with your permission, I can take them now and leave immediately.'

'Well, I may need you for the next few days, but I guess someone else can stand in for you. As I said if that's what you want to do –'

'It is. I've made my decision. I just wanted to say goodbye before I go.'

'OK, Emma, if that's your decision. I'll get it sorted. You take care of yourself, and if you need anything, just say.'

'I will.' Booth then started crying, got up and hurriedly left the office. The others in the main office looked at Booth leaving Patterson's office in tears and wondered what was happening. Patterson came round from his desk

and gave his colleagues a sheepish look before closing the office door.
Patterson sat back down, trying to concentrate on working out the rota for that day and assigning his team specific tasks. Yet, it was almost impossible. His mind was whirring with a thousand thoughts and worries. He thought about Booth and her leaving for Stirling. Should he try one more time to make her stay? Apart from anything else, she was a good officer. He thought about Stephanie. Would she be all right? He thought about his kids. Would they ever visit again? In addition, he thought about the case and Louis Gallacher. Would they be able to find him before he murdered someone else?

Patterson rested his head in his hands, trying to ease the mental pressure. He felt sweaty and cold at the same time. He noticed his hands were shaking again and put them on the desk, stretching his fingers out, trying to steady them. With despair, he heard someone knocking on his office door again. It was Brian.

'What the hell is it now?!' Patterson snapped, raising his voice to a level that everyone in the office turned to look in his direction. 'Sorry, Brian, just please tell me some good news.'

'Not sure if it is. We've just had a call from Central. They've pulled a body from the Clyde, and apparently, the victim resembles Louis Gallacher.'

'Whereabouts?'

'Just past the Gorbals Street Bridge. Northside.'

'Come on, get the others and let's get down to Gorbals Street Bridge.'

Chapter 54

The Bird That Never Flew

Forty minutes later, Patterson stood by the side of the River Clyde, just down from Gorbals Street Bridge. With it being Christmas Eve, the roads were full of cars carrying Christmas Eve shoppers to and from the city centre.

As he continued to stand on the riverbank and look around, Patterson could only feel an overwhelming sense of disappointment. A black body bag lay a few yards away. It didn't just remind him of Cheryl Kerr's murder – it reminded him that a serial killer hadn't been brought to justice.

Patterson eventually walked over to the body bag. It was an act he didn't want to do, but he knew he had to. He kneeled down and drew back the zip. It was Louis Gallacher, all right. Gallacher's face reminded him of Cheryl Kerr's. Not so much that there was a physical resemblance, but he had the same washed, clean look of someone freshly fished out of a river. His black hair was swept back, only one long strand falling over his forehead. If it wasn't for the fact he was deceased, you would have sworn he was in good health. Gallacher wore a grey T-shirt, black tracksuit bottoms, and blue trainers. Lifting up the T-shirt and tracksuit bottoms, Patterson saw no visible marks on the body. No immediate signs of foul play. By all accounts, Louis Gallacher looked like an accidental drowning or a suicide victim. If it was suicide, then no doubt CCTV would turn up footage of him silently jumping off an upriver bridge.

It didn't seem right that Gallacher should get to decide his own fate. Patterson zipped up the body bag and stood up, again feeling a little dizzy as he did so. That was that, then. End of story. He walked away from the body bag towards his fellow officers. It seemed as if all around him, life was carrying on, as usual, those last-minute Christmas shoppers unaware a major police investigation was coming to a close. He looked across at the cars crossing Gorbals Street Bridge, the innocent blue sky, the proud, impressive buildings lining the Clyde and the bridge itself.

On either side of the elegantly curved bridge was a rather garishly painted shield that displayed the Glasgow Coat of Arms. The shield had a tree in the centre on which a bird and a bell sat while two fish framed the tree.

Here is the bird that never flew
Here is the tree that never grew
Here is the bell that never rang
Here is the fish that never swam
Let Glasgow flourish

The verse referred to a legend associated with Glasgow's founding father, St Mungo. Patterson thought about his own view of city life. All the murders, heartache, and grief he had seen over the years. He thought about the Cheryl Kerrs, Lucas Rybas, Sally Flemings, and Sarah McKays. Those birds that never flew, those trees that never grew, those bells that never rang, and fish that never swam - that was the Glasgow Patterson knew. So many lives unnecessarily ended before they truly had a chance to live. Patterson bowed his head and went to rejoin his fellow officers.

Then he stopped.

Patterson looked back at the body bag and thought for a moment. He walked back, knelt down and once more unzipped the bag.

Suddenly he knew the answer to one question.

The answer to that first question led him to the answer to a second question and then a third, and then another. A followed B followed C followed D. Suddenly, all the pieces of the jigsaw started falling into place. Patterson had experienced revelations throughout his career, and this was another. When the fog suddenly lifts, and you can see all that once had been shrouded in mist.

Patterson knelt down further until his face was almost touching that of Gallacher. He prised open Gallacher's mouth.

Everything made sense in a few moments, and Patterson knew Louis Gallacher was not the Glasgow Subway Murderer.

Chapter 55

A Mosaic of Murder

Patterson strode away from the body bag and towards his fellow officers, still gripped by his revelation. To his colleague's surprise, he walked past them without stopping.

'Sir? Is something wrong?' Pettigrew called after him.

'I need to meet someone; I'll see you back at the station.' Patterson said, turning his head and putting a hand in the air but still not stopping. Pettigrew and Simpson looked at each other confused.

As Patterson got into his car, he brought out his phone. He called to arrange a meeting with the person he felt could hold the last piece of information that could finally reveal who was the real Glasgow Subway Murderer.

After the call ended, Patterson looked at his phone and noticed a message from Callum.

'Hey dad, hope you're all right. Sorry about other night but had to get away. Will see you

sometime x'

This immediately made Patterson feel better, and he realised how much the situation with his kids and Stephanie was also playing on his mind. Patterson drove on, refocusing on the case and reviewing all the events of the last few weeks. It was like he was rearranging all the little shards of information that had fallen his way in the past few weeks.

As the minutes passed, in his mind, he was arranging a mosaic that hopefully, when put together, would form an image of whoever was the Glasgow Subway Murderer.

Chapter 56

A Lovely Cup of Tea

Patterson parked his car on George Street, near Queen Street Station, and then walked down to the Glasgow Museum of Modern Art. The museum was housed in a very unmodern, one-time Victorian mansion house complete with a grand portico as its entrance. Patterson walked up the wide stone steps and entered the main gallery and reception area. He then walked down some stairs to where a library was housed. The library had a trademark hush, like a neat, calming whisper in the heart of loud and untidy city noise.

Passing through the library, Patterson arrived at the café at the back of the building. It was a simple, open-plan designed area that, apart from the odd clicking of teaspoon on saucer, carried over the quietness of the library. Patterson looked over and saw who he was going to meet, already sitting at a table. He had his back to the entrance and studied a small laminated menu with apparent intense interest. Now and then, he would take a sip from the cup before him on the table.

Tempted by the strong aroma of freshly ground beans, Patterson ordered a coffee. He waited, paid for his drink, and then walked to the table. The man at the table looked up and smiled as Patterson came round and sat opposite him.

'I'm glad you could make it at such short notice,' Patterson said.

'Not at all, not at all,' said Professor Brodie. 'I asked to meet here because I was attending a meeting of the Glasgow Debating Society.'

'Really? Unusual to have a meeting on Christmas Eve, is it not?'

'On the contrary, it's a tradition they have. I always attend.'

'I'm surprised this place is also open on Christmas Eve.'

'I expect they want to cash in on the Christmas shoppers.'

'Right,' Patterson put a teaspoon of sugar into his coffee and looked around, which Brodie noticed.

'Did you know this building was once owned by a tobacco baron?'

'Was it indeed?'

'Yes, and did you see the statue of Wellington outside with the traffic cone on its head? It always makes me chuckle.'

'Yes, it's very funny,' Patterson said

solemnly.

'I must admit I'm rather curious as to why you wanted to meet me?'

'Oh, there's no specific reason; it's really just to thank you for your help, what with me disrupting your historical society on more than one occasion. Oh, and to let you know about the latest developments regarding the case.'

'That's kind of you – and have there been any developments?'

'Yes. A few hours ago, we apprehended a suspect. To be more exact, we dragged Louis Gallacher out of the Clyde. Not that far from here, in fact. You may have heard on the news we were trying to locate him. Well, we have, unfortunately, drowned in the river.'

Professor Brodie looked shocked.

'Gosh! When I first heard you were looking for Louis, I couldn't believe it. I thought there had to be some kind of mistake. Of course, I know Louis could be a bit obnoxious at times, but a murderer? I didn't think it was possible. I suppose it shows you can't really know anyone nowadays.'

'No,' said Patterson, sipping his strong coffee in the wide cup. 'I guess we all have our secrets.'

'And you say you just found him not long ago? Dead? Isn't that awful? I mean, I know he murdered all these people but drowned? It wouldn't surprise me if he's taken his own life.'

'That's what I thought. My guess is he probably got drunk, very drunk and then threw himself in the river.'

Professor Brodie nodded. 'More than likely. Still, it's a terrible business. I don't envy your job one little bit. Having to deal with that kind of thing every day.' Professor Brodie looked around him, smiling as if admiring the café. 'You know, I do like this place. I really should come more often when I'm in town. This is a lovely cup of tea. I'm rather tempted to have a scone and jam. The price is a bit steep, but I am rather peckish.'

'Why don't you? You only live once.'

'True. No, no, mustn't give in to temptation. I think I'll wait; It'll only spoil my dinner. So do you know why Louis carried out these awful murders?'

'I believe so. We received a video from Louis this morning in which he as good as confessed to the murders. He said Strathclyde Transport was planning an extension to the Glasgow Subway, which would mean demolishing some historic buildings. Something Louis was against. So, he carried out this campaign of murder to damage the Glasgow Subway and stop the extension. To some degree, he succeeded; by all accounts, passenger numbers are way down, and plans for the extension have been put on hold.'

'Well, I never,' said Professor Brodie shaking his head. 'So, I guess that's that. Job done. I mean, as far as you're concerned.'

'Almost, but not quite.'

'Not quite?'

Patterson took another sip of his coffee. 'There are still one or two loose ends that need to be tied up. One or two things I need to understand before I can truly say the case is closed.'

'What sort of loose ends, if you don't mind me asking?'

'Well, for instance, Gallacher said stopping the demolition of these buildings was his sole motive, but I'm not convinced. At least to the extent he would commit a series of murders for that cause.'

'Yet, surely... if he has said that is the motive, why wouldn't you believe that?'

'Because the victims were not just murdered but tortured and sexually assaulted.'

'I don't see your point.'

'Well, why do that? To deter passengers from the subway, all he had to do was murder. That would be more than enough of a statement, I would think. So why the torture and sexual assault? I believe this hokum about trying to save a few old buildings was simply a cover, if you like, an excuse. First and foremost, Louis wanted to torture, sexually assault, and murder. Maybe he had to convince himself he was doing it all for some grand deed. Maybe he had to believe that he was somehow on the side of right and not wrong. In reality, it was nonsense. He simply wanted to murder, sexually assault, to cause pain; that was the real reason behind the killings. Not trying to save a few old buildings.'

'A few old buildings? Far be it for me to contradict you, but it seems to me that these old buildings, as you call them, were probably of great historical value and worth trying to save. Of course, Louis may have been in the wrong. However, I feel you're probably mistaken as to his motive. Surely, trying to save our heritage is a cause that could be described as worthy and certainly can't be dismissed out of hand.'

'No, you're wrong. See, I found out which buildings would be demolished if this extension went ahead. Regardless of the extension, they would probably have needed to be pulled down at some point. Perhaps one building had some architectural value, I think it was near Bridgeton Cross, but even that was touch and go. None of the buildings had any real chance of survival. No, in my view, Louis Gallacher carried out these killings because of his sexual appetite, his desire to torture and murder, and nothing more. That's how he should be remembered, and that's how he will be remembered. Five people died because of this so-called campaign. Five human beings whose lives were ended before their time. All for some bricks and mortar that no one would miss. Besides, Gallacher's dead now. Mark my words, I'll see that The Glasgow Subway Murderer, as the press have so eloquently named him, will go down in history as a sexual pervert, nothing more. He was a monster who used Glasgow's history as an excuse to satisfy his own sexual desires. That's the truth of the matter.'

'I'm not so sure, Inspector. But then again, you're the detective.'

'Actually, you really want to know the truth?' said Patterson. 'I'm not even sure it was Louis Gallacher who carried out the murders. I believe someone else set him up to be the fall guy.'

'You're not serious?' Brodie said, shocked. 'My God. Have you any idea who that someone could be?'

'Well, to begin with, it's someone who knows these murder locations well. Say a member of your historical society. It was someone with an excellent knowledge of history in general and, in particular, the history of Glasgow. It was also someone who befriended Gallacher. Because –'

'You mean, Father Gillespie? Eugene?'

'No, his alibis check out for all the murders.'

'Then who?'

Patterson didn't answer but continued to study Brodie until the realisation hit.

'Oh, come now, Inspector, you're not seriously suggesting I had anything to do with these murders? That's preposterous.'

'I don't suspect you, Professor Brodie. I

know it was you.'

Brodie didn't react but looked at the menu as if he was again contemplating buying himself a scone and jam. He looked back at Patterson. 'Me? Really? Even if what you say is true, you forget one thing. How could a frail old man like me possibly carry out such crimes? It's impossible.'

'Because you're not a frail old man, as you put it. You see, I first suspected you were exaggerating your condition when I saw you on top of that hill in Ruchill Park. How could you manage such a climb in your condition? I mean, I'm not in that bad shape myself, but it still took me a fair effort to reach you. I didn't think too much of it at the time, but it did make me wonder. Then remember when I visited the Friends of Old Glasgow that night? When I dropped my pen? The speed and ease you bent down to pick it up surprised me. Again, I found it curious but nothing more. Of course, we had already checked with your doctor, who confirmed your condition. So, as I say, I didn't think that much more about it. Then, this afternoon, as I was looking down at the body of Louis Gallacher on the riverbank, I had a revelation. Have you ever had one of those professor? Suddenly, everything becomes clear and fits into place. First, I realised that Gallacher was not the murderer. That being the case, it, of course, meant someone else was.

That someone had to also want the extension stopped. Someone who had a love of history and knowledge of Glasgow. Someone who knew Gallacher. There was one person who fitted all the criteria I went through. You. You ticked all the boxes. Every single one. And for every single murder, you had the means along with the motive.'

'Did I really? It all sounds a bit fanciful to me.'

'Not fanciful at all. You persuaded Tommy Beaton to get a set of keys cut because, no doubt, you persuaded him you were a history buff and just wanted to look around the tunnel when it was quiet. Along with the financial incentive, Tommy thought, what harm could it do? Little did he know. You met Lucas Ryba when you went to Father Gillespie's Sunday mass. So when Lucas came out of the subway that afternoon at his regular time, as you knew he would, you said you would give him a lift home. Yet, first of all, you took a detour to visit Glasgow Cathedral, again you no doubt made an excuse about wanting to show him one of Glasgow's most famous landmarks. Poor Sarah McKay and Sally Fleming were just in the wrong place at the wrong time. As was Alec Donaldson in your first botched attempt at abduction.'

'My, my Inspector, you have it all worked out, don't you. However, I'm not exaggerating my condition. You said yourself you checked with my doctor. The fact remains how could a frail old man like me have carried out these murders.'

'That's what I wondered. Everything else made sense, yet, as you say, how could a frail old man like yourself carry out these murders? After I saw the body of Louis Gallacher this afternoon, that was the one piece of information I couldn't fit in with everything else. So just before I came here, I arranged a meeting with your doctor. With a little more pressing, he freely admitted the truth. You see, helping you to get more assistance from the health authority is one thing, but aiding a murderer is quite another. He soon admitted there's nothing wrong with you. In fact, he said you're in reasonably good health for your age. At least your mobility is good enough to carry out these murders. That was the last piece of information I needed to know it was you.'

Brodie still didn't react and looked around him as if he was continuing to admire the architecture. Patterson continued.

'He did tell me about one condition you have. He said you are impotent. Which probably explains why you sexually assaulted your victims instead of raping them.'

'So, I have more mobility than I make out. Oh, and I'm impotent. You really think that's evidence?'

'Not on its own, but we'll sooner have other

evidence. For instance, I was intrigued by why you wanted to meet here when I said it would be far easier to meet later on tonight at your home. I was quite insistent, yet you were even more so. Are you really sure the debating society is meeting today on Christmas Eve?'

'Once again, I don't get your point?'

'I think that's another lie which will easily be proven. The point is you insisted we couldn't meet at your home because you were afraid I would notice that wallpaper.'

'Wallpaper?'

'The wallpaper that was the background to Louis Gallacher's video.'

'Oh, you mean that video where Louis confessed to the murders?'

'But he didn't confess to the murders. With you helping to write his script and with some subtle editing, he just said enough to make people watching think he was talking about the murders and for Louis to think he was only talking about a campaign to boycott the subway. See, I think Louis Gallacher did care about Glasgow. Yet unlike you, he had a conscience, not an evil heart. Unlike yourself, he's not a murderer.'

Professor Brodie's smile was long gone. 'Well, all I can say is you're completely wrong. I know you appear to have worked all this out in your silly little mind, but I swear I am not the murderer. For instance, Louis couldn't have made that video without already knowing about the murders. Therefore, he couldn't have thought the video was solely about boycotting the subway, could he?'

'I said we received the video this morning. I didn't say the video was made this morning or even in the past few days. No, I believe the video was made around five, say, six weeks ago. Just when Louis thought his contract wouldn't be renewed. Just when he was angry enough at Strathclyde Transport to make that video. He made that video just before he was offered a new contract by Strathclyde Transport.'

'Inspector, please don't play games. There is no way you could know when that video was made.'

'But there is. I would say there is irrefutable evidence to show that video was made a few weeks ago. As I say, it was made around six weeks ago. At the same time, you helped convince Louis his contract with Strathclyde Passenger Transport wouldn't be renewed. You see, Louis did love his job. You persuaded him to make that video to get his revenge. You helped write the script. Yet, when Louis did have his contract renewed, you said you would get rid of the video, but you didn't, did you? You waited until this morning to upload it just after you threw him into the Clyde. After he was pulled from the Clyde, I smelled his breath, and there was still the distinct smell of alcohol.'

'So Louis had a drink before committing suicide, throwing himself into the Clyde. Is that so surprising?'

'Louis hated alcohol. Couldn't touch the stuff.'

'So he made an exception. Dutch courage.'

'Possibly, but I don't think so. I think it's far more likely that somehow you forced alcohol down his throat until Louis was barely conscious and then threw him into the river.'

'That really is the most absurd load of nonsense I have ever heard. Apart from anything else, it still doesn't alter the fact you can't have known when that video was made.'

Patterson took another sip of his coffee which was now lukewarm but still tasted nice. 'Around three hours ago, Gallacher's body was pulled from the Clyde.'

'You've said that.'

'What I didn't say was what initially sparked my revelation. You see, I noticed something curious about Louis. His hair was quite long. So long it was swept back. Yet, in the video we received this morning, his hair was short, very short. How do you account for that? I account for that by estimating his hair had grown that long in the last five to six weeks. From the time he made the video to this afternoon when he was pulled from the Clyde. As I said, that video was made just before these murders started. To be exact, it was also made just before you murdered Alec Donaldson in that first botched kidnap attempt at St George's Cross. And then you successfully, as it were, murdered Cheryl Kerr. It will also be shown the video was filmed in your house. I noticed you didn't deny that wallpaper is in your house. I'm sure we'll find other evidence, including DNA, linking you to all six victims, including Tommy Beaton. Since he was probably stabbed with the same knife that you murdered Alec Donaldson with, it leads me to suspect you kept that knife, and it will be found in your house,'

'I told you, you're completely wrong,' said Professor Brodie.

'Am I?'

'Yes. For one thing. I didn't murder those people because of some kind of sexual desire, as you put it. What utter nonsense. I murdered those people because I truly believe we need to save those buildings. We need to save our history, our heritage, whatever the cost.'

'Even at the cost of murdering six innocent people?'

'Of course, it's unfortunate people had to die. Don't you think I regret that? Regardless of what you believe, I do have a conscience. I'm not a bad person. Yet, I had to do what I believe is right. Whether you agree with it or not, the ends justify the means. That's the truth of the matter. Someone needed to take a stand, and I'm proud of what I did.'

'Proud? I'm sure you are.' Patterson stood up. 'Professor Malcolm Brodie, I'm arresting you for the murder of Cheryl Kerr, Lucas Ryba, Tommy Beaton, Sarah McKay, Sally Fleming, and Louis Gallacher. You do not have to say anything, but it may harm your defence if you do not mention something when questioned that you later rely on in court. Anything you do say may be given in evidence. Do you understand?'

'Yes, I fully understand.'

Patterson brought out a pair of bright silver handcuffs and cuffed Brodie with his hands behind his back.

'Is this really necessary?'

'You may as well as get used to it. Welcome to the rest of your life. Come on, let's go.'

Patterson took Brodie by the elbow and led him out of the café. Brodie walked defiantly upright by Patterson's side through the library and the museum.

They exited the calm and warmth of the building into the cold and noise of the city. The centre of town was still packed with Christmas Eve shoppers. Walking down the museum steps, Brodie stopped and nodded towards the Duke of Wellington's statue with the traffic cone on its head.

'Look, so funny.'

'Yes, hilarious,' answered Patterson as he led Brodie down the steps.'

Chapter 57

Buchanan Street

Even though Patterson's car was parked on George Street, which was only a few minutes away, Patterson thought about calling for a car to take him back to the station. However, he realised even for a police car, it would be hard to get through the streets that were already full of traffic. He decided he might as well take Brodie back in his own vehicle.

As Patterson and Brodie started to walk towards the car, from somewhere in the distance, folk music could be heard, a familiar Christmas song. Patterson realised it was probably a Christmas market somewhere. Patterson was suddenly aware there were so many people around him. He hadn't quite realised how many there were. Christmas shoppers by their hundreds, thousands even, all around. Many walked past the museum from the large Argyle Street stores up towards Queen Street train station. Patterson hesitated. Maybe it would be best to call for assistance. Yet, he found himself still walking towards George Street and his car; he kept going, reminding himself it was five minutes at most to reach his vehicle.

It had been a while since Patterson had found himself in such a crowded environment. He tried not to think about it, but the more he tried not to think about it, the more he thought about it. His anxiety hadn't crept up on him as it often did. Now, it unexpectedly beat him over the head with a Bratwurst while singing a Christmas carol. The traffic on Queen Street was now at a standstill, jammed solid. Still, Patterson walked onward, Brodie cuffed by his side, both being pushed along by the weight of the crowd. His car was only three minutes away. Yet, Patterson found he suddenly couldn't think straight. It wasn't just anxiety; the tiredness and stress he had been trying to keep in check the last few days were catching up on him again. He didn't feel right, but his legs still moved forward as part of the crowd. He heard a voice to his right and realised it was Brodie.

'Are you all right, Inspector? You look a bit lost.'

Professor Brodie was annoying. Patterson didn't answer but took a deep breath and grabbed Brodie tighter by the elbow. George Street and his car were only two minutes away.

Patterson and Brodie were now fully part of the throng moving along the pavement as a deafening noise assaulted Patterson's ears.

People talking, chattering, laughing, shouting. It was unbearable, but the two men were still progressing steadily toward George Street. In less than a minute, they would be in the safety of Patterson's car. Walking up Queen Street, they passed George Square on the right. Christmas lights shone brightly, flashing and streaming, all with determined, brutal jollity. Patterson and Brodie were squeezed by what seemed a thousand bodies, and Patterson now found it difficult to catch his breath.

'Look around you, Inspector.' Even though he was right next to Patterson, Brodie had to shout to be heard. The professor nodded towards the statues in George Square and the surrounding buildings. 'These statues and buildings are not just bricks and stone; they're living beings. Symbols of lives past and present, they're the people who built them; they're the millions of people who have simply walked past them over hundreds of years. These buildings are the lives of Glaswegians, they're us, and you think our history is not worth saving? Ha! These buildings have souls and feelings just as much as we have.'

Patterson tried to concentrate. He still couldn't catch his breath. He felt dizzy. So many people. The words of Brodie were only half heard as he kept a firm grip on his arm. 'Save your speeches for the court, Brodie; I'm not interested.' Yet, Brodie was enjoying his moment and still shouting above the clamour of people.

'This great city is its history. We are all history. You say the end doesn't justify the means, well I beg to differ; sometimes the end very much justifies the means.' Brodie was a maniac, thought Patterson. he looked around him, but it was difficult to see above the crowds of bobbing heads. He felt as if he was drowning under waves of bodies.

As they neared the junction of Queen Street and George Street, opposite the railway station, it was becoming impossible to move forward. Patterson was sweating in the cold, worried he would pass out amidst the imprisoning entanglement of bodies. There was a constant beeping of car horns as the stationary traffic showed its frustration. Patterson still felt dizzy, nauseous and still, Brodie spoke.

'At least I can look back and say I did my part. I did what I could. Someone had to take a stand.'

Then, in a split second, Patterson felt himself lose hold of Brodie. Brodie was being pushed away from him by the weight of the crowd. Patterson looked to his side, but he couldn't see Brodie anywhere.

'Brodie! Brodie!' There was no answer, and Patterson started aggressively pushing his way out of the crowd onto the road. Patterson still couldn't see the professor and ran around the cars on the road, all pointed towards George

Street but stationary. There. Patterson saw Brodie running across the road, still with his wrists cuffed behind him, towards the pavement outside Queen Street station. Patterson tried to follow as all the time, the beeping of cars and shouts and cries of people were ringing in his ears. He could now see Brodie running towards Buchanan Street. The professor really wasn't as immobile as he had been making out.

Patterson ran in pursuit and started to gain on him. Patterson was still gaining but suddenly stopped in front of a taxi that came out by the side of Queen Street station. Patterson looked at the taxi driver, who was mouthing some obscenity. When Patterson looked up again, the professor had already reached Buchanan Street. Patterson ran on, and by the time he got to Buchanan Street himself, he saw Brodie turn left and descend into Buchanan Street subway station. As Patterson reached the top of the main stairway entrance, he saw Brodie running into the station down below. Patterson followed, running down the wide main stairs, the escalators on either side crammed with people moving up and down. As Patterson reached the bottom of the stairway, he saw Brodie manoeuvre over a turnstile and make his way down towards the platform. Patterson followed, dodging around people, pushing some out of the way as he tried to catch up with Brodie.

As Patterson reached the station platform,

there was a loud murmur of voices as the crowds waited patiently for the next train to arrive. Most were waiting in small groups against the platform wall, allowing Patterson to see Brodie in the middle of the platform, bent over and breathing heavily; Patterson, himself breathing heavily, walked towards him.

'You should have known better to run down here, Brodie; what are you running away for anyway? It's over. There's nowhere to go.'

There was a low rumble behind Patterson as a train approached the station.

'I told you, I did what I thought was right. I have no regrets.'

'That's great. Now come with me, and I'll drive you back to the station.' Patterson was mindful of what Brodie could do. He was aware of the train approaching. The rest of the passengers on the platform looked on as the two men shouted their conversation over the noise of the approaching train. 'Come on, professor, don't do anything daft; you can tell your side of the story to the court; just come with me.' Patterson moved towards the professor.

As the train entered the station, it gave its usual childish toot.

'You know, Inspector, you should always do what's right and let history be the judge.' Brodie stepped back and fell onto the rails in front of the train. There was a large whack as the train hit Brodie's body. As he fell under the wheels, a mix of slicing and crushing and then a loud popping sound was heard, Brodie's head going directly under the wheels. A screeching of the train braking mixed with passengers' screams on the platform was then heard. As the train came to a halt, couples held each other, parents covered their children's eyes, and Patterson collapsed onto his knees before completely passing out.

Chapter 58

An Ending

It was Christmas Day, and an overbearing silence permeated every inch of Patterson's home. Multicoloured presents lay unwrapped under the tree, and Stephanie lay wrapped in bed upstairs. Patterson sat half-slouched on the settee, resting on his elbow and looking at the TV, which was on mute. It was showing a James Bond film Patterson couldn't remember the name of. As he absent-mindedly watched the screen, his brain tried to unscramble a thousand jumbled thoughts about the day before.

He knew he had made the wrong decision; that was at the heart of what eventually happened. His ego had managed to convince him to take Professor Brodie back to the station in his car. Yes, Patterson had misjudged the crowds, had suddenly felt anxious and possibly wasn't thinking straight, yet, that was no excuse. Once Brodie confessed, Patterson should have called for Pettigrew or Simpson or any police car and waited for them to securely take Brodie to the cells. Instead, Patterson wanted to be the cowboy hero riding back to the sheriff's office with the outlaw strapped over the back of his horse.

After returning to the station and receiving a deserved bollocking from Dunard, Patterson arrived home around eight o'clock to find Stephanie in one of her foulest, most drunken moods. Her anger about being drunk, especially when Callum and Aisling were there in the previous days, was now taken out on Patterson. Patterson was too exhausted to put up any sort of fight and instead listened to the constant tirade of abuse until Stephanie inevitably fell asleep on the settee. Once confident she was suitably unconscious, he draped her arm over his shoulder and walked/dragged her upstairs to the bedroom. After pulling her dress up and off over her shoulders, he dropped her onto the bed and pulled the covers over her. Patterson then went back downstairs and slept on the settee in his clothes.

It was now four o'clock in the afternoon on Christmas Day, and Patterson watched as Bond ran across an oil rig avoiding silent explosions. Stephanie had stayed in bed all day, avoiding everything she could. Patterson went up to talk to her in the morning, but she stayed resolutely asleep or resolutely determined to appear asleep. Patterson let her be. He couldn't say it was a happy Christmas; maybe it was never going to be a happy Christmas.

The doorbell rang.

Patterson wondered who it could be. There was no close family to speak of who would visit apart from Callum and Aisling. Besides, Boxing Day was usually the accepted time for any visits. Patterson lifted himself up off the settee with tiredness still penetrating his bones. He opened the front door to see Pettigrew.

'Claire.' Patterson's first thought was that something had happened. Perhaps it was the investigation. Perhaps there had been another murder. Perhaps –.

'Sorry to turn up unannounced. I was just passing and thought I'd drop by.' As she spoke, her breath vapourised in the fading light and the cold late afternoon air. Only now did Patterson notice she was smiling and holding a box wrapped in bright Christmas paper.

Patterson moved to the side and opened the door a little bit more. 'Come in; you'll catch your death out there.'

'No, really, I can't stay. I was just passing; I'm on my way to my parents; I –'

'Don't be daft; come inside for five minutes.'

Pettigrew stepped inside smiling, stopping in the hallway as if she hadn't been given permission to go any further.

'Go through to the living room.'

Pettigrew did so, noticing the untouched presents under the tree and the TV on mute. She perceived a curious atmosphere as if Christmas was a day of mourning, not celebration.

'I didn't want to intrude,' Pettigrew said. 'Is Stephanie not around?'

'No, she's feeling a bit tired; she's upstairs having a nap.'

Pettigrew nodded and looked at the TV screen. 'Is that film on again? It was just on last week.'

'Aye, I know. Sit down.' Pettigrew sat down stiffly on the settee.

'Oh, here,' Pettigrew said, holding out the box, 'It's not a present as such, just some shortbread. I thought you might like it. I'm drowning in the stuff.'

'Thanks,' said Patterson taking the box and putting it by the side of his chair. 'How's your Christmas been?'

'Fine. I hate family get-togethers, though. Don't know why, but I'm quite nervous about it.'

'Ach, it's not my cup of tea either, but just enjoy the food and think it'll be another year before you have to do it all again.'

'Aye. So, how's yourself, anyway?'

'Me?' Patterson looked away from Pettigrew. 'Oh fine, bit tired, well exhausted actually. You know how it is just after an investigation is completed.'

'Aye. Takes me about a week at least to get back to normal. I would much rather be in bed right now. And how are you, you know, emotionally? It must have been a bit traumatic yesterday.'

'You could say that. I kind of messed up, and it certainly wasn't pleasant seeing Brodie go under that train. I feel more for the people standing on the platform. At least I have some experience of seeing bad events. Says me, who passed out. I was told a few had to be treated for shock. Not surprised. No, fair to say it wasn't the nicest Christmas Eve.'

'I can imagine. So did you know Brodie was who we were after when you went to meet him?'

'As good as.'

'How come?'

'After I saw Louis Gallacher pulled from the Clyde, some things didn't add up. The length of Louis's hair and the smell of alcohol for a start. I realised Gallacher may be innocent, and if that was the case, someone else was guilty. I thought of Professor Brodie. However, only after I visited his doctor and he confessed to lying about Brodie's condition was I almost certain Brodie was guilty.'

'Why Brodie, though? Why not someone else?'

'Oh, it was little things. A lot of little things. They kept popping up and pointing me toward our professor friend. Like you remember the video Gallacher made? I noticed in the video Gallacher said "exceedingly so" It just didn't seem like a phrase Gallacher would use.

Plus, I knew I'd heard it before but couldn't think where. Then I remembered. Brodie. Brodie used it the night I went to the Friends of Old Glasgow and when I met him at Ruchill Park. He said *Exceedingly so.* It was a very Brodie phrase. It made me think Louis had help writing his speech, and perhaps Brodie was the one who had been helping. It's strange how your mind works sometimes. It was the tiniest thing, but once I knew Gallacher was innocent, my intuition was telling me Brodie was behind all this. Plus, I met Brodie in Ruchill park, he also suggested that I should keep an eye on Gallacher. He subtly wanted Louis Gallacher to be our main suspect. He has it planned all along for Louis Gallacher to be the fall guy. '

'Yet, Brodie wanted to disrupt the subway?'

'Aye, that's why Brodie deliberately targeted a wide range of people. Male and female of varying ages. He wanted to scare as many subway passengers as possible instead of targeting one demographic.'

There was another moment of silence before Patterson sat upright as if remembering something. 'Oh, would you like a drink, coffee, tea?'

'No, I'm fine, thanks, really,' said Pettigrew

'Brodie justified his actions to himself by believing he was saving Glasgow's history or heritage or some nonsense like that.'

The two officers stopped talking again, and

the overhanging silence took its opportunity to make itself known.

'Well, I guess I better get going,' said Pettigrew, 'the family will be waiting.' Pettigrew raised her eyes to the ceiling, and Patterson smiled.

They both rose, and Patterson followed Pettigrew to the front door. Once outside, Pettigrew turned and gave Patterson a hug and a peck on the cheek.

'Merry Christmas, sir, and say Merry Christmas to Stephanie too for me.'

'Will do; you take care, Claire, and thanks for visiting.'

Pettigrew nodded, got in her car, and drove away, giving a little wave out the side window as she did so. Patterson waved back and then shut the front door. When he sat back on the settee, he noticed the Bond film had finished, and a sitcom had started. A *Christmas Special*. It was nice of Pettigrew to come round, thought Patterson. Then he thought of Stephanie and went upstairs.

Stephanie still had the duvet half covering her face. Patterson pulled it downwards, and he could tell from her reddened eyes that she had been crying.

'Stephanie.' He shook her by the shoulder and, taking a tissue from his pocket, wiped her eyes.

Stephanie blinked her eyes open and looked up at Patterson like a remorseful child.

'I'm sorry, I'm really sorry,' Stephanie said the words between gulps and sobs.

'It's OK; there's nothing to be sorry for. It is as it is. You've got better before, and you'll get better again. Now, why not come downstairs and we can have something to eat? Christmas isn't over yet, although you've missed the James Bond film.'

'Good,' Stephanie said and, taking the hankie from Patterson, wiped her nose.

'Come on, get dressed; I'll see what there is to eat. There's still time to have Christmas dinner, even if it is a sandwich. Coming down?'

'I will. Just give me five minutes, promise.'

'OK,' Patterson bent down and kissed her on the cheek. 'Love you.'

'Love you too.'

Patterson rose from the bed and went downstairs. For all that had happened, for all that ever happened, he knew he still had Stephanie in his life, and for that, he would always be eternally grateful. It may just be a happy Christmas, after all.

Printed in Great Britain
by Amazon